BARGO LYNDEN:
ADVENTURE OF A LIFETIME

By

Nicholas T. Davis

Hope you enjoy
this intriguing
fantasy!

Nicholas T. Davis

<u>Dedication</u>

This tale of magic and faith is dedicated to Ronald Short, my seventh grade English teacher, who with his help and insight inspired me to become a writer.

TABLE OF CONTENTS   PG

CHAPTER ONE:THE NEWS COMES IN

Bargo Lynden was a young Woblo at the ripe age of twenty nine, and the son of Jeremiah Lynden, a blacksmith in Woblo Town, a small village which neighbored the Forbian forest, Northwest of the Swift River. Bargo lived and worked as an apprentice under his father, and although it wasn't the job he wanted, it paid his rent, and fed him well. He had no wife or children, no desire to have any, and preferred his privacy. He liked to play his banjo in his spare time, and also liked to collect precious gems. It was the latter avocation which enticed him into the adventure of a lifetime.

It was on a far away world not much different than our own, in a land called the Shudolin where the Woblos resided; four feet tall furry creatures with the beak of an eagle, and ears of a rabbit. Their feet and lower legs were rigid and bird-like, while their hands were more like humans'. They also possessed the ability to speak like humans, and often did, as humans were their faithful caretakers of the land, protecting them from dangerous outsiders. Woblos were somewhat peaceful, unless provoked, and seldom traveled outside their comfort zones. They loved to have celebrations involving food and music, and were very fond of dancing and singing. They were totally oblivious to the perils beyond their harmonious land.

To their South, past Short and Great Lakes, were the Licarions; five feet tall reptilian beings who thrived on war and conquest. If not for the power of the Shudolin militia and navy, which contained humans and wood elves, they would have surely became rulers of the land. Glamara, the lizard king, fantasized of the day he could destroy the Shudolin Kingdom, and break the Royal Council of their peaceful ways.

One day, Bargo sluggishly carried some metal to the forge to make horseshoes, and turned his head quick towards the door, when he heard a sound.

"Did you hear that?" he asked his father.

"What?" his father asked, and dropped his hammer on a nearby table.

"I thought I heard someone scream for help."

His father laughed at the inference.

"Nonsense. I heard nothing. You must be getting heatstroke, and need a rest from labor. Perhaps you'd like a break?"

"No, I'm fine. But I could use a sip of water. It's very hot today. I will return in a short time."

"Very well. Then maybe you can finish Mr. Bellow's shoes by this afternoon?"

"Of course, Papa."

"It certainly is a hot one today," Jeremiah said to himself aloud, as his son exited the shop, and headed toward the local community well. He pulled up the bucket, and dipped the metal ladle into it, which hung from the well. He drank from the ladle, then dropped the bucket back in the well, as he heard a voice from behind him.

"Morning, Bargo, " a young human woman said. He turned around to greet her.

It was Lilly, a local farmer's wife, who brought some vegetables to sell in the local market. She was a woman in her young twenties with long, braided, blonde hair, and a thin, supple face which inundated her beauty. Her hands weren't quite as appealing, and showed signs of hard, grueling labor.

"Morning, Ms. Lilly. How are you doing on this fine morning?"

"Well, Lawerence and I were hoping it would rain soon. Our crops have all but dried up. If we don't get some soon, I fear we'll have none to sell, or even eat."

"Could be the wizards of the East putting a spell upon us. I hear they often do that."

"You believe in those mystical stories? It's just silly Elven folklore."

"Is it just folklore no one's ever returned from Bereuka Island alive? They say sailors often tell of monstrous beasts that live across the ocean, and demon like creatures."

Lilly laughed at his stories, as she dismissed such misguided parables.

"Who have you been talking to? That's the most ridiculous thing I've ever heard. The only monsters are in your mind, Bargo Lynden."

She patted him on the head, and walked away. Bargo, disgusted she didn't believe him, went back to the Blacksmith shop. He didn't think the legends were false, and if there was some way he could prove it, he would; he just didn't relish the thought of having to go there. The stories told to him by his Aunt Catherine spoke of demonic creatures under the rule of a dark sorcerer named Garlock. He had a large castle on Bereuka Island, which was surrounded by serpents in the oceans, which could swallow a ship whole.

He didn't live near an ocean, and never saw anyone around the village perform magic, so he had no idea if the stories were true or not. He hoped one day to at least see the ocean for himself. The sea port of Riverton was located about three hundred miles North of Licarion City, home of the Licarion Kingdom, and Glamara himself. There were often sea battles in between, and although the Licarion Navy was small, they weren't permitted to cross into the Shudolin's waters without starting a war. Bargo knew his father fought in the battles twenty years earlier, and injured his right leg in a sword fight, which caused him to walk with a limp. Still one of the toughest wobloes in the village, Bargo always admired his father's bravery, but had no desire to follow in those footsteps. Woblo Town was somewhat removed from battle territory, and the few Woblos who lived there kept to themselves to avoid conflict.

The truth was, he didn't know what he wanted to do with his life. He wasn't really happy in his current line of work, and other than music and minerals, had no other interests. Musicians performed throughout the area, but the pay wasn't very much, usually just meals or lodging, and maybe a little pocket change for the local pub. Rocks and minerals weren't very valuable to most people, unless they were gold, diamonds, sapphires, quartz, or crystal. With the nearest mine at least sixty miles to the North, travel proved difficult on the northwest end of Garlo Lake without a boat, or mule.

It's not that he didn't like to work with his father; he did, and there was mutual respect in this area. He would much rather have his own son work for him than to have to pay somebody else twice as much for less professional work, and the Blacksmithing craft took years to learn properly. The village mostly used his services for horseshoes, tools, and things like metal kettles, bowls, and cups. Occasionally, soldiers would come to the village to have swords or knives made, and even sometimes maces or calthrops, but these weren't his main items. That beautiful sunny March day, or the month of "Calla", as the Elves, men, and Woblos called it, would be pivotal to the future of all of the Shudolin.

Bargo returned to the shop after his drink, and finished the shoes just as he said he would.

"Son, make sure when you lock up, and lock the back door as well," his father said, as he prepared to go home. "I'm going to stop by your mother's grave."

Bargo nodded, reminded of the affliction which took his mother just two years earlier, in the darkness of a cold winter. A sweet woman, she cherished her husband's craft, for he would often make metal lamps and candleholders for her.

Bargo had no brothers and sisters, only cousins, and most were near Riverton or Dragginbuck. Two of his cousins, Barlow Lynden, and Joeseph Garkee, were both under the king's service in the Shudolin Militia and the Royal Naval Guard respectively, and stationed there. He admired their bravery, for he felt he would never be able to become a soldier as they were. Barlow's father was Joeseph Lynden, a former high ranking official of the Shudolin Royal Guard, which was a special unit of the militia, and used to often address the issues of coastal territories.

The Woblo cleaned up for the evening, as he felt a strange feeling come over him. He guessed maybe the heat of the forge, or the heat of the early summer air was too blame for his sudden dizziness, and tried to go back to what he was doing. He stared at the bright orange glow of the forge, and thought maybe he was hallucinating from some bad mushrooms he ate the day before.

He saw two red eyes staring at him from the fire, and felt an evil presence. 'You're starting to believe your own stories, you silly twit,' he said to himself, and grabbed his broom again.

"Bargo Lynden," a deep voice said to him from the fire.

"Bargo Lynden?"

"Yes," he reluctantly said, as he faced the forge.

"Beware the evil which awaits you."

"What evil?"

"The evil of the disciple."

"What disciple?"

"The disciple of Garlock."

"But he's just a silly legend!"

"He is no legend, for his presence is real."

"And who are you?"

"Who I am is not important. I am the voice of good, and the arm of righteousness."

"I like to know where I'm getting my information from, if you don't mind."

"You need not know who I am at this moment. Your town will be visited by a young Elf, who calls himself Glam, who brings devastating news to the land. You will follow his instructions, and he will guide you to Riverton."

"Riverton? Whatever for?"

"I cannot divulge that information now. He will be at the Braeca pub tonight, you must bring your father as well."

"But he just left for the night! And he'll never go to the pub."

"That doesn't matter. You must convince him his presence is needed. The future of the Shudolin is depending on you both."

"Depending on me? You've got to be kidding?"

"No, now wait for Glam. He will arrive at 7:00 pm. Goodbye, and good luck."

He grew dizzy again, having felt like he just woke up from a nap and a bad dream. He shrugged it off, as if he'd worked too hard and let his imagination run away from him. After he put all the tools back, he locked the front and back doors, and swept up the metal shavings on the floor. It was 6:00 pm, and he knew his father just sat down to his dinner of veal stew. He walked to his house, knocked on the door, and Saraphine, an older woman who was his maid, answered it.

"Come in, Master Bargo," she said, as her silvery, bound hair glittered in the candlelight from the chandelier. "He just sat down to dinner."

BARGO LYNDEN

"Thank you, Sara," he said, and walked into the dining room, which was fifteen feet long and twenty feet wide. The walls possessed candleholders about them, ten in all, and there were two windows in the front of the room. The dining table revealed its finished solid oak, fine china porcelain dinnerware, and a crystal glass, which he drank from.

"Bargo," he said. "Please sit and have some stew with your father."

"I'd love too, Dad, but for some strange reason, I feel I need to be at the pub tonight. I was wondering if you'd join me?"

"Are you playing music there tonight?"

"Well, ah, no."

"Then why the heck would I want to go there? You know I don't drink anymore."

"I just feel we need to both be there."

"You're talking crazy talk again. Are you sure you're okay, Bargo?"

"Just trust me, Papa, please."

"All right," he said, and shook his head. "I'll go if it makes you feel any better. Just let me finish my dinner first."

"Of course. I'll get your pony ready."

"Thank you, Son," he said, and took a bite of the stew.

In the evening, they arrived at the crowded pub just before 7:00pm. There seemed to be more soldiers than usual in the establishment, and all drank heavily. As the two four feet creatures entered, some of the soldiers ridiculed them.

"Who opened the pub to pets?" one tall, black haired man with an eye patch said.

"They don't carry rabies, do they?" another jested.

The two of them shrugged it off, walked to the bar where the bartender, Robert, poured drinks for others. A burly man of five feet, his dark gray beard and mustache covered his weary face, and his ears heard too many sad tales of despair from drunken travelers from the east. He greeted them with a wide grin and an open hand.

"Jeremiah," he said, as he shook his hand. "What a pleasure it is to see you! What can I get you?"

"Give my son an ale, and I'll just have some water, if you don't mind."

"Where's your sense of adventure? I remember when you used to be quite fond of the Strawberry ale."

"That was years ago. And I'm afraid my son's the one with the sense of adventure. In fact, he still hasn't explained to me why he dragged me here tonight?"

"I'm not quite sure myself," Bargo said. "But I know there was a good reason."

He glanced over at the soldiers near the entrance, who continued to laugh at them.

"Don't mind them," Robert said. "Most of those guys are from Riverton, and they're not used to seeing Woblos, and most Elves are about the same height as them. They're harmless."

"I could care less about them," Jeremiah said, as he dropped some gold coins on the bar.

Within minutes, a tall dark haired Elf entered the bar, and walked over to the mayor, who was a thin, brown haired man with blue eyes. He whispered something in his ear, the mayor stood up, and raised his arm to address the crowd.

"May I have your attention, please?" he asked. "This is Glam, a messenger from the Royal Council in Riverton. He has some news he must share with us."

The crowd settled down, as the elf pushed his cloak to the side. When the room grew silent, he pulled out a scroll, and began to read it.

"We, the members of the Royal Council of the Shudolin, have some disturbing news for the people of the land. The Licarion armies and navies have advanced on our land, and our defenses are faltering. They have been assisted by the Grassmen, and we can no longer maintain a stable control of the region. For this reason, the council has declared war on the Licarions, and we are now all at risk. I, Glam, messenger of the council, have been sent here to ask for five volunteers to return with me for a mission of utmost importance. It appears King Timothy was abducted by the Licarion Army and transported into their territory. We need to find him, and return him to the council unharmed."

He glared about the room as no one raised their hand, not even the soldiers. One soldier stood up to address him.

"Why should we help a king who doesn't care about the common man?" he asked.

"Yea," another said. "When our crops dried up last year, was he there to bring us water?"

"He has done his best," Glam said. "He can only do so much with the resources he has. You must understand, this war has affected all of us, and now we're without a leader."

"What's in it for us?" a civilian Elf asked.

"Fifty gold pieces, food, lodging, and weapons."

"Hardly enough. You'd have to pay me twice as much to get me to go into Licarion Territory.

"I am authorized to pay up to one hundred gold pieces for each man who will go. But for that, you will have to supply your own weapons."

One man stepped up to the front of the crowd. His wavy, brown hair was a silhouette in the darkness of the pub, but his face became more visible as he approached the candlelight of the bar. It was weathered from years of hard living, and battered with a few scars on it. His eyes were dark blue, and his teeth were chipped in the front. It was obvious he'd been in a fight or two.

"Count me in," he said. "Don't worry about weapons, I have plenty of my own."

"Anyone else?" Glam asked, but there was no answer.

Jeremiah turned towards his son.

"Is this why you brought me here, to take you on some crazy military mission? I'm sorry, Son, but I'm afraid my soldier days are over."

"I didn't think anything like this was going to happen," Bargo said. "I didn't know why he was going to be here. I just had to satisfy my curiosity. When I saw the eyes in the fire, I just thought I was having a dream."

"Eyes in the fire? What in the Shudolin are you talking about?"

"Last night when I was cleaning up around the shop, I saw these eyes in the forge staring at me, and then they spoke to me."

"Okay, I'll play along. What did they say?"

"They said to come here because there was an evil presence coming, and this Elf would bring the news."

"Well, it's probably just a coincidence. There isn't anything such as an evil presence, only evil hearts in men."

A drunk patron turned around to face Jeremiah, ready to start trouble.

"Who you calling an evil man?" he asked, as he swayed back and forth. "Huh, Rabbit face!"

"Not you, Sir. I was talking about the Licarions."

"What about you? Are you going on the great quest to save our wonderful king?"

"No, I'm afraid my fighting days are over."

"You're sure about that?"

"Positive."

"I don't think you could fight your way out of a chicken coop. In fact, you'd probably feel at home with the chickens!"

"I don't wish to quarrel about it, so if that's what you believe, then so be it."

"Sounds like you're insulting me!"

"I'm not. Please can we not do this?"

"Sounds like you're afraid to fight me."

"I just see no reason to."

"I've got five big ones right here," he said, as he took a swing for his head. The woblo ducked, and punched him in the midsection. He bent over, Jeremiah took his metal water cup, and knocked him over the head with it. He then kicked him to the floor while he was still trying to catch his breath.

"Hey, the creatures can fight!" one of the soldiers laughed.

Glam stepped away from the door, and walked over to Jeremiah.

"You're Lieutenant Jeremiah Lynden, aren't you?"

"Was Lieutenant. How do you know who I am?

"I've heard stories of a great Woblo fighter, but I never thought I'd meet him face to face. What are you doing these days?"

"I'm retired from the military, if that's what you mean. I'm a Blacksmith now. I'll make your weapons, but I won't use them."

"Not even for 200 gold pieces?"

"Hey," another man said in anger. "Why are you giving him twice as much?"

BARGO LYNDEN

"Because he's twice the fighter you are, even if he is smaller," Glam replied.

"No," Jeremiah said.

"I'll do it," Bargo blurted out.

"What? No, absolutely not! I won't allow you to go get yourself killed."

"But it's 100 gold pieces. I don't even make that in a month."

"I don't care. The answer is still no!"

"Why don't we discuss it over a drink, Mr. Lynden," Glam asked.

"I don't drink anymore."

"Come on, just one for the old times. It's on me. What's your favor?"

"Well, if you put it that way, how can I resist? I'll have a cup of the Winterberry wine."

The bartender poured a cup for the both of them, and Glam raised his glass to make a toast.

"Here's to old battles, fallen comrades, and the smell of Licarion blood."

"Here, here," Bargo said, as they toasted, and then drank their beverages.

"There is one thing I think you should know, however. Your brother and Bargo's uncle, Joeseph Lynden, and your nephew, Joeseph Garkee, have agreed to help us. They spoke rather highly of you; it would be a shame to prove them wrong."

"What's that supposed to mean?" Jeremiah asked.

"I meant simply, they spoke highly of you, and said you were a great soldier and fighter."

"Not anymore, and they know that."

"There is another development."

"What's that?" Jeremiah could tell he was edging him to come along, when he really just wanted to go home, smoke his pipe on his porch, and look up at the night stars.

"Joeseph's son was among those captured."

"Barlow?" Bargo asked in shock.

"Yes," Glam said. "He was among the troop transporting the king to Bashworth when they were attacked."

"Well, he doesn't expect me to rescue him, especially when he knew the risks."

"But he's our cousin!" Bargo insisted.

"I'm sorry, Bargo. But when all of them joined the service, they knew what they were getting into."

"But Barlow wasn't actually on duty," Glam said. "He was just at the wrong place in the wrong time."

Jeremiah slammed his fist on the bar.

"Damn it! Well, I still can't help you. I'm sorry, but Joeseph will have to find his own son."

"Well, I'll be at his place in Dragginbuck for a couple of days if you change your mind. Then we'll be leaving for Riverton, once we find a boat. Take care, and enjoy your retirement."

"But Papa," Bargo interrupted.

"Enough!" He slammed his cup on the bar. "You better get home and get some rest. I don't want to have to dock you a day's pay for being late."

"You know I wouldn't do that."

"Go home!" Bargo left the pub disgusted and embarrassed, as several men laughed at him.

"He's not as brave as his father," one laughed. "Perhaps, he became a chicken?" The men giggled at the silly joke.

"That's my son you're talking about," Jeremiah announced, and the pub grew silent. "Show him a little respect. Robert, I'm heading home myself, I've got a busy day tomorrow. "

"Take care, Jeremiah. And be careful out there. I hear the Licarions have violated the treaties and are crossing into Shudolin territories. They could be anywhere."

"Thanks for the concern, Robert, but I think I can handle myself quite well. I'm still pretty skillful with just a hunting knife. Good night."

"Goodnight, Master Jeremiah." The Woblo left the pub, and the men still grinned at him, but settled down to the point where they dare not say anything.

He walked his horse through the dark streets of the town, and thought about everything said at the forum. He didn't believe in the nonsense Bargo babbled on about; such as voices from the fire or evil eyes. He began to think his son finally went insane from his own wild tales, and the rubbish he heard from others about wizards and evil creatures, such as dragons. He knew the Licarions were real, however, and were themselves, night creatures. If Robert was right about them crossing territories, he'd better learn to keep one eye open, and his right hand ready on his trusty sword.

CHAPTER TWO: THE DEPARTURE

The next morning, Bargo neither heeded his father's warning, nor cared what he thought about the whole matter; he was a grown woblo, and didn't need supervision. He packed up some needed gear; three days change of clothes, some biscuits and honey to tie him over until he caught some fish for dinner, a couple of small daggers his father gave him for his last two birthdays, and a small magnifying glass used to inspect stones and minerals with. He also brought a canteen of water, and a small bottle of Blackberry wine.

He raced through the village streets to get to the stable before his father saw him. Lilly waved and smiled, as he passed her by the community well. When he got there, Glam packed his gear onto his horse, and greeted the scraggly fighter he met the night before as well as Bargo, and introduced two other wood Elves, Tamarka and Pocor. Glam was surprised to see the Woblo, and extended his hand in glee.

"Master Bargo," he said. "I didn't expect to see you here after what your father said last night."

"I'm my own Woblo," he stated. "My father can't tell me what to do, or where to go."

"But he can fire you," the man said, and smiled.

"Are you sure this is what you want?" Glam asked. "I don't need any tagalongs that are going to have regrets halfway through our mission?"

"I'm certain. I've been living in this dull town for too long. I need some excitement in my life."

"You'll be wise to change your attitude, Son, " the man said. "Or you won't be living at all. Get this straight, young Woblo. This is going to be an extremely dangerous venture, and you'll do exactly what people tell you to do, if you want to survive it."

"Relax, Barton," Glam told him, laughed, and placed his hand on Bargo's shoulder. "I'm sure his father has taught him to fight well."

"When are we leaving?"

"As soon as everyone is here. We're expecting one more person to show."

"What' s your rush, half pint?" Barton asked the Woblo.

"No rush, just excited to get started."

"You didn't tell him, did you?"

"I don't know what you're talking about."

"He didn't tell his daddy he was coming with us. I guess you'll be in trouble now by the Lieutenant."

"That'll be enough, Barton," Glam snapped. "As soon as she shows up we'll go."

"She?" Barton asked, annoyed. "You didn't say anything about a woman coming along."

"She can handle herself with a sword as well as you. Perhaps better."

"What is she, another Elf?"

"She's a person, just like you."

"Can't wait to meet her."

"Ah, here she comes now," Glam said, as the woman approached. Bargo, just as surprised to see her as the rest of them, was used to seeing her in a dress, not dark gray pants, and found himself in complete awe.

"Lilly?"

"Bargo Lynden," she said. "What in the Shudolin are you doing here? Does your father know you're here?"

"I should be asking you the same question. Does you husband know you're here?"

"Yes he does. And he is in full support of me as a warrior. He's my love and provider, and I am his protector."

"Great," Barton grumbled. "Now we have to worry about pets and women! This is going to be a fabulous adventure!"

"I'm not a pet!" Bargo snapped, offended.

"Let's go," Glam said. "We're wasting time bickering. We have to be at Dragginbuck by sundown, so we can get a boat down the Swift River to Riverton."

"If your father knows you left, he'll be onto us a lot quicker than that," Lilly said. "And he'll be dragging you back by the ears!"

"I'd like to see that!" Barton laughed. "He's got such big ears!"

"Look here, Barton," Glam said, and pointed his finger at him. "There is no room for bigotry on this venture. You'll learn to treat everyone with respect here, be they Woblo, woman, or Elf. Understood?"

Barton spit on the ground next to his horse.

"Perfectly. I'll try to curb my tongue in the future."

Glam reached inside a wagon next to the horses. "Here are your weapons," he said, as he handed each of them a sword, a bow, and a bundle of ten arrows each in a holder.

"How are you with a sword, Woblo?" Barton asked.

"I've never really had to use one."

"What about a bow?"

"I scored a 70 out of a hundred on the archery games last year."

"That isn't the same as a moving target, Kid. So Mr. Glam, you're allowing us to bring an apprentice with us as well?"

"I'm sure he'll hold his own if the circumstances call for it," Lilly defended.

"Will you hold your own too, Lassie?" He asked, as he got closer to her young, pretty face.

She pointed the sword at his chin, inches from his jugular vein.

"You best to believe that, Mr."

"Enough," Glam said, and mounted his horse.

There was a smaller, white pony for the Woblo, which he mounted. He hadn't ridden a horse or pony much before this, so it took him a few minutes to adjust himself on the saddle of the animal, and the sword tended to be a little heavy to his liking, which left him slightly unbalanced. Once he got his bearing, he followed the others down the stone path which led to Dragginbuck. After about a mile up the road, while they rode their horses along the path, Barton turned towards Bargo.

"What do you normally do for a living, Woblo?"

"I'm a Blacksmith apprentice."

"Isn't that rather dangerous with all the fur you have?"

"I wear gloves, and I keep back a distance from the forge."

"Sounds like you know your business."

21

"I'm learning. My father's much better at it than myself. I'm much better at it than fighting, if that's what you mean."

"Just making conversation. It's going to be a long journey, and it's nice to get to know who's going to watch your back."

"And what's your story, Mr. Barton?" Lilly asked.

"Not much to tell. My parents broke up when I was young, and I guess I've been on my own since then, working various jobs, mostly as a fisherman, and as a farmhand."

"So what qualifies you to be on this journey?"

"Should I tell her, or are you going to?" Glam asked.

"I will," Barton said. "About twenty years ago, I was in the Shudolin Naval Brigade, and was sailing on a ship called the Astenonia. When it was attacked by Licarion forces, I saved some men from drowning. It wasn't anything anybody else wouldn't have done in my position."

"That's not the whole story, however. After he saved the men, he climbed onboard the enemy ship, and single handedly did away with the whole Licarion crew of thirty."

"Remind me not to get on your bad side," Bargo laughed.

"What about you, Lassie, what's your tale?" Barton asked the young woman.

"I've been married to my husband, Lawrence, for 10 years, and we have a farm near Woblo Town. And I'm pretty good with a sword."

"Ever seen battle?"

"Eight years ago, our farm was attacked by Grassmen. My father trained me some before he died, but my real training was that night. There were eight of them; my husband held off three, until he was struck unconscious. I held off the others."

"Did you kill any of them?" Bargo asked, surprised at her aggressiveness.

"Of course. I killed all of them." Bargo looked astonished at the statement, and Barton just laughed.

"It's seems there's more to the Lassie than meets the eye!"

"I'd prefer you don't call me that anymore." He could tell she already didn't like him much, just like other woman he met of her stature.

"Okay, you win. What would you like me to call you?"

"Lilly's fine. Or you can call me Mrs. Tumberhill."

"Married, huh? Okay, Lilly, it is."

"We'd better pick up the pace if we want to reach Dragginbuck by sundown," Glam said. "The Licarions will be out after dark, and we're more vulnerable on the trail. Besides, I believe we're being watched and tracked."

"By the Licarions?" Bargo asked.

"By somebody."

"Probably your father," Lilly laughed. "I still can't believe you didn't tell him about it."

"He did," Glam answered, as he turned away. "He just wouldn't listen; the same way he wouldn't listen to his superior officer twenty years ago."

"What do you mean?" Bargo asked.

"Forgive me. I misspoke when I shouldn't have. That was the past, and I should bury it, along with my grievances. I merely meant your father can be a stubborn man."

"Don't I know that."

"Well if it's him, you think he would just come and take Bargo home," Lilly stated.

"That's why I don't believe it's him," Glam said. "Let's just get there before dark, shall we?"

While the horses galloped down the long and twisting trail, Bargo couldn't help but sense something more than the Licarions; something which drew him towards it, but had no idea what it was. He felt an evil, dark feeling again, like someone or something watched him from afar, even beyond the Shudolin, and across the sea. It was the same feeling he had back in the Blacksmith shop the day before. In fear, he kept close to Lilly's side, her being the most familiar to him.

By sunset, they reached Dragginbuck without an incident. They approached the large town, as the glow of orange light from the street candles dotted the landscape of cobblestone paths and rustic old stone buildings. Glam led the way, greeted by several of the townspeople, who knew him as an ambassador for the Elven folk, and a leader from the Shudolin Royal Guard.

Barton followed behind him, as several people gazed at his rough appearance with indifference; reminding them of homeless people. It was when they saw Lilly, and then Bargo, they stared insistently, as if they never saw women carrying swords, or a Woblo for that matter. Woblos simply didn't travel this far east, and certainly didn't congregate much with humans,-at least around here. There were a few exceptions, such as Joeseph Lynden, who they were on their way to see.

They ventured down a couple of side roads, until they came to the back door of a place called the Collena Inn. Glam dismounted his horse and tied the reigns around the post provided. The others followed, as Glam knocked loudly three times, and then once more. The door was answered by a tall, burly fellow with long, dark brown hair who was missing several front teeth from a few brawls he recently got into.

"Is he in?" Glam asked.

"Yea, but they have to wait out here," he said, referring to the rest of them. "Except the Woblo."

The others were surprised they allowed him to go in.

"Keep a close watch," Glam told Pocor. "You never know what scum is lurking in the night. Saboteurs, thieves, and of course, Licarions."

The tall man opened the door, and Bargo walked in with Glam. Sitting at a tall table with a tall glass of Winterburry ale was an older, gray colored woblo. This was his Uncle Joeseph, who once fought along side his father. He looked as rugged as his father, although quite a few years older.

"Bargo, my Boy. I'm so glad to see you! It's been such a long time."

"About fifteen years, Uncle. You look well."

"As you do. I must admit, you're the last one I'd expect to see here. Does your father know you're here?"

"By now he does, I'm sure."

"Come on, sit down, sit down." He turned to the Elf who brought him in. "Glam, why don't you fetch a couple of ales for you and my nephew here?" He nodded, and left the back room towards the bar. "You know your father would kill me if I allowed you to help us?"

"Like I told the others, I'm my own Woblo."

"How's your father doing these days?"

"He's well. He works hard everyday in his shop. He's been a little bitter since I moved out, however."

"It's the first time since your mother died he's had to deal with being alone. He'll deal with it one way or another. He hasn't been drinking, has he?"

"No, no."

Glam returned with drinks, and sat down next to Joeseph. "Well, here's to forming an alliance," he said, as he raised his glass. The others clinked their glasses together with him. "To the son of Jeremiah Lynden. May he be as ruthless and fierce a fighter as his father."

"Here, here," Joeseph said, as he took a sip. "Has Glam told you anything about the nature of the mission?"

"Yes, some," Bargo answered. "He told me Barlow and the king were kidnapped by the Licarions."

"Yes. And it's up to us to get them back. The last information we received was from Riverton, from a reliable source there. They said they were heading south towards North Licarion City."

"So we're heading to Riverton?"

"Yes, in a day or two, when we can charter a boat," Glam said. "We'll have to be on our toes tonight. The Licarions have spies everywhere, and some are even humans and Elves."

"You can bed downstairs in the store room," Joeseph said. "Glam will keep guard, half the night, and I'll take the other half. The rest of you will need your rest for training."

"Training?" Bargo asked Glam in confusion.

"You don't expect to go out there without training, do you?"

"Well, I suppose not. I just thought we were leaving right away."

"I have a man tracking them as we speak. He's been advised to do nothing but observe. If Jeremiah shows up tomorrow, though, we could have a problem."

"I'll deal with my brother," Joeseph said. "I'll convince him I haven't seen him. The boy has to become a man someday."

"Good luck. My father's not so easily convinced," Bargo said.

"He'll listen to me."

"I hope you're right," Glam said, as he smirked. "You should've seen what he did to this big guy in the pub."

"I have a way with my brother. He never gets mad at me, and even if he did, I'm twice as fast with a right hook than he is, even at my age."

"I had no idea you wobloes were so feisty. It's a refreshing trait."

"I'm glad you enjoy it. Call your friends in, and show them to their quarters."

The small troop was shown to the cold, dark cobblestone basement, with just the light of an oil lamp, which the older Woblo carried. There were various wood crates throughout the fifty by thirty feet wide space, as well as barrels of wine and ale. Joeseph prepared a corner for them with some straw, as well as a few quilts.

"I'm sorry for the accommodations," he stated. "But the less attention we draw, the better."

"It's not raining or snowing in here, so we're fine," Barton said.

"I've had worse," Lilly added.

"Very well, then," Glam said. "I'll be at the top of the stairs if you need anything. Do not leave here without checking with me or Joeseph first."

"What if we have to relieve ourselves?" Barton asked.

"Let me know, and I'll follow you."

"Sounds no different than the militia to me."

"It's for your own protection. Sleep well. and we'll see you in the morning."

Joeseph and Glam left the basement, as the small party got comfortable with their lodgings. Lilly laid out one quilt to lie on, and another to cover herself with, as Barton lit his pipe, and watched her.

"Would you mind not smoking while we're down here?"

He took a puff, blew it out, and put his finger in it to extinguish it.

"Sorry. I wouldn't want to offend you."

"You're damn right you wouldn't."

"Ah yes, and the lady curses as well. Splendid."

"And don't get any ideas in the night. You know what they do to men who attack women around here."

"Don't worry about that. I wouldn't want to feel the other end of your sword."

"Well, I'm happy for that. Bargo, how well do you know your uncle?"

"Fairly well, although I haven't seen him in a long time."

"Can we trust him?"

"Of course, I trust him with my life!"

"Well, we may have to," one of the Elves said.

"And what's your story?" Barton asked him.

"I am a member of the Elven Royal Guard, as well as Pocor here.," Tamarka said. "We were sent here as backup, and are both skilled with a bow and sword."

"I don't understand why this Glam didn't get more of your own people, instead of recruiting everyday town folk."

"What, Elves? Because the Licarions are sly and resourceful adversaries, and can detect soldiers and Elves coming a mile away," Tamarka answered.

"A Woblo will be the last thing they'd be looking for," Pocor said. "Did Glam tell you why you're really here, Mr. Lynden?"

"To help get the king and my cousin Barlow back."

"Yes, but there's more," Tamarka said. "He needs you to find something for him."

"What?"

"We don't know," Pocor said. "He won't tell us."

"Where is this item he wants me to find?" Bargo didn't like where this conversation was going, and for the first time since he left, felt like he wanted to give up, and go back to Woblo Town.

"In the heart of the Licarion Territory," Tamarka said. "I'm surprised he didn't tell you yet."

"He probably figured if he did, you'd refuse," Lilly said. "You can't do this, Bargo, it's too dangerous!"

"Did you come along as a fellow soldier, or as his mother?" Barton asked.

Lilly grew angry with his attitude.

"Unlike you, Mr. Barton, I care about Bargo. I've known him since we were both young, and I would hate to see him get involved in something which may cost him his life. I thought we were all in this together."

"We are," Tamarka said. "That's why you're going to help him find it."

Barton laughed at her.

"You asked for it."

"What about your father?" she asked Bargo.

"What about him?"

"Have you thought about what you're going to say when he gets here?"

"He'll say nothing to him," Pocor said. "Joeseph and Glam will deny ever seeing him."

"I hope you're right," she said. "If I know Jeremiah, he'll tear the place apart until he finds him, and won't give up until he does."

CHAPTER THREE: LEGENDS OF OLD

Bargo, the last to wake up the next morning, rubbed his eyes, and watched Lilly sharpen her knife, which she kept on her belt in a sheath, while Barton smoked his pipe. The two Elves practiced with their swords under Glam's supervision. Once he noticed the Woblo was awake, he walked over to him, and offered him a cup of tea, as he sat down on the steps of the cellar.

"When Tamarka and Pocor are finished, you and I will practice."

"I'm no match for you."

"It's only training. I will go easy on you, I promise."

"There isn't much room down here."

"There's enough to serve our purpose. Besides, you need to learn to fight in enclosed spaces. Once we reach Licarion Territory, much of our fighting will be underground."

"The others mentioned something about finding something for you."

"That's nothing you need to be concerned about right now. I will explain more once we reach our destination. Shall we begin?"

The two Elves moved out of the way so Bargo could have his turn. Glam held out his sword to initiate the simulated conflict, and Bargo mimicked his actions. Due to the weight of the weapon, he had trouble lifting it to swing it, which made Barton laugh.

"He can't even lift the damn thing, let alone swing it at you."

Glam looked at him, annoyed by his remark.

"Try this one," he said, and handed him a shorter, thinner sword with Elven markings on it. "It was given to me by my father, Slamondra. It is said to have belonged to the great Elven king Fioratu, who gave it to my father for saving his life with it. If you can learn to use it, I'll give it to you."

"I'll do my best," he said, as he handed his old sword to Lilly. "Now, pay attention. "When I go high, and come down, you hold

29

your sword low and close to your body, but above your head. When I come low, block my swing. Let's try, shall we?"

Glam swung his sword down, Bargo pressed the Elven blade against it, and backed up, until he fell over into the crates. Barton shook his head, and waved his arm.

"Bargo, concentrate. Get up, and we'll try again."

"I don't know. Maybe my father was right. Maybe I'm not cut out for this."

"You are as only as brave as you believe, Master Bargo," Lilly said. "Even though you're small, I have faith, and know you can do this."

Bargo again raised his sword with both hands, and positioned himself for defense. Glam did the same, and swung high, as the blades met in mid air. Glam pressed it hard against his, as the Woblo exerted all his force to push him successfully away. He then swung several times, as the Elf blocked his sword.

"Good, good. Now you're getting the hang of it."

The Elf went to swing at his head, and the Woblo ducked, placing his leg behind his trainer's. He then knocked him to the floor, as he fell into a crate, and onto his behind. Barton laughed loudly at the spectacle.

"Look's like the teacher needs a refresher course himself."

"He got lucky on that one. But tripping me was a very good tactic. Why don't we take a break?"

He sat down on the crate next to him, while Bargo sat down on the steps, and stared at the sword he used, and the Elven writing on its blade.

"You talked about your father getting this sword from the Elven king. What does the writing on it say?"

"From duty comes honor, from honor comes everlasting life. He who possesses everlasting life, possesses tranquility. It is a very old style of language, and is seldom used anymore."

"What was the Elven Kingdom like? What was Fioratu like?"

"He was a great king of his land, a protector of his people, a father to his children, and a great warrior. The Elven kingdom was attacked by Garlock, the sorcerer. and his evil army of Glorcs. Fioratu and his army defeated them, and crushed their evil influence."

"Glorcs?"

"Yes, they are bipedal, hairy creatures, similar to wolves, with inch long claws, and razor sharp teeth. They are five feet tall, and very quick. They were also assisted by the Licarions, but were forced out of the land by the Elves and men who bravely stood by their king's side to abolish them. Garlock had no choice but to flee the land and take to the sea, and Bereuka Island, where he was said to be exiled."

"We've heard of this sorcerer called Garlock," Lilly remarked. "I've also heard they are nothing but silly fairytales. Everyone knows there's no such thing as magic."

"Ah, but that's where you're wrong," Glam corrected her. "The stories are real. It's said that if one travels to Bereuka Island, the home of Garlock's castle, they'll be plagued by violent storms, sea serpents, and the spirits of those he imprisoned for eternity. They are said to live in the sea as Fishmen, who climb the side of a ship and pull on the mooring lines, until the ship is pulled under the sea."

"Like I said, fairytales," Lilly laughed.

"I think not. I know someone who's been there."

"They say nobody's ever returned from there," Barton said.

"This man has, and swore to me Garlock was still alive."

"I knew it!" Bargo said, as he realized his premonition was right.

"If he is, why hasn't he attacked the Shudolin?" Barton asked.

"The Elven king crushed his reign by finding his source of power, and destroying it."

"And what was that?" Bargo asked.

"It was called the 'Staff of Varlana,' named after the land it came from. It contained a large blue stone called 'The Zahara stone,' or better known as 'the Gem of Rebolin,' and a spear tip forged from the Volcano Rebolin by Rhiatu himself. Gootok, an evil Glorcion king, who was said to be Garlok's father, stole the staff, and used it for his own evil purposes. His mother was an Elven princess named Giariak. Once the staff's power was said to be destroyed, Garlock became limited to only simple magic."

"How was it destroyed?" Bargo asked.

"Actually, it can never be truly destroyed. It's needed in the

31

fight against evil. It was only scattered about the lands in various parts and unknown places; the staff in one, the tip and stone in another. Nobody knows where the staff and tip are."

"But you know where the stone is?" Barton asked.

"No, not personally. But I know someone who may."

"Is this really still about saving the king, or something else?" Lilly asked.

"Yes, of course it is. Bargo asked me a question, and I'm just answering it."

"I still think it's just a bunch of stories. Until you prove different, I don't believe in those old Elven fables."

"Fioratu was no fable. He was a great king and warrior. Garlock stole his bride and threw her into the sea, and he vowed his revenge. He gave his life to save this great land from Glorcion rule."

"I wasn't referring to him. I was referring to the magic rubbish."

"You will see that you shouldn't make a mockery of the legends when the warlock returns. It is said he sends his mercenaries throughout the lands and sea to find the weapon to rebuild it, in hopes he may one day rule the Shudolin again."

"Well, when that day comes," Barton jested. "I'll be the first one to put an arrow in his eye."

"Silly fool. Do you think an arrow can stop a sorcerer?"

"I don't know, I've never tried to shoot one."

"Foolish notion, Barton. Garlock once had powers far beyond anything you've ever seen. He could turn a river to blood, make a whole town burn to the ground, and plunge the country into an eternal darkness."

"And now?" Lilly asked.

"He's confined to the island with only the power to keep invaders away."

"Why doesn't anyone try to finish him off completely?" Bargo asked.

"Many have tried, but all have failed."

"Well, if you decide to try, count me out," Barton sneered.

"What's the matter, Laddy?" Lilly asked him. "A little scared of superstitions?"

Barton scratched his face, and smiled at her, as his missing tooth caught her attention.

"No. It's just not what I signed up for."

"Don't worry," Glam said. "If I ever undertake that mission, I'll make sure we come equipped with the Shudolin Navy. That's not the focus of why we're here."

Lilly looked deep into the Elf's eyes, and walked towards him until they were face to face.

"For some strange reason I feel you're lying to us, and you're hiding something. I'm not sure what it is, but by the time we get to Riverton, I'll find out."

"When we get to Riverton, everything will be explained to you."

"Is that the Elven way, or the kingdom's way?" Barton asked.

He frowned, looked up the stairway, and then back at the troop.

"It's getting late; it's time to see about getting a boat for tomorrow, and provisions at the market. It'll be a two day trip up the river."

"Aren't you forgetting something?" Lilly asked. "What about Bargo's father? He'll be coming here."

"If he does, Bargo will have to face him, and tell him, that's all."

"That's all?" Bargo sighed, nervous. "You have no idea how mad he'll get."

"Well, we'll cross that bridge when we get to it."

They walked up into the pantry, where Joeseph prepared breakfast for some of his guests who slept the night off upstairs. He scrambled some eggs in a pan on a hot plate which rested over the fireplace.

"Morning, gentlemen, and Lady," he said.

"Morning, Joeseph," Glam answered. "Listen, if Bargo's father shows up, could you possibly steer him in the wrong direction?"

"Of course. I think I can handle my younger brother. He won't give you any trouble."

"Thanks, Uncle Joeseph."

"Don't mention it, Bargo. I was young and spirited once my self."

"What about my father? What was he like?"

"Oh, the stories I can tell about your father and I. I remember when we were fighting the Licarions down in Fort Shendlekend, and your father was captured."

"Really, Joeseph," interrupted Glam. "We must get-"

"My father was captured by the Licarions?" Bargo asked.

"Yes. He and I were part of an operation to sustain a base down there when the Licarions attacked. They don't have much of a naval force, but there were a sufficient amount of ships that we were outnumbered. They overtook us, and captured or killed all of our crews. Bargo and I were taken to North Licarion City to be executed."

"How did you escape?"

"It was your father who helped us escape."

"Joeseph, he doesn't need to hear about days of glory passed," Glam said, rather annoyed he was wasting time.

"But he needs to hear about fairytales?" Lilly quipped.

"Anyway," the older Woblo continued. "He was taken down to the dungeon, where he was left with no food or water, until the king decided when he was to be killed."

"So how'd he escape?" the impatient young Woblo asked.

"The bars were rather loose around the stone, so he was able to dig his way out with the bar he pried loose. By the time they found him, he successfully killed two of the guards, and stole their swords. The skilled swordsman he was, it wasn't long before he freed all of us, we overtook the royal chambers, and escaped."

"I knew my father was a great warrior. So why is he so against me having a little fun and adventure?"

"He only wants what's best for you," Lilly answered. "He doesn't want you to make the same mistakes he made in the past."

"Like his leg?"

"Exactly. But have no fear, you are with some of the best warriors the Shudolin has to offer."

"Do you really mean that?" Barton asked.

"Of course I do," Lilly said. "But don't take that as an invitation for a courtship or anything."

"Duly noted, Mrs. Lilly."

"We are wasting valuable time," Glam reminded them.

"Glam is right, we best get going," Barton said.

They said goodbye to Joeseph, headed out the door and down the cobblestone path, which was now flooded with people. The crowd again stared at the unlikely bunch, especially Bargo, which made him extremely uncomfortable. It was as if he were an outcast of some kind; back home Woblos were common, and here they were some kind of freak of nature. As he stared back at their faces, he saw bewilderment, curiosity, pity, anger, and even indifference.

They walked four blocks, until they were at the waterline of Garlo lake, where there were several small river ships under 20 feet, with single sails supported by single masts. They had a cabin underneath which bedded maybe ten people at the most. Glam approached a man at the docks with a thick black beard who appeared weathered from his life as a man of the sea. He shook his strong, burly hand, and looked up at his six feet frame.

"Hello, Walter," he said. "Any chance we could barter for a ship?"

"Depends on what you have to barter."

"How about 100 gold pieces?"

Walter rolled his eyes at the offer, and glanced over to a twenty feet open boat with no cabin, and a single sail. "That's what 100 will get you. It is a very fast boat, however. It will get you to Riverton in a day or two."

"Yes, if the rain don't sink us first. Especially this time of year. How about giving us one of the other ones for 50 more?"

"I'm sorry but that just isn't going to work for me. I need at least 500 on those."

"Very well, then, we'll take the long boat. You drive a hard bargain, Walter." He handed the gold pieces to the man, and then walked back to his colleagues. "Here are twenty five gold pieces to buy what we need for our trip. Pocor knows what provisions to pick up. I will meet you back at Joeseph's Inn in a couple of hours. I have some other business to attend to while I'm here. Please, stay out of trouble while we're here, and if you see Jeremiah, don't let him drag Bargo back without talking to myself or Joeseph first.?"

"Don't worry, we'll keep an eye on him," Barton said.

"That's what I'm worried about," Glam said in a half-smile.

Barton smiled back, as they proceeded to walk the seven

blocks to the market. He turned to Pocor, as the Elf kept his right hand on his sword sheath as he strolled.

"How long have you known Glam?" he asked him, when he knew they were out of his hearing distance.

"A long time," he answered. "I know he seems a little secretive sometimes, but in his job, it's necessary to conceal the truth when needed."

"This stone he claims his friend has found, what do you know about it?"

"He never said he found it, only that he knows where he might be able to find it."

"Is that the reason he wants us to do this, is to find the stone?"

"You ask too many questions, Mr. Barton. Why can't you just accept you're on a mission for king and country?"

"Cause king and country haven't done much for me lately."

"The market's just up here around the corner. Please don't say anything to anyone, even if they speak to you. I'll do all the talking, is that clear?"

"Of course," Barton answered.

Once they entered the large square where the market was, they were inundated by hundreds of people who scavenged through the various fruits and vegetables to find the best pick of the day. Pocor grabbed some apples, grapes, berries, as well as some carrots and beets, paid the merchant, and placed them into a burlap sack. They walked further, where the Elf picked up some rope, some canteens, an oil lamp, and some bows and arrows. He noticed two men behind Bargo who taunted him.

"Hey rabbit-face," one said to him, as he pushed him. "Turn around."

"Please leave me alone," Bargo told him.

"You better do what he says," the other said. "Or he'll peck you to death."

Pocor turned around to face the men.

"Is there a problem, Gentlemen?"

"Yes," the first man said. "We don't allow pets to roam free around the market."

"He's not a pet," Pocor answered. "He's a friend."

"You have a poor choice in friends," the second man said.

"Perhaps as outsiders, you think you have a special privilege around here. Perhaps we should turn you over to the constable."

"If you believe I've broken the law, that is your right."

"Well," the second man said. "Let this just be a warning to you. We don't want any freaks around here."

Bargo grew angry at his remark, and pushed the man, which knocked him into the apple crate, causing the fruit to scatter around the ground. As his friend lay in the pile, the other man became angered by the Woblo.

"You little beast!" he yelled.

Pocor jumped in front of him and drew his sword, placing it at the man's throat.

"Let it go."

Bargo and the others backed away, as the man did the same, and the Elf helped his friend to his feet. The others proceeded to walk away, but Pocor faced the men until they were out of sight. They thought they lost them while they looked through the rest of the market, but as Bargo looked over some stone jewelry, he was shoved back, this time to the ground. When he rose to his feet, he was faced by his own father.

"Bargo?" the surprised Woblo said.

"You know this squab, Fur face?" the first man, now alone, asked.

"He's my son, and don't call me Fur face."

"What are you going to do about it?"

Before the man could move, Jeremiah punched him in the stomach, and then in the face. He then turned to face his son, who already left the area. He started to walk towards the direction he believed he ventured, but was intercepted by his brother, Joeseph.

"Jeremiah," Joeseph said, as he acted surprised. "What brings you to Dragginbuck?"

"You know damn well why I'm here. Where is he?"

"Who?"

"You know damn well who-Bargo."

"Why would he be here?"

"Come on, Brother. I know you're still connected with the king."

"I gave up that kind of work years ago. I just run the inn now.

Perhaps you and I can go back there and have a cup of tea. It's been a while since we've talked."

"I don't believe you're condoning this. He's just a young Woblo. He has his whole life ahead of him."

"Whatever are you talking about, Brother? Come, let's have some tea."

"Well, I could use something warm to drink after my journey. But after that, I want some answers."

"As you wish, Jeremiah. Ah, it's so nice to see you again. I miss the good old days."

"They weren't so good to me. The tortures of fellow soldiers, and comrades fallen isn't something I relish about the good old days. You're a sentimentalist, Joeseph."

"And you are a stubborn old Woblo who refuses to let his son grow up."

"If growing up means him dying in the process, then I hope he never comes of age."

CHAPTER FOUR: ON THE RIVER

Joeseph prepared the kettle of water in the fireplace, and poured a cup of tea for each of them. "Have a seat, Jeremiah," he told him, as he directed him to the seat which faced away from the back door. He purposely did this, so he would know when his friends returned. He sat, and took a sip of the tea.

"Delicious. You certainly are the accommodating host, Joeseph. How is business going these days?"

"Fairly well. But a lot of my guests in the inn are guys sleeping off the night with hardly any money. I don't get many paying guests anymore, and most of the money is from the bar."

"Well, I'll pay for the night, if you can tell me where to find my son."

"Jeremiah, he's a strong willed boy, why don't you give him a little leeway?"

"Did you give Barlow any leeway?"

"Well, you know the circumstances were a little different with him."

"And now I hear he's missing. And you want to lecture me on parenting?"

"Forgive me, Jeremiah, I don't want to start our visit on a bad note. I'm just concerned making him follow in your footsteps by keeping him at the shop might make him go wayward anyway. We all get bored with our jobs, even me."

"Bargo knows I need his help. He's always been a good boy."

"Which is precisely why you should trust him to make the right decisions. He needs his freedom right now."

"Does he now?" Bargo chuckled. "I thought what he really needed was a good beating."

"Jeremiah, don't talk like that, you know you're not that way."

He saw Glam's face in the doorway, and the Elf quickly backed a way, and pushed the others back as well. Jeremiah noticed his brother looking at the window, and turned around to

BARGO LYNDEN

see what he was looking at.

"Something wrong?"

"No, just thinking about what to serve for dinner tonight."

"How about my son on a silver platter?"

The older Woblo laughed at his quip.

"Why don't we take a trip up front so I can show you around the place, maybe find you a room?"

"You're not going to tell me where he is, are you?"

"Jeremiah, you know me better than that."

"If I find him, he's coming home with me."

"Shouldn't that be his own decision?"

"He's got delusions this adventure is all going to be fun and games. You and I both know how war can end up."

"He's a grown Woblo, and he'll have to learn to defend himself sooner or later."

"I know that, but I need to teach him those things, not some Elf from the Royal Guard."

"But you haven't, only how to shoe horses."

"Being an Iron smith is important to me, and it gives me pride to know my son will carry on the business."

"It seems to me I once knew a young Woblo who also sought out excitement and adventure, and refused to follow his parents' wishes as well."

"I know, I know. But ever since Elizabeth died, I vowed to her he wouldn't lead that kind of life."

"You shouldn't promise something you can't deliver on."

"Perhaps you're right, and maybe someday I'll let him join the academy. But not on this trip. It's a job for mercenaries and soldiers, not a small group of amateurs. Bargo is no swordsman."

"And neither were you, but you learned quickly, as he will too."

"I was different."

"In what way? You were just as stubborn, pigheaded, and difficult as he is."

"Yea, yea, don't remind me. Well, if you do see him, don't tell him I'm here. I don't want you scaring him off."

"Now why would I do that?"

"Because, my older brother, it's the way you are."

"Come on, let me show you around, and we'll find you a room for the night." He nodded, they left the pantry, and walked into the tavern.

The others slipped through the door unnoticed with their provisions, and headed down into the cobblestone basement. Glam peeked through the tavern door to make sure Joeseph kept his brother away, then followed.

Bargo sighed in relief, as he dropped one of the burlap sacks to the floor.

"That was close."

"Why would Joeseph bring him here?" Lilly asked their Elf commander.

"Because he would have came here anyway. What better hiding place than right under his nose."

"I see your point. But what's to prevent him from coming down here?"

"Joeseph, that's what. He'll do his best to keep him occupied until we leave in the morning."

Lilly glanced at the worried look Bargo had on his face. "What's wrong, Bargo? Having second thoughts?"

"Just a little nervous is all, with my father right upstairs."

"By the time he gets up in the morning, we'll be halfway down the lake," Glam said.

"I hope you're right. My father can be very persistent."

"Well, it'll be dark soon, so it'll be best we light some lamps. I'll keep the first watch, then Barton, then Pocor. So far we haven't run into any spies, but that may change the closer we get to Riverton."

The next morning, they were out of the basement before sunrise, and walked the three blocks to the pier. Barton looked at the vessels, which were lined up two in a row on each dock.

"Which one's ours?" he asked, as Glam pointed to the longboat on the near end.

"That one."

"You've got to be kidding. We'll get soaked in that thing,"

"Do you have 500 gold pieces to charter the others?"

"No."

"Then keep your opinion to yourself, and find a way to stay

dry on our voyage."

"I don't know how we're going to do that," Bargo said. "It already looks like rain."

"Pocor and Tamarka will load the provisions, and we'll be on our way."

The two Elves loaded the gear into the longboat, as the others climbed on board. When Bargo got in, he noticed the small bag with his magnifying glass was missing. He looked all around, but couldn't find it.

"I lost my magnifying glass. I must have dropped it."

"We don't have time to look for it," Glam said, while he untied the bow and aft lines.

"You don't understand. I need it."

"And your father is on his way right now to stop you. In fact, here he comes up the road now."

They could see the faint figure of the patriarchal Woblo hobble down the road. He stopped and picked up Bargo's bag that he dropped. He yelled to them, but they could only faintly hear him, as the boat quickly drifted from his sight, until he was like an ant on the landscape.

Glam and Pocor raised the single sail onto the mast, as the others positioned themselves in the boat. The wind picked up, and they took advantage of the direction it was blowing, which was downstream towards the river. After they raised it to full mast, Glam turned towards Bargo.

"Grab that jackline rope, and tie it around each of your waists. We're probably going to run into some rough weather in a couple of hours, due to the storm coming. It's better if you go overboard to have something to hang onto still attached to the boat."

"Go overboard?" Bargo asked. "Glam, there's something I have to tell you."

"What is it?"

"I can't swim."

"That's just great," Barton sneered. "Not only does the Woblo not know how to fight or shoot, he can't even swim!"

"As I told you once before," Glam barked at him. "There is no room for bigotry on this quest, or any other kind of nonsense. If you do it again, you'll be swimming back to Dragginbuck. With a little luck, we can reach Sanctin Creek by morning, depending on the storm. If the Woblo falls in, I'll fish him out myself."

"You did it again," Lilly said to him.

"Did what?"

"You referred to our mission as a quest, as if you were looking for something. A blue stone, perhaps?"

"I'm sorry. I misspoke."

"Yea, right," Barton said, as he pulled out his knife to sharpen it. He stroked the knife against the sharpening stone four or fives times, put it back in his sheath, and smiled at the Woblo. "I like to keep it razor sharp. That way I can slice off an ear or two if necessary."

Bargo gave a nervous smile, and then handed him the rope. He tied it around his waist, and handed it to Lilly, who did the same. The Elves, who commandeered the boat, remained line free.

"The Licarion and Grassmen attacks have been occurring close to the Monko Peninsula, so once we reach there, stay alert. We'll need to have bows ready, because they are expert marksmen, they're quick, and can also swim extremely well."

"I never shot an arrow at someone before either," Bargo stated.

"Stay down then, on the floor of the boat. We'll cover you."

"Useless," Barton muttered, loud enough for the Woblo to hear, but quiet enough where Glam didn't.

Lilly just gave him a disgusted look, and stared at the scenery of the lakeshore. The oak and maple trees just started to grow leaves, and the sea of wild daffodils and petunias blanketed the landscape. The cattails just emerged from the water, due to the high level of the lake. She turned to Bargo, who was just as entranced by it, having never left his small town near the Forbian forest.

"Pretty, isn't it?" she asked.

"Yes. I never been on the lake before. It's beautiful."

"The storm doesn't look too beautiful," Glam said. "It'll be coming up quicker than I thought. Pocor, you're the sailing expert, how high do you think the waves will be if the wind is forty knots?"

"Four feet, possibly, perhaps five."

"Which is it, four or five?" Barton asked, as he rolled his eyes.

"It's hard to say, but I would guess four."

"How deep is the hull?"

"Five feet," Glam said. "It'll be a little rough, but we should be okay. The rest of you might want to sit on the floor of the boat, and not on the seats. You can be thrown from the seat."

They followed his orders, as the waves slowly increased in roughness, and it rained heavily. "Great," Barton snarled. "I'm getting wet without even leaving the boat."

"Get used to it," Glam told him. "This whole journey is going to be a fight against the weather."

"Now look who's whining," Lilly said, as she smiled, her rosy red cheeks accentuating her dimples.

The Woblo was the most scared and kept quiet, trying to keep himself warm, while the cold, bitter rain pelted his soft, brown fur. His ears stung from the loud thunder bursts all around them. Pocor adjusted the rudder to steer the boat to the right, and closer to land, as he tried to direct the lightning strikes towards the shoreline and not the boat.

"Steady as she goes," Glam said. "We don't want to end up on the rocks."

"Glam, can I ask you something?" Bargo asked.

"Sure, Kid. What is it?"

"My cousin Joe Garkee is in the navy, and he started when he was twenty. How long is the term you must serve as a seaman, before you can become an officer?"

He laughed at the creature's question.

""Four years. Why? Are you thinking about becoming a sailor?"

"No. I was just wondering how he could be on a boat for such long periods of time, that's all."

"It isn't easy. This is just a little squall that'll pass, some storms at sea can be man killers."

Just as he said that, a gust of wind blew the boom to the right, and Bargo fell to the floor so it wouldn't hit him in the head. Tamarka held on tight to the kicking strap, as the boat leaned to the right, just above the waterline. After he finally gained control of the boat, when the wind died down a bit, he was able to pull it back over and tacked in another direction. In the quiet calm, Glam placed his hand on Tamarka's shoulder.

"Good job," he said in praise.

"Thanks, Sir."

By this time, the clouds passed, the sun reappeared and began to set in the west. Licarions were nocturnal creatures, couldn't stand the daylight, and seldom left their underground caverns. These were desperate times, however, and they became bolder, and took more risks, including entering into Shudolin Kingdom territory for their attacks.

When Bargo thought about the story his uncle told him earlier, he understood why he should fear them. They were quick and clever, struck at the most vulnerable point, and showed no mercy. He saw why his father no longer wanted any part of battle, and settled down to a quiet life. What he didn't understand is why he didn't want him to pursue his own dreams, and expected him to live the same, dull life he currently led.

Scared and fascinated of what was to come, he knew his newfound friends would protect him from harm. He felt somewhat safe he had a weapon himself, even if he only was a beginner with it, and figured it only took one good strike to put an enemy down.

Glam suggested they sail to the south of Vork Island, where the passage was the most narrow, and also the most dangerous. He normally wouldn't have taken this route, but the other way was another fifty miles around the north end of the island. This meant they risked an attack from either of the enemy factions. The Grassmen, most prevalent in the area, were green, vicious, hairy creatures, with two inch razor sharp claws, and a taste for human flesh. They often hunted local townspeople who happened to accidentally enter their territory, which was limited to the grasslands south of the Swift River.

It was said an evil Elf named Ang was their leader, and the negotiator between them and the Licarions. They banded together several times to try to overcome the Shudolin Kingdom, but always failed. Ang lost an eye in a battle near Jarod, and wore an eye patch over his left eye. He also had a two inch scar from Glam's blade, which left him very distinguishable from other Elves. He never forgave his long time classmate of the academy, and vowed to someday seek revenge against him. Glam knew this, and always stayed prepared for his return.

The evening descended upon the rain soaked crew, and as the sun dropped, so did the temperature. Just as the Woblo began to dry off, the cold spring night reminded him how nice it was to be in front of a warm fire. He already had second thoughts, and wished he was in a cozy, comfortable flat. The others didn't seem to mind it as much, except Lilly, who threw her maroon colored, hand sewn quilt around herself to stay warm. She saw Bargo chilled as well, and invited him to share it with him, putting her arm around him. He obliged, while Barton smiled, still fixed on the idea he was nothing more than a glorified pet.

The water calmed down a bit, and the moonless night became quiet, except for the sound of a far off owl, or the splash of a fish jumping out for a nighttime meal. Glam and Pocor watched closely, while each of the group dozed off, until only the two of them remained awake.

"If we travel through the strait, we may get attacked," he whispered to him, as he placed his hand on his shoulder. "If you can, take evasive action closer to the island."

"What if they're already on the island?" Pocor asked him.

"I doubt it. Licarions can swim well, but it's a good mile between the island and the peninsula. I believe they'd drown by then."

"Unless they're Fishmen."

"Don't be ridiculous. That story only pertains to Bereuka Island. At any rate, if we stay closer to the land, we should be all right. It's once we get closer to the river I'm worried about. Just be alert, and I'll do the same. If we get through the night, we'll stand a better chance."

"I hope you're right. I'm not sure this bunch will be able to hold off a full scale attack."

"Have faith, my brother. They may be more powerful a faction than you're willing to accept."

"We'll see. Why don't you wake Tamarka up to relieve you in a little while, and you can get some sleep at least?"

"Maybe later. I want to see us at least through most of the strait. With no wind, it'll be a slow process. We may have to use the oars."

They passed into the strait, and there was a loud crack on the island in the distance, which woke the others up. Glam drew his bow fast, and waited to see if he could see an object moving on the shoreline. After hearing nothing for a minute or two, they dismissed it as an animal, such as a fox on its nightly prowl. Glam kept his bow ready just in case, and the others went back to their slumber.

By morning, they made it halfway through the strait, and the wind again picked up enough for them to raise the sail, and continue on their path. The shorelines between the bodies of land started to narrow, however, and Glam grew concerned for everyone's safety. He only caught a couple hours of sleep, but for him this was enough to keep moving.

"Have your bows ready," he told his two Elven subordinates. "We're heading near Grassmen Territory, and they can be ruthless fighters."

"That's what I've heard too," Barton stated. "I once heard about a guy who tried to kill one, and he bit his whole hand off."

"Stay alert, and none of us will lose a hand, finger, or anything else. The three of us should be able to pick off most of them with arrows. That is, if they don't get us first. We'll be coming up on the river in about an hour."

Once they approached the river, the land was about a quarter mile apart, and the water was much shallower there, about ten feet deep, with a stronger current. At the tributary, the elevation dropped, it became much deeper there, and was less rough. Until then, they faced upcoming rapids which could possibly capsize or destroy the boat. Glam wanted to tie the jackline to the others again, but this would also leave them vulnerable to immobility.

They rounded the end of the peninsula, and the current carried them even faster. Glam knew there were small falls they needed to pass over before getting to the rest of the river. Bargo grabbed the side of the boat, as it rocked and bounced on the waves. Pocor took down the sail until they could pass through the rapids. While they swiftly moved down the river, Lilly noticed a figure move through the rocks above. She couldn't make out what it was, but it traveled rather quickly. She gestured for Tamarka to get ready with his bow, but he saw nothing. The waves began to go over the boat the further they ventured downstream. At one point, it seemed like the hull cracked upon some rocks, but upon further inspection, there wasn't any visible damage. They descended down the small waterfall with relative ease; the boat was immersed at one point, however, and there was at least an inch of water on the floor, but not enough to be concerned about sinking. Glam made sure everyone weathered the event safely, and checked the rocks above to make sure no one followed them.

At the very top of a cliff, he noticed a familiar figure in a dark cloak who stared down at him-Ang. He dropped his arm, and several Grassmen shot arrows at them. "Get down!" Glam yelled to the others, as he drew his long bow. He and the other Elves fired back, as three of the Grassmen fell dead into the water below. When they realized they were out numbered, Glam gave the command. "Get us out of here, Pocor, as fast as you can."

Pocor raised the sail and the boat continued down the river, while the arrows quickly followed behind them. Three or four hit the boat, and several entered onto the floor. Bargo hid under the security of Lilly's quilt, as several of the attackers threw rocks as well. They could see two other long boats coming towards them, full of Grassmen holding swords and bows. It was obvious they were trapped with no way out.

"What do we do now?" Bargo asked, as he poked his frightened head out from under the quilt.

"We prepare to fight," Lilly said, as she stood up and drew her sword.

"I don't think that would be wise at this point," Glam said. "If we do, we'll surely die, there are too many of them. We'll have to wait for a more opportune time. If I know my old friend Ang, he won't kill us right away."

He could see the one eyed Elf, as he came down the hill to where the land leveled out into a grass plain. "Don't kill them," he yelled from the shoreline. "Bring them to me."

The Grassmen boarded their boat, took their weapons, and tied them up. They then navigated the boat to the shoreline, where they tied it to a tree. They were led off the boat, and directed to walk in a westerly direction. After about a mile, they came to a small village which used to be inhabited, until the beasts killed the townspeople. They were led into a log and sod building, where Ang sat in a wicker chair, with one of the creatures at each side of him. He smiled, as Glam was brought before him.

"Good to see you again, my friend. What has it been, ten years?"

"Fifteen to be exact."

"Seems like just yesterday to me. Just yesterday that you scarred me for life."

"I did what I had to do."

"Just like I'm about to do what I have to." He glanced at the woblo. "Why do you have a Woblo with you?"

"It's a long story, and I haven't got the time."

"You're so right you haven't got the time. You'll be dead by sundown. That's about the time my friends get hungry."

"What happened to you, Ang? You used to speak proudly of the kingdom."

"Gold, my friend, and lots of it. More than you'll ever see in the Shudolin."

"Why have you broken the treaty by attacking this village and kidnapping us?"

"The Grassmen don't recognize treaties or laws. They take what they can conquer. As a spy for the Royal Guard, you should know that by now."

"Well, once the kingdom finds out what you've done here, they will send in the militia."

"And how will they make decisions without their king?"

"How did you know about that? Perhaps you had something to do with that?"

"Perhaps. Or maybe it's just that Glamara keeps me informed on what his plans are."

"My cousin is Barlow Lynden," Bargo blurted. "He was with the king. Is he okay?"

"Your rabbit friend here seems to have a little gumption to him," Ang said. "Unfortunately, I'm not aware of who your cousin is, his whereabouts, or his status. I'm not paid to be an informant, just an executioner. Your friends will become tonight's main course, but I have special plans for you. I'm going to make you suffer for a long time before I finally kill you."

"I can't say I'm looking forward to it," Glam said. "But if I can just get free, I'll definitely make sure I'll repay your act of kindness."

Ang laughed wildly at his remark.

"A fighter right to the end, huh? Well, when I get through with you, you'll be begging me to kill you."

Glam handled the situation well, considering he was out of options. It was at that particular moment, he wished Jeremiah came along after all. He was small, but he killed more Grassmen than anyone he ever heard of, and was the only one who could help them at this point. Somehow in his mind, he knew the lieutenant wouldn't give up looking for his son, and he would surely not let him die such a horrible death without a fight.

CHAPTER FIVE: THE PROFESSIONAL

By this time, Jeremiah saddled one of his ponies, and headed out to look for his son. He knew they had the advantage by boat, but his blessing was knowing their destination. He brought his old war sword; as well as a bow, and about twenty arrows. As he followed the river, he knew they were headed into dangerous territory, due to the fact he tracked Grassmen many times, and knew their migratory habits. They were nomads, and took whatever they could find or steal.

The last time he encountered them was towards the end of the last battle with the Licarions. There was an Elf with them who had an eye patch, but he was at a loss to remember his name. He knew he worked for both the Licarions and the Grassmen, although he didn't know the nature of his work. Jeremiah fought and killed many of the beasts, who invaded a small town near Bacon Hills, southwest of Riverton that left many of the townspeople dead.

He knew it would rain again soon, and he couldn't get too close to the embankment or he'd fall at least fifty feet into the river, or die on the way down. He kept back a bit, stayed in the woods, and used his pocket compass for direction. He reached the strait about noon, but they had a considerable jump on him, and in a way, he thought it was fruitless to follow them. His fatherly instinct, however, told him not to give up, for fear the group was already in trouble.

When they left, he saw the figure of a woman from the shoreline, and guessed it was Lilly. If anybody could take care of his son it would be her, but even though she was skilled with a sword, he still felt the Grassmen would get the better of them, due to shear numbers. They were vicious, cannibalistic killers, and trained to fight, conquer, and destroy everything in their path.

Once he reached the beginning of the river, he dismounted, and crouched down to the ground. Finding Grassmen tracks, he decided to walk a bit to follow them, and led his white pony behind him. He brought enough provisions for three days; the time he believed it would take to find the party.

Traveling further, he saw several more tracks, until the area was flooded with them. He noticed some tracks which were different from the others, possibly a man or Elf print. He believed this was their leader, and the Elf he saw many years back. He drew his sword for protection and glanced through the trees down the river, where he saw a 20 feet long boat with a single sail. He surmised this was the boat his son's friends used, but it was docked at the shoreline, and empty. He decided to investigate it, so he mounted the pony, and climbed down the embankment at a less steep angle.

At the bottom of the hill, there was a huge field stretching at least a mile. While on the hill, he noticed there was a village about two miles away, and guessed they may have gone there for supplies. When he reached the boat, and found it abandoned, this seemed a bit peculiar. He again dismounted the pony, and climbed into the boat. Inside it, he found packs, quilts, and weapons that were just left. He saw nothing inside had been taken, which also seemed strange. He placed Bargo's small bag with the magnifying glass in his larger sack, in case he might come back to the boat.

He climbed back out, mounted his pony again, and headed to the west towards the village of Old Monko, where he believed they headed. He again followed several tracks in a path towards the village. He approached with caution, for he wasn't protected by trees; only a few large bushes and tall grass, his enemy were notorious for using their greenish color for camouflage in grasslands. He used his sword to cut through the high vegetation, until he reached a solitary oak tree in the middle of the field. He dismounted again, hid behind the tree, pulled out his periscope, and looked through it at the village. He could see several Grassmen took the small village, and probably killed or ate the inhabitants.

He didn't see any sign of his friends, and wanted to get a closer look, but figured if he did, they would spot him in a minute. He put the periscope away in his pocket, looked at the hill to his south, and tried to figure out what to do to rescue his friends. He thought maybe he could get a better strategic position on the hill, but it would be difficult, for there were several of them, and he only had twenty arrows. He trotted over to the back of the hill and to the top, where he hid behind some bushes and trees, and got into position. He was at a good vantage point to shoot several of them, and would have no problem doing so, having the ability to shoot accurately up to four hundred yards.

While he surveyed the village, he saw something which gave him an idea. Next to one of the buildings was a fire pit with a roaring fire, probably for the night's dinner. If he could get close enough, he could spread the fire as a diversion, and rescue his friends in the process. He noticed a Grassman guard just outside the village, and this was his first target. He pulled back his bow, and got ready to fire, when he heard a voice behind him, and the point of a sword touching his back.

"Uk tor ukton," it said, which meant 'lower your weapon. He began to follow his order, lowered his head, and then fell to the ground, reaching for his knife. The Grassman swung his sword down, and missed him, as he rolled out of the way. Jeremiah kicked his feet out from under him, and he fell on his back on some rocks. The Woblo went to stab him, and the creature struggled with him, making him drop his knife. He grabbed the bow next to him, pulled it around the Grassman's neck tight, and strangled him until he was no longer breathing.

He picked his knife and bow up, and then went back into position. None of the others heard the commotion, so he still was at an advantage. He pulled his bow back, and fired, as he dropped the guard. He then scurried down the hill, until he was behind the last building next to the fire pit.

Most of his aggressors were busy making arrows, sharpening their swords, carrying wood for the fire, and gloating over the gold and silver they acquired from their invasion. While one dropped the wood on the fire, Jeremiah ran behind him, and plunged his knife into his side. He Grabbed a log, set it on fire, and then lit the roof of one of the small buildings. He ran behind another building, as the Grassmen noticed the fire, and ran to the well to fetch water to put out the flames.

When most of them vacated the buildings, he noticed two guards out in front of one particular structure. He figured this was where his friends were being kept, and slipped behind it in quiet. He came around the side, and threw both his knives at the two of them, and they dropped to the ground in pain. He pulled out his sword, and decapitated one of their heads, while he stabbed the other in the chest. He then retrieved his knives, made sure no one else was around, and walked inside.

"Father!" Bargo yelled, in relief, as he untied his son and Lilly, and then she untied the others.

"How did you find us?" asked Glam.

"By our tracks. My father is an excellent tracker."

"You Woblos are full of surprises, aren't you?"

"Right now you have to get out of here before they catch on," Jeremiah said. "Sneak around the back, and up the hill to the south. From there, you can backtrack to the boat. Now get going, and I'll meet you at the boat."

"No, Father. You'll get killed."

"Don't worry about me. I was killing Grassmen before you were born."

"Won't the boat be the first place they look?' Barton asked.

"I'll divert them away from there. Now get going."

They followed his order, and ran up the hill. A couple of the creatures spotted them and yelled, but the Woblo quickly silenced them by throwing his knife at one, and striking the other with his sword. He ran back up the hill to fetch his pony. By this time, Ang and the others realized their prisoners escaped, and saw Jeremiah grab the pony. They ran towards the hill, so he jumped on, and charged a full gallop, his sword raised for battle.

Upon entering the group, Jeremiah swung with a fury of a knight, hacking and slicing as he went. After charging them, he and his pony ran away across the field, as the rest of the Grassmen chased behind him. Ang realized his tactical plan, and yelled to the group to change direction, and head towards the boat. The sub-humans, being primitive in knowledge, ignored his command, and continued to chase the Woblo. The Elf decided to head towards the boat on his own, and ran towards the river. Jeremiah saw this, veered to his left, and paralleled his move. The Grassmen followed him until they were at the riverbank.

By this time, the others were back in the boat, and waiting for

Jeremiah. Glam was just about to get in, when Ang came up from behind him, and held a knife to his throat.

"You were saying about killing me," he said to his long time foe.

They could see Jeremiah, as he rode up towards the boat from behind. Ang turned, and was caught off guard because of his bad eye. He found the Woblo's eagle-like claw in his face, which left another infamous scar on the Elf, crossing his other wound to form an X fashion on his face. The force knocked him to the ground, and before he could move, Glam drew his sword, pointing at the one-eyed Elf's chest.

"Don't move a muscle, or I'll cut you where you lie."

Ang smiled at his once old time friend.

"You win, for now."

His sarcasm was biting, and Glam would have loved to kill him, but had orders to follow. He jumped in the boat, as several of the Grassman ran from the brush. Jeremiah turned towards them with his sword drawn, and Ang rose to his feet in defiance.

"Caiu Mok Tor goj," he told them, which meant 'cut him into little pieces.

"Go," Jeremiah told them, as he faced the crowd of bloodthirsty creatures.

Glam untied the boat as fast as he could, and pushed off the shoreline, as the courageous Woblo drew both his swords against the group. He clashed his weapons against theirs, the sound of clanging metal heard for a mile, and fought until he could no longer fight. His worried son watched from the boat, as his father succumbed to his attackers.

"We have to go back," Bargo pleaded in tears, as Lilly grabbed him tight.

He watched in horror, as his father fell to the ground in a pool of blood. The evil Ang laughed from the shoreline, as he watched the craft depart. He pointed his finger at Glam, and warned him.

"I'll find you one day again, Glam, and you will pay for crossing me, just as your animal friend paid today. And you will remember the day I put my sword into your heart with vengeance."

Bargo cried in despair, and fell into Lilly's chest. He then stood up in anger, as she tried to stop him.

"And you'll remember the day I repay you for killing my father!" he yelled back.

Lilly pulled him back to the floor of the boat, as it drifted down the river, and out of sight of the Grassmen. Glam placed his hand on his shoulder in comfort.

"He was an honorable Woblo. And a good friend to help us."

"He will pay for this," Bargo muttered in anger.

"You cannot defeat Ang. And it would foolish to try. You must let it go."

"Let it go? If he killed your father, would you let it go?"

"Bargo," Pocor said, who was hoisting the sail to the mast. "He did kill his father."

"What?"

"Many years ago, when I was just a young man, as you are," Glam explained. "I chased him for years after I found out, until I finally faced him, and tried to kill him. I have yet to succeed. He is a powerful adversary, and one Elf or Woblo alone won't defeat him."

"So what do we do now?"

"We move on for what we came for. Your father must have reconciled with your decision, so he would want you to carry on."

"How do you know?"

"Because he gave his life for us. And there is no greater man, than one who gives his life for his friends."

"Then I will make him proud."

"I think you already have," Lilly told him.

Barton bowed his head, as he sat next to the young Woblo in remorse.

"I just want you to know everything bad I said about you I take back. You are truly a Woblo of great character, just as your father was."

"Isn't this your bag?" Lilly asked, and handed it to Bargo.

"Yes, thanks, Lilly. Hey, my magnifying glass is back in here. And there's a note. Lilly, could you read it to me?"

"Of course. Bargo, I'm writing this to you, because I don't believe I'll ever see you again, and I don't expect to get out of this alive. If I somehow manage to save you, I just want you to know how I struggled with your decision, and prayed you'd made the right one. I was young like you once, and longed for the excitement, spoils, and luxuries of adventure and exploration, just as you are now. I just didn't want you to go through the pain it caused me in life, especially with your mother and you. I regret not taking care of my family sooner, and the sorted life I left behind. Now you have grown up as you should, don't worry about me. Live your life to the fullest, and if you need the inspiration to fight for a cause, fight for me. Your father, Jeremiah Lynden."

Bargo thought about his words for a minute, and then turned to their Elven leader.

"How soon before we get to Riverton?"

"About two more days. We have to stop at Sanctin Creek for supplies. Why?"

"I want to get started as soon as possible."

"Bargo, you aren't thinking about revenge, are you?"

"My father said I should fight for him, and I intend on doing just that."

"Seeking revenge on Ang and his army of Grassmen is a foolish mistake."

"Didn't you say Ang is actually helping the Licarions in North Licarion City?"

"Yes, but I don't see why-"

"Then eventually he'll need to return there, and I'll be waiting for him."

"Bargo, aren't you listening to me? You can't and won't jeopardize this mission for a bitter feeling such as revenge. Maybe Jeremiah was right. I can drop you off in Sanctin Creek, and maybe you can get a new start there in a Blacksmith shop."

"Bargo, he's right," Lilly said. "You have to stay focused or you'll risk all of our lives."

"Please," he said. "I want to stay, please don't make me go back to my old, boring life."

"Then there will be no more talk of revenge," Glam said. "Once we get to Sanctin Creek, we'll take the night off, get cleaned up, and have some dinner and ale."

The remainder of the evening was quiet on the river, but still rather cold. Bargo once again nestled next to Lilly, who put her arm around him to keep him warm. She saw now he was all alone, and furiously bitter about the incident. She always looked out for him when his father couldn't, and wasn't about to stop now. She hadn't planned on coming in the first place, but the offer of 100 gold pieces, and the fact this year's crop pretty much was a disaster, influenced her to change her mind. Now glad she did, it helped knowing it kept her Woblo friend safe, which made her all the more secure.

She missed her husband, but knew someday she would come back to him. She wasn't scared of a few Grassmen or Licarions; a sharp, quick sword could solve that problem. She was afraid of what Glam got them into, and whether the mysticism of this evil wizard actually existed, or if it had been just an old fable thought up to keep others away from island. Lilly was curious about this gem Pocor spoke of, and if it was as powerful as they said it was.

Another concern of hers was if Ang survived. She had a strange feeling he would be up the river in a few miles, waiting to attack them from the shoreline. Although Jeremiah eliminated many of the opposition, Ang still had a large enough group to stop them. Now night fell upon them, and it was even more crucial they stay alert, and ready for adversaries.

Bargo fell asleep soundly for the first time in three days, as Lilly gazed up at the beautiful full moon, and wished all the more for her husband's company. He wouldn't survive the journey, however, being incredibly clumsy, and somewhat unskilled with weapons. A farmer, like his father, and his father before that, he wasn't raised to wield a sword, or even draw a bow. If it wasn't for Lilly, he never would have lived through the attack on their home.

Pocor also stared at the clearing sky in amazement. The wind calmed to a lull, and the water flowed in a slow, but steady pace.

"Looks like tomorrow will be a nice day after all," he said. "If we get a good headwind, we'll reach Sanctin Creek by midday or so."

"Unless Ang gets to us first," Lilly said.

"Glam is prepared for that," Pocor answered, as his superior heard his name in his light sleep. Barton also asleep, placed his hand tight on his sword sheath. Tamarka kept his bow loaded and ready to shoot at anything that moved, and monitored the shorelines to make sure they weren't ambushed.

By daylight, they traveled twenty miles up the river, and were close to the end of the tributary they started from. The areas close to the body of water used to be relatively safe, but due to the recent attacks, it meant travelers needed to be much more cautious. Places less populated were vulnerable to being invaded, and most villages didn't have royal militia protection.

Bargo awoke and gave himself a good stretch, while he noticed Lilly dozed off. By this time, Glam, wide awake, pulled out some sharp, star shaped weapons, and placed them in a bag which hung from his shoulder.

"What are those?" the Woblo asked.

"They are called 'stars of death. When you throw them, they travel about 25 yards, and instantly kill the enemy. I hoped to not have to use them right away, but if we get attacked by Ang again, we might need them."

"Will they kill him?"

"Probably not, but they'll slow him down a bit. Ang is from royalty, and only a true Elven blade from a king will kill him. Your Elven blade."

"Are you saying I'm the only one who can kill him?"

"No, your blade is the only thing that will kill him. When the time comes, I'll borrow your blade, and kill him myself."

"Are you telling him more fairy tales?" Lilly asked, as she awoke from her long nap.

"I speak the truth. What do you know about the Elven beliefs and history?"

"You're the expert," she said, and smiled, her rosy cheeks raw from the wind. "I'm just along for the gold, which we have yet to see."

"I will pay you when the job is finished, as we agreed."

"This job so far hasn't been worth it," Barton added. "You can't pay me enough to be somebody else's dinner. And I haven't even had one good sword fight yet."

"Do we have a mutiny within our midst?" Glam became annoyed at the remarks. "It's Bargo's cousin who's been captured, how does he feel about it?"

"I say continue. You can keep your gold, and give my share to the others."

BARGO LYNDEN

"No. You will get your share to do with what you want. If you don't want it, give it to those who need it, and I know you will, Mr. Lynden, because it's the right thing to do."

"Sir," Pocor said to his superior. "There appears to be something moving up by the rocks about a half mile upstream."

He handed the periscope to the Elf, who raised it to his right eye and looked through it. "Ah yes, more Grassmen," he said. "No sign of Ang, but that doesn't mean he isn't close. Okay, men, and woman, let's get prepared. Once we get by them, we'll be Riverton bound."

"There's at least ten to twenty that I saw," Pocor said.

"Then the odds will be even. Everyone but Bargo, get ready with your bows. If they get too close, draw your swords, and fight them on the rocks. Bargo, if Ang comes out, I want you to throw your sword to me when I tell you to, and stay in the boat."

Everyone complied to their orders, and as soon as they were within sight, they launched arrows from the boat, sending at least six of the Grassmen off the rocks and into the water. There was just enough time to launch a second set, and kill three more, before several on the land prepared to attack from the shore.

Once the boat passed through the twenty feet wide passage, it was pushed to the shore, as an arrow landed into Pocor's shoulder. He was forced to let go of the jib line, which caused the keel of the small sailboat to hit a rock on the bottom. It forced them to jerk forward, and Tamarka fell into the water, while Barton found himself on the rocks, with three bloodthirsty Grassmen staring down at him. He was forced to fight them where he lay, and he swung his sword into one's leg, then rose to his feet.

Lilly and Glam also jumped onto the rocks, and clashed their swords against their aggressors'. Bargo remained in the boat and held onto Pocor, who was in extreme pain, as he tried to pull the arrow from his own shoulder. Bargo helped him remove it, as human blood dripped onto the brown fur of his hand, and then threw the projectile overboard.

By this time, Barton subdued the two other Grassmen, and was helping the others fight off the remainder. When he saw his forces were being depleted, Ang emerged from the woods with both swords drawn against the three of them. Lilly and Barton attacked Ang, as he quickly fought the two of them off, knocking Barton down the hill, into the river, where he sprained his right arm. Lilly tripped when Ang pushed her over the boat into the water, and she hit her head on a rock, which knocked her unconscious. Tamarka waded to her, and with Bargo's help, got her back in the boat. Barton struggled to get into the boat, as he lay next to Pocor in extreme pain. Ang now faced his long time friend alone.

"Finally, it's down to you and me, my old friend. You'll pay for what you did to me, but I won't kill you immediately, just a piece at a time."

"Give it your best shot. Now, Bargo!"

The Woblo didn't hear him because he was too busy helping his friends, but thankfully Tamarka did, and reached for the sword sheath on Bargo's waist. He threw the sword to the Elf, but it landed directly in front of their foe instead. Glam went to reach for it, as Ang kicked him onto the rocks. Glam lost his regular sword into the river, as the evil Elf stepped on the special sword, and smiled down at his adversary.

"Get out of here now," Glam yelled to his friends. Tamarka quickly pushed the boat away, until it was loose again.

"Now," Ang said to his foe, who was lying at his mercy, and faced a blade to his chest. "Do you prefer I start with an ear first, or a much more vital organ?"

"Go through my heart and get it over with."

"No, I prefer an eye. The same eye you took from me."

"Maybe I should take the other one as well." Glam threw his dagger into Ang's leg. He backed up, Glam grabbed the Elven sword, and swung it randomly at the other Elf. Ang, with two swords, had the advantage, which forced Glam to lose balance, and send both of them in the river.

The others watched from a distance, as they rounded a bend, and the two struggled in the water, with neither Elf resurfacing from the river. Bargo and Tamarka watched in fear, while their friend disappeared from sight. They now lost their leader, their navigator, and any chance of recovering their 100 gold pieces.

CHAPTER SIX: SAFEHAVEN

Two hours passed since they last saw Glam. Pocor lost blood quickly, and Lilly was still unconscious, but alive. Tamarka helped Barton with a makeshift sling around his arm, and Bargo used a wet cloth to wipe Lilly's forehead.

"What are we to do now? he asked Tamarka. "We have no money to even get a place to stay once we reach Sanctin Creek. Good thing I brought my banjo along, maybe I can find somewhere to play there."

"Let's not hope in comes down to that."

"Glam's come out of situations like this before. He'll survive."

Tamarka watched, as his friend gasped for air, and his blood dripped to the floor of the boat.

"You save your energy, Pocor."

"They were in the water a long time," Barton said, also trying to fight back his agony. "There's no way either could have survived."

"You're wrong," Tamarka said. "It is a little known fact Elves can hold their breath a long time under water, longer than most humans."

"Well," Bargo said. "If he did survive, I hope he was able to kill Ang."

"So do I, Bargo. So do I."

"Tamarka," Pocor called to his friend. He came to him, and sat on the floor of the boat next to him. "If you get back to Elf City, tell my wife and kids I love them. Promise you'll take care of them for me."

"You're going to make it, Friend. Just hang in there."

"Just promise." He grabbed his arm tight.

"Okay, I promise."

"Thank you, you're my best-" Before he could finish the sentence, his friend slipped into an eternal peace only Elves understand. Tamarka bowed his head in sorrow, as the Woblo did the same. While Bargo held Lilly's head on his lap, she began to awake, and looked up at her friend's smiling beak.

"Good afternoon," he told her, as she tried to lift her head, still groggy from the blow.

"Hi. We're still alive?"

"Yes," Tamarka said. "But not for long, if I don't navigate the boat through the next set of rapids. Bargo, tie the tagline around everyone, and throw Pocor over the side.

"What in the name?" Barton asked. "That's how you treat your friends, just throw them over the side?"

"We don't have time to argue about it."

"Can't we at least bring him to Sanctin Creek for a decent burial?"

"We can't afford him dragging the rest of us under. We're about to reach the roughest part of the river."

"Well, I don't care if he is an Elf, he should still get a decent burial."

"You've had an interesting change of heart," Lilly remarked.

"It just isn't right," Barton insisted.

"Very well. You tie him to a separate tagline then," Tamarka said. "If the boat starts to lean and sink us, I'm cutting the rope, understand?"

"Whatever you say. As long as he gets to Sanctin Creek."

The river grew gradually rougher, and with the sail no longer useful, Tamarka pulled it down, and wrapped it around the boom. They were at the mercy of the river, and just prayed they'd stay in one piece, as waves battered the boat, and flooded the inside deck. Soon the water grew four inches deep inside, and Bargo's banjo began to float. He grabbed it and tied it to his pack, as a large wave almost knocked him out of the boat. Tamarka grabbed his arm, and threw him back to the floor.

"Stay down."

Tamarka ducked himself, as the boom swung towards him, and almost struck him in the head. Another wave hit the boat, and the vessel leaned to the portside, which caused Pocor's limp body to fall out of the boat. Tamarka pulled out his knife to cut the rope, but Barton put his good arm up to stop him.

"Let go of my arm," the Elf said. "You'll kill us all."

"No," Barton said in defiance.

"Let me cut the rope, or I'll be forced to cut your throat." Barton complied, and released his arm.

He then cut the jackline, and Pocor's body raced ahead of them down the river. There were a few large waves after that, but it settled down the closer they got to the end of the tributary. When things calmed down completely, he turned towards Barton again.

"Don't you ever disobey an order from me again. When Glam's not in charge, I am, is that understood?"

"Yes." Barton bowed his head. "I understand. Sorry."

"Well, at least the rest of us made it through alive. No thanks to you."

"Yes," Bargo said. "But in no condition to do any fighting. I myself, am without a sword."

"Well, we're safe for now. It's very doubtful there will be any Licarions or Grassmen near the next part of the river, especially with the Shudolin Navy patrolling it. When we get to Sanctin Creek we can attend to the injuries."

"I think I'll be fine," Lilly stated. "I'm a little groggy, and have a bump on my head, but I think I'll survive."

"I was referring to Mr. Barton's arm," the Elf said. "Sanctin Creek is probably another fifty miles up the river, or about a day if we move at a steady pace, say around ten knots. Bargo, can you help me to raise the sail?"

Bargo agreed, and held the sail, as Tamarka untied the knotted rope, which was battered by the wind and waves. Once he got it untangled, they again raised it to full mast, despite some holes ripped through it. It would slow the sail down a bit, but at least it would still be navigable.

Lilly sat up, rubbed her forehead, and tried to gain her composure. She reached for her sword, which was missing from when she fell over the boat, and realized Barton and Tamarka still had theirs.

"What do you suggest we do once we get to Sanctin Creek as far as lodging goes?" Barton asked.

"I have a few connections there," Tamarka said. "I have a friend who owes me a favor."

"Where is this place?"

"I'd prefer not to say at this point. For our own protection."

"Whatever you say is fine," Bargo said. "I think we need a little anonymity right now."

"And a little peace and quiet for a day or two," Lilly said.

"Two days is about all we'll have left to reach Riverton," the Elf said. "After that, I'm afraid it'll be too late."

"You can leave me in Sanctin Creek, if I'm going to slow you up," Barton said.

"Giving up, Mr. Barton?"

"No. I'll catch up with all of you later. I'm not going to give up the money that quick. I'll take a couple of days for my arm to heal, and then I'll catch up."

"It's a big countryside. Are you sure you'll find us?"

"I'll find you."

"Don't worry about it. We should be safe in this part of the territory. And you won't slow us up."

Once they reached the main part of the Swift River, the surroundings were more docile to them. Fishermen and navy patrol boats alike traveled up and down the river, where the calmer part of the body of water was, the tributary which led to the sea, and to the naval port of Riverton. Many of the travelers waved a friendly greeting, and with no Licarions or Grassmen in sight, for the first time on their journey they felt at ease.

They reached Sanctin Creek by sundown, and were greeted by another Elf, with brown hair, a mustache, and a beard. Tamarka reached out his right hand to give him a shake, and he grabbed it tight, pulled him from the boat, and then wrapped his other arm around his friend.

"Tamarka, so good to see you again."

""Good to see you again, too, Gimgo. Tie the aft line, Bargo." The Woblo followed his order, and climbed out of the boat. Lilly grabbed the bow line, tied it to the cleat, and came ashore as well.

"Where is Pocor and Glam?"

"Pocor has left us, and I fear Glam may have done the same. The fact is, he got in a battle with Ang, and now he's missing."

"It's hard to believe someone got the better of him," the brown haired bearded Elf said. "Well anyway, I've managed to get you two rooms in the Charlatan Inn, just a few blocks from here. I see you have a few rips in your sail, I'll have one of my men look after it. Were you followed here at all?"

"The Grassmen kept us on the run for a while, but eventually we shook them. Unless Ang survived, we should be all right."

"Very well. The Woblo should be okay, as long as he stays outside. The inn frowns on animals in their establishment."

"Then where is he supposed to sleep?" Lilly asked.

"In the boat, of course."

"Now wait just a minute," the angered Woblo said. "I live in a house just the same as anyone else in this town. Why can't I stay there?"

"Those are the inn's rules. I'm sorry."

"Can't you get Belinda to bend the rules just this one time, Gimgo?" Tamarka asked him.

"Well, she's kind of funny about it, but considering we're engaged to be married, I might be able to persuade her."

"Thank you," Lilly said. "You can't let him sleep out in the cold, he'll die of pneumonia."

"Thanks again, Gimgo," Tamarka said. "I'm afraid we lost some of our weapons on the way. Could we possibly pick up some tomorrow at the Blacksmith's?"

"Yes, you can talk to Maurice tonight, and he'll probably have them ready in a day or two."

Gimgo had a couple of his men take turns as they watched after the boat, and the supplies left in it. The party walked down the street, into the back door of the inn, and climbed up a steep stairway, which led to four rooms from the main hallway.

"Lilly, you and Bargo can take the room on the end, and Barton and I will take the room next to that," Tamarka said. "Gimgo, could you have one of the maids bring us up something to eat?"

"I'll see what I can do. They're not used to giving room service around here. And, besides, Belinda said the Woblo could stay here, but if anyone saw him, he'd have to go."

"Well, we'll only be here a day or two. We'll just have to make sure Bargo stays out of sight. Although, I would like you to meet Maurice."

"Why?" he asked. "So you can get me to change my mind?"

BARGO LYNDEN

"No," Tamarka said. "I wasn't thinking that at all. I need your expert opinion."

"I'm no expert. You must be thinking of my father."

"I still value your opinion, and would like you to be there. If you're half the journeyman your father was, you should know a good sword when you see it."

"Very well. But I think you're wasting both of our time."

"Don't underestimate yourself, my small friend."

Lilly and Bargo started to walk towards their room, when Gimgo stopped them.

"Perhaps Ms. Lilly would like to join Tamarka and I later for a couple of drinks down at the pub?"

"No, I don't think so," she said. "But maybe Mr. Barton would?"

"Are you up to it, Mr. Barton?"

"Why not? I need something to kill this throbbing pain in my arm."

"Very well. I'll send up some food for you, and we'll meet Mr. Barton downstairs about eight o'clock sharp."

"Thanks for letting us stay here," Lilly said.

"Just make sure he stays out of sight," Gimgo said, and turned to the stairway. Lilly directed Bargo into the room, and then shut the door, as Barton and Tamarka went in the room next to them.

Bargo turned towards Lilly, as she dropped her pack on the bed.

"Why do humans and Elves hate me?"

"They just don't think of you as an equal, only an animal."

"In other words, a freak of nature."

"Don't call yourself that. You're a better being than most humans I know."

"Do you think of me as an equal?"

Lilly smiled, as her rosy cheeks glimmered in the light of the oil lamp, and put her hand on his cheek.

"Of course I do. You are my dearest and oldest friend in Woblo Town. You're not only my equal, but my salvation."

"In what way?"

"It's because of you and your father I decided to come along. With our crops almost gone, we would have surely starved. Now,

68

I'll be able to feed us, and buy us both new clothes."

"With what money? That left with Glam."

"I don't think so. I don't know of anyone who walks around with 800 pieces of gold in their pockets. I think we're supposed to be paid by the king himself."

"Like I said, I don't care about the gold. I just want Ang dead."

"Bargo Lynden, hasn't your father taught you anything? If you continue this vendetta, you will die. You're no match for Ang, and you know it."

"But now he's killed Glam as well."

"We don't know that yet," she said, as she took her clothes from her pack and placed them in a drawer.

Bargo started to pace about the room, and then looked out the window and down at the road, which was only lit by one or two oil lamps. He watched as several people passed by, then the street became vacant, except for an Elf who wore a bowler hat, dressed in an animal skin vest, wool pants and dark, black shoes.

"Do you think we have any hope of finding my cousin and the king?" he asked. "They do, after all, have a big head start on us."

"I don't think you need worry yourself, Master Bargo. The Royal Council will know what to do."

"I guess you're right." He looked down at the Elf, who was still there, this time lighting his pipe. He glanced up at the Woblo, smiled an evil grin, as his eyes narrowed, and glowed dark red. This wasn't normal to Bargo, and he sensed the same evil presence he felt the night in the Blacksmith shop. He turned in fear to his female companion. "Lilly, come quick."

By the time she got there, the stranger disappeared around the corner and out of sight.

"I don't see anything. Really, Bargo, you need to relax."

"There was an Elf out there with glowing red eyes."

"Glowing red eyes? Like a dragon, or something?"

"Yes, I'm not fooling around, I'm telling the truth."

"Okay, okay. What do you think it means?"

"I don't know. I had the same thing happen when I looked into the forge the night before Glam came into town. I saw the same glowing red eyes. It warned me of a coming evil over the land."

"Well, if that's so, we'll have to stay on our toes. What did this

Elf look like?"

"He wore a hat, a vest made from beaver pelts, and shiny black shoes. He also had a mustache."

"Well, we'll have to keep an eye out for him."

A maid came up to the room carrying a large tray with apples, nuts, berries, potatoes, bread, and a small cooked goose. The four of them ate in Tamarka's room, which was the largest of the two, and had a table. Bargo especially liked berries, particularly strawberries, and was also fond of goose. Being not much of a hunter, he seldom got to enjoy it, except at his father's, and other special occasions, such as the Woblo Town Annual celebration.

After dinner, Bargo and Lilly turned in early, while the men went down to the pub. Tamarka properly wrapped Barton's arm to protect it from any more damage, and looked forward to an ale or two. He sat down at the bar, as Gimgo greeted them.

"Evening, Gentlemen." He took a seat as well, and waved for the bartender. "A round of ale for my friends, Michael." He nodded, and within a few minutes returned with the beverages.

Tamarka took a sip, licked his lips, and removed the froth from them.

"So, Gimgo, how have things been going here lately?"

"Pretty good, like I said earlier, Belinda and I are going to be married in a year or so, and of course, you'll be invited."

"That is if I'm back by then, and still alive."

"You'll survive, you always do. And I'm sure Glam will as well."

"So tell me, Gimgo," Barton said. "What do you know about the Licarions?"

"Probably a lot more than you do. They've managed to take control of a good portion of Shudolin Territory lately, including Bendlecheck, and part of Bacon Hills. They are savage fighters, and take no prisoners, unless they have a purpose for them."

"But we're safe here, right?"

"Yes, for the moment. This place is heavily patrolled by the Shudolin Navy and Militia. So far, we've managed to keep them out. Tamarka, what's the Woblo's story?"

"His father was Jeremiah Lynden."

"Jeremiah Lynden? I haven't heard that name in years. Isn't he the one who broke out of North Licarion City's prison?"

"Yes, that's the one."

"You said 'was' his father. Did something happen to him?"

"Yes," Barton said. "He was just killed by Ang and the Grassmen."

"Ah yes, Ang. Is that why Glam went after him?"

"Yes," Tamarka answered. "We lost track of them after we passed a bend in the river."

The Elf noticed a stranger in the crowd, who wore a hat and watched the trio, and slowly drank a bottle of rye. Tamarka knew him as an agent of Ang's, and met him several times before in other places. It was more than a coincidence he showed up here.

"Excuse me, Gentlemen, I have to talk to a rat who needs to be exterminated," he said, and walked over to him. The other two looked at each other in bewilderment of his statement.

"Hello, Kain." He placed his hand on the Elf's shoulder.

"Hello, Tamarka, long time, no see."

"Not long enough, apparently. Tell me, just why are you here, anyway?"

"To deliver a message."

"Okay, so deliver it, and leave."

"Ang isn't dead, and he wanted me to tell you, he's on his way here now."

"I don't believe it, and why would he warn us anyway?"

"Because he knows there's nothing you can do to stop him. Without the Elven sword, you cannot kill him."

"How did you know about that?"

"Do you think I was born yesterday? I didn't get to be one of his best men without knowing everything there is to know about him."

"Why not kill him yourself then?"

"Why bite the hand that feeds me? He pays me very well, and I've no desire to control everything. Besides, he's given me a little bonus to bring back the Woblo alive."

"What does Ang suddenly want with the Woblo? Wasn't it enough he left him without a father?"

"I don't know what he wants with him. I just follow orders. I was told to deliver him, as soon as you turned him over to me."

"And why should I turn him over to you?"

"Because, if you don't," he explained, as four other Elves surrounded his friends at the bar, with knives drawn on them. "I will kill your friends. Shall we take a walk upstairs?"

The seven of them walked out of the crowded pub, and into the back hallway, where the stairs led up to the rooms. Tamarka knocked on the door, and Lilly answered, her sword drawn. She was shocked to see the crowd of Elves in the hallway took them hostage.

"Drop the sword," Kain said, and Lilly complied immediately. "Grab him, and let's go. Ang will be expecting us." One of the Elves grabbed the Woblo by the arm, as he struggled.

"Where are you taking me?" he cried, as he tried to fight them off, and was lifted off the ground by the larger beings.

They released Tamarka and Barton and backed up, when they heard a noise in the far room. Before they could turn, the door bust open, and Bargo turned to face Glam in amazement, with both swords drawn and ready to fight.

"Glam, you're alive!" he yelled.

"Bargo, get out of here, now." The Woblo ducked out of the way, and darted down the stairway.

"Hello, Gentlemen," Glam remarked. "Did you miss me?"

Kain and two of the Elves went after Glam, while Tamarka and Lilly fought the others. Glam wielded both of his swords to fight off his aggressors, as the metal clanged together. He fought two of them at once, as he stabbed one of them in the shoulder, and the other in the stomach. Kain watched Tamarka and Lilly defeat their adversaries, and found himself alone to face Glam.

Knowing his odds diminished, he himself ran down the stairs, and out the back door. Bargo watched, as he ran down the street and out of sight. Glam came down and found him outside, scared and in shock.

"Are you all right?"

"Yes. Thanks to you."

The others soon joined him in the back alley, and Lilly placed her hand on the Woblo's shoulder.

"Are you all right?"

"He's fine," Tamarka said. "Glam, what happened back on the

river? How'd you manage to escape Ang?"

"I didn't. After we fell in the river, we struggled, and Ang hit his head on a rock. I dragged him to shore, and left him there."

"Why didn't you kill him?" Bargo asked.

"He's the only one who can lead us to where the king is. I can't kill him just yet."

"And what makes you think he'll lead us to him?" Barton asked.

"Because I know Ang, and Kain, and know they are informed about everything the Licarions are planning. They want our Woblo friend for some unknown reason."

"If you're hiding something, now is the time to tell us." Lilly said.

"He spoke to me," Bargo said, as the others looked at him, confused.

"Who spoke to you?" Glam asked.

"Ang, when you were upstairs, I ran out, and he was at the door. His eye was burning bright red, and I found myself unable to move."

"What did he say to you?" Lilly asked.

"I don't remember," Bargo said, as he began to cry. "All I remember was his evil eye staring at me."

"It's all right, Bargo," Glam said. "I'm just glad I was able to get down here in time before he abducted you. Tamarka, what's our weapon situation?"

"I talked to Maurice, and he's going to have them ready in a day or two."

"Very good. After that, we'll head upstream to Riverton. Bargo, here's your sword back, you might need it, if Ang returns."

"Thank you." The Woblo placed it back in his sheath. "I just wish I could remember what he said, it might help you more."

"Don't worry, my friend. We'll find out sooner or later. Try to get some rest. Tamarka and I will stand guard in the hallway tonight. If you hear anything, give us a holler."

They walked back into the inn, and up the stairs to their respective rooms. Bargo found himself at a loss to what Ang told him, and he didn't know why; it was almost as if he had no memory of it, or was in a trance of some kind. He knew whatever the message was, it left an evil feeling in his heart, and he knew his life would now be forever changed because of it.

CHAPTER SEVEN: TRICKS OF THE TRADE

The next morning they were up early, and Glam rested while the others ate their breakfast. It was a much nicer day than the previous day, about 70° out, and sunny. After Bargo and Lilly ate in their room, she went to dress in the bathroom, and came out wearing a dark blue dress, along with black leather boots. Her hair was brushed and braided, and she had the most beautiful smile Bargo ever saw.

"How are you today, Master Bargo?"

"I'm fine. Lilly, you look beautiful this morning."

"I feel beautiful, and blessed to be alive. Are you ready to face the day?"

"Not really. I couldn't sleep, and I had nightmares."

"Nightmares?"

"Yes. I dreamed I was in a large tower, surrounded by evil, glowing, red eyes, hundreds of them, and they kept coming closer until they were all around me."

"Bargo, these stories are starting to get to your head. Ang and his friend with the hat are nothing more than spies sent by the Licarions. When are you going to stop believing in evil wizards, magic, and demons?"

"Glam believes me."

"He's a silly old Elf, even if he can fight like a Licarion."

"I don't think so. You don't know what it's been like. I never would have came on this journey unless a voice told me to. I've never defied my father's wishes before."

"Okay, Bargo, we'll talk more about it later. Tamarka's expecting you to come with him to the Blacksmith shop."

"I still don't see why he wants me, I'm just an apprentice."

"Enlighten him, Bargo. You may learn something."

"What's the point? I'm done with that part of my life."

"Bargo Lynden, don't say such a thing. With your father gone, it's your responsibility to take over for him when you get back. This is an opportunity for you to finish your training, and become a journeyman."

"In a day?"

"Perhaps you know more than you think you do."

"Come on, Lilly, you know I'll never be as good a Blacksmith as my father was."

"Negativity will bring you negative results."

"But I hate being a Blacksmith."

"We all perform jobs we hate sometimes, we just have to make the best of it. Now, get yourself together, and let's get going, okay?"

"Yes, Maam," Bargo complied, picked up the Elven sword, and eyed it over.

"It's a good thing Glam was able to recover it from the river. We may need it later on."

"Yes." He placed it in the sheath around his waist. "I'd like to put it right through Ang's heart."

She gave him a look of disgust, and pushed him lightly through the doorway. Tamarka and Barton were waiting in the hallway. Barton puffed on his pipe with his left hand, and Tamarka leaned against the wall.

"Gimgo told me a couple of Ang's men were hanging down by the docks last night, trying to mess with the boat," he said. "His men scared them away."

"What were they looking for?" Lilly asked.

"He didn't say. At first I thought maybe Bargo, but it was after they came here."

"The sword, perhaps?" Barton suggested.

"Maybe. Well, Maurice is waiting for us down at his shop, and I have a large order for him, and not a lot of time. I thought maybe Bargo could help."

"I'll do my best," the Woblo said.

When they arrived at the Blacksmith shop, the man named Maurice was already busy at work, hammering a piece of red hot steel against the anvil. He had wavy, gray hair and a mustache, and wore a pair of round glasses, which rested on his nose. He stood about four feet ten inches, just a little taller than Bargo. When he saw the party enter, he used the tongs to dip the steel in a barrel of water, set it down, and then removed his gloves. He walked over to Tamarka and offered his hand to greet him.

"Tamarka, Good to see you again." The two shook hands, firmly, as friends sometimes do.

"Hi, Maurice, I'd like to introduce you to my friends. This is Barton, Lilly Tumberhill, and Bargo Lynden."

"Please to meet you all," the Blacksmith said, as he shook each of their hands. "Tamarka, I'm willing to fill Glam's order, but it will take time. I told him tomorrow, but I'm not sure I can have it all done. I have other orders as well, even though yours is top priority, and two of my guys took the day off."

"Which is why I brought you a helper." He put his hand on Bargo's shoulder.

"You're joking? The Woblo?"

"Not just any Woblo, the son of Jeremiah Lynden."

"The Blacksmith in Woblo Town?"

"Yes," Bargo said. "You know of my father?"

"Son, there isn't a Blacksmith around who doesn't know or hasn't heard of your father. He's the best there is. Well, that's different. Tell me, are you a journeyman, or are you still an apprentice?"

"Just an apprentice, Sir."

"And how long have you been an apprentice?"

"Ten years."

"That's awful long time to be an apprentice."

"My father didn't feel I was ready."

Maurice smiled and shook his head in disapproval.

"If you haven't gotten that far in ten years, you might as well find another line of work."

"That's what I told him."

"His father is, let's say, a little strict in procedures," Tamarka said. "He was, after all, a lieutenant in the Shudolin Militia."

"Very well," Maurice said. "You can start by finishing up the pile of horseshoes over there."

Bargo walked over reluctantly; the thought of more horseshoes didn't appeal to his liking, but he didn't want to argue about it. He really wanted to make something he could be more proud of, such a fine saber or arming sword, or even some calthrops.

"We'll be back later today to pick Bargo up," Tamarka said. "We have to get some more supplies, and talk with a couple of Gimgo's men about an incident last night. Have fun."

'Fun?' Bargo thought to himself. There was nothing fun about slaving over a hot forge to make horseshoes, even if it was only late spring. He hated it and wished he never worked as a Blacksmith, but he also knew Lilly was right, and expected him to drop everything he was doing, and go back to his old life. Glam painted a picture that his father expected him to finish this mission, but he knew in his heart it was against his father's beliefs; and he wanted nothing to do with battles which left him wounded and bitter.

Maurice was an easy man to work for compared to Jeremiah, but it didn't mean he wasn't picky. One of the shoes Bargo finished lacked a couple of punched nail holes, and he was quick to point it out to him. He apologized, and tried to concentrate more on what he was doing rather than what was going on in the world around him. The last time he'd been at a forge was the night before he left, when he saw the red eyes, and heard the voice from the flames.

He noticed a few things about his teacher which bothered him, particularly his lackadaisical attitude towards embers falling on the floor. Horses frequently walked through the larger back entrance to be fitted, leaving straw, and dry grass, which could ignite. His father was much more diligent towards safety, and kept his shop amazingly clean.

He also left a hot pair of tongs lying somewhere that could've easily burned someone, himself included. He noticed he used copper and tin a lot to make brass, then would blend iron with it after. This cut on costs for iron, but left the sword less effective and brittle. His father always prided himself on strictly using iron, no matter what the cost. He ended up charging more, and they took longer to sell, but in the end he knew he produced a superior product. He questioned Maurice on this process.

"I'm just trying to make a living," he said. "Iron's expensive, and I can't afford that much overhead. I sell more of these swords due to their weight and power."

NICHOLAS T. DAVIS

"What good is a powerful sword if it breaks in battle? What if I can show you a way to use just as much iron, but make it just as effective as your heavier sword?"

"I say show me what you got. If you have a better way, I'd love to see it."

Bargo pulled a two feet long iron bar and began to heat it on the forge, until it was just shy of red hot. He placed it on the anvil, and pounded it until it was slightly flatter. He then placed it back in the forge, and repeated the process, until it was a flat bar of metal. He used a chisel and hammer to break away the excess metal, until it was about five inches wide. He heated it one more time, used the chisel to shape the pointed end of the sword, and brought it over to the grinder, pumped by pedals, and ground it into shape. This process took him four hours, with another hour to make the tine for the sword. He took the scrap iron and placed it in a bucket. By the time he was finished, it was near nightfall.

His teacher looked over the iron sword, most impressed. "This is a fine sword, young man," he said. "A much better job than the apprentices I've had in the past. Your father has taught you well. You wouldn't want a job working for me, would you?"

"As much as it pains me, I have to decline your offer. I'm only passing through, and once I get back, I have to figure out what to do with my father's shop."

"Of course. Well, thank you for all your help today. With what you've taught me today, I'm sure with you, the other two guys, and myself, we'll have that order done in no time tomorrow."

"Remember what I told you. Don't throw the metal away, it can be reheated and used again for shoes, calthrops, or other items."

"I will," he said.

By late afternoon, Tamarka, Lilly, and Barton returned to pick up their friend. They brought a wagon full of supplies; including food, water, wine, necessities such as mail armor, shields, more bows and arrows, a box with lamp oil, rope, new blankets, and some clothing. Maurice and Bargo came out to greet them, as Tamarka helped the Woblo into the wagon.

"Thanks for letting Bargo help out, Maurice," he said.

"It was my pleasure," the Blacksmith said. "It's nice for an old

79

dog like me to learn a few new tricks. I even offered him a job, but he refused. Said something about getting back to his father's shop."

"Glad to hear that," Lilly giggled. Bargo gave her a slightly annoyed look, and found a place to sit on the wagon.

"Bargo, I want you to try this on," Tamarka said, and handed him a mail vest, which he put on.

"It's a little heavy."

"It's supposed to be, it's made of chain metal, and will stop most swords from going completely through you."

"Well, it's uncomfortable."

"Well, it's the best protection from Ang you have for the moment."

"He has our protection," Barton replied.

"As long as he isn't left alone. And at this point, I don't believe it's wise to leave him alone."

"He made no attempt to grab me today," Bargo remarked.

"He won't in broad daylight. Ang's not fool enough to draw attention to himself. He'd attack at night."

"You mean tonight?" Lilly asked.

"Yes, he knows we're leaving tomorrow. If he makes a move, it will be tonight, which is why we need to be ready for him. We'll discuss it, once we get back to the inn. There may be spies running about."

The wagon with two horses rolled down the road, and around the corner, as Maurice waved goodbye, and walked back into his shop to close up. Once he walked through the door, and shut it, he felt a sharp blade at his throat.

"What business do you have with the Woblo and his friends?" a voice asked.

"He just came to help me with an order today," the frightened Blacksmith answered.

"What kind of an order?"

"Let's see now. Seven swords, or was it six?"

"Don't play with me, old man, or I'll bleed you dry."

"Yes, it was six swords, ten calthrops, ten stars of death, and a couple of knives."

"Very good," he said, and released his grip. Maurice turned to face the Elf, who wore a bowler hat. He grinned, as he grabbed the man's apron, and tightened it around his neck. "If you tell anyone I was here, I'll stuff your head in your own forge until your face burns off."

"Yes, Sir. Please don't hurt me, I'm just a poor old Blacksmith."

"Who has a poor choice of friends. Tell me, did they say where they were going?"

"Riverton, I think."

"Ah, to see the council," Ang's subordinate said to himself. "Well, you won't get hurt today, poor old Blacksmith." He then left as quick as he came out the back door, the man relieved his life was spared.

They dined on roast pheasant, potatoes and carrots that evening at the inn, and prepared for an night of surveillance. Tamarka positioned himself on the roof, after he climbed out a window, and carefully climbed up a drain pipe. He drew his bow, crouched down, and waited for anyone who came through the back. Barton took the hallway, with his sword drawn, in case anyone came up the stairway. Lilly stayed in the room with Bargo, and Glam waited just around the corner from the front entrance, to see if anyone came through there.

It was a rather long wait before there was any action, about four and a half hours. Tamarka found it hard to keep his eyes open, and began to doze off. It wasn't until he saw a dark figure emerge from a back alley, just around the corner from the back door of the inn, he became fully alert. He knew right away it was the overzealous Kain; he could spot his silly hat anywhere, and he made no bones to hide his presence, almost like he wanted to be seen. To Tamarka it didn't make sense because he strolled right past the inn, and around the corner.

While he had the bow aimed at his foe, he could sense someone behind him. Turning quick, a sword swung at him, and he ducked just in time. It was a hooded figure, and he couldn't make out exactly who it was, but he had a good idea. He dropped his bow, and drew the two daggers he had, protecting himself from the sword, but found it difficult to fight him off. He fell to the ground on his back, as his aggressor kicked him until he was at the edge of the building. He held his sword at his throat.

BARGO LYNDEN

"You'll pay dearly for interfering," the figure said, as he raised the sword to remove his head. When he did, a star of death flew, and bounced off the blade. He turned to face Glam, who threw another into his leg, which he pulled out with little painful response.

"You'll never win, Ang," the heroic Elf jeered. "Let him go."

"If you wish," he said, and kicked Tamarka over the side. He grabbed the ledge just in time, and hung onto it with one hand. He then approached Glam with great fury, as the Ang pulled out his sword to defend himself.

"It's time to finish this."

"What's the point, you know you can't kill me."

"No, but I can make you suffer a little." He swung his sword at him, Ang blocked it, and aimed lower, as Glam mimicked his action. The two pushed the swords away, and fought until they were both near the edge. Glam sliced into Ang's arm, and he screamed in pain, only to return the favor by cutting Glam's left hand. He fell to the ground, and rolled, as Ang's sword hit the stone roof. Glam threw another star, which caught him in the face, and he screamed until he removed it. Tamarka climbed back onto the roof about then, tripped him, and he fell off the roof. Tamarka then helped his friend to his feet. The two of them looked over the side, and there was neither a sign of Kain or Ang.

"You better get downstairs. He may try to have Kain run around the front, and Barton's no match for him with only one good arm."

"Yes, Sir," he said, and slid down the drainpipe, and back in the window. Bargo and Lilly woke up as he entered. "He's back. Stay put, and keep on guard."

Lilly drew her sword, as the Elf went into the hallway, where Barton was supposed to be, but was nowhere to be found. 'Damn,' he thought, and opened the door to the empty room. When he did, he heard a commotion in the other room next to him. He ran into his room, and found Kain choking Barton. He grabbed the Elf by the arm, and punched him in the face, which knocked him to the floor. He then kicked him until he was unconscious. He helped Barton to his feet.

"Are you okay?"

"Yea, he just caught me off guard."

"Tie him up, I'm going to check on our Woblo friend."

He picked up their hostage, and placed him in a chair.

"You bet," he said, and tied him to it with some rope.

Tamarka went into Bargo's room, only to be faced with Ang again, who threw Lilly across the room, which gave her a black eye. Glam flew in through the window behind him, and Barton came in from the next room when he heard the commotion. Realizing he was outnumbered, he dropped his sword to the floor.

"As I said, Ang," Glam said. "You won't win this fight. Bargo, the sword, if you please?" The Woblo handed him the sword. "You can leave now, and stay out of our way, or I can pierce you now, your choice."

"Perhaps you are right. I've done my share for the Licarions, maybe it's time to retire. I'll help you in any way I can. All I ask is that you don't kill me, and let me go in peace."

"Do I have your word you'll help us find the king?"

"You have my word."

Tamarka reached to grab his arm, and Ang threw some powder on the floor, which caused an explosion, causing smoke to fill the room. When the smoked cleared, he was gone, and took his sword with him as well. The others choked until the gas dissipated, and realized Bargo was still among them.

"Is everyone okay?" Tamarka asked. After everyone answered, they all sat down in relief. "So much for his word."

"Well, I don't think he'll be back tonight," Glam said. "Between my sword, and the stars, I've cut him up pretty bad. He'll need to heal. Barton, go to the other room and keep an eye on our hostage. We'll talk to him in the morning. You guys, better get some rest. We need to be out of here by sundown tomorrow."

"We're leaving at night?" Bargo asked.

"This part of the river is safe at night. Ang knows better than to attack in patrol areas. He'll try again after we leave Riverton, but by then we should have some reinforcement."

"There's something about these two that really bothers me," the Woblo said.

"Oh?" asked Glam. "What's that?"

"Their eyes are pure evil. When I look at them, I see

evil."

"Like the evil of a sorcerer?"

"Please," Lilly snarled. "Haven't we had enough problems without bringing up the magic nonsense."

"If you saw what I did, you wouldn't think it was nonsense." Bargo stated.

"Well," Glam said. "Whether it's true or not, I think we should heed Bargo's warnings. He seems to be of great value to them, although I'm not sure why yet, and we wouldn't want them to be disappointed if we didn't at least try to give them what they wanted. Little do they know that they'll end up getting more than they bargained for."

CHAPER EIGHT: INQUISITIONS AND BETRAYALS

The next morning after breakfast, Tamarka escorted Bargo up to the Blacksmith shop to finish their order, and Glam stayed back with the others to interrogate their prisoner. He knew Kain would tighten his lip like a live clam being pried open by a fisherman's knife, but had to figure out a way to get him to talk. He entered the room, grabbed a chair, and sat down across from the tied up, mustached prisoner.

"Good morning, Kain. Can I get you anything, a little water, or perhaps some wine?"

"Tea would be nice. But don't get me anything if you think it's too much trouble."

"Oh, no trouble at all. Barton, why don't you call down the hall, and have Lilly bring up some tea for our guest."

"Yes, Sir," Barton said, now able to move his arm a little. He left the room, and the Elf turned back to his captive.

"If I'm your guest, why am I still tied up?" Kain asked.

"Because as my guest, I like to make sure you're not harmful to yourself or anyone else."

"Very funny. Tell me, Glam, do your friends know of the real reason you're dragging the Woblo halfway across the countryside?"

"I don't know what you're talking about. Besides, I'm supposed to be asking the questions, not you."

"You can ask me whatever you want, it doesn't mean I'll answer it. You answer mine, and I'll answer one of yours."

"How about you answer mine, or I'll use you as an anchor for our boat."

"Getting irritated, are we?"

"Very well, I'll play along. But you do realize any information I give you is strictly public information, and I'll not disclose any of our mission."

"You can skip the double talk. We both know you brought the Woblo along because he's a gem collector who knows his stones."

"If you already knew the answer, why'd you ask?"

"To see what your reaction would be."

"I see no point in this line of questioning. Let me get to my own. Where did the Licarions take the king and his party?"

"How do you know it was the Licarions?"

"Who else could it have been?"

"The Grassmen."

"The Grassmen wouldn't know what to do with them if they had them. They'd be more likely just to make a dinner out of them."

"How do you know they haven't?"

Barton returned with his cup of tea, as Glam told him to set it down, but not give it to him.

"Stop playing games, Mr. Vortella."

"You're going to deny a dying man his last cup of hot tea?"

"You're not dying yet. Tell me where they're hiding, and I'll let you have your cup of tea, and go."

Kain laughed a hearty laugh.

"You, an agent for the Royal Guard, would just let me go? I doubt that. Besides, I think I decided the Calamine tea is more to my liking." His sarcasm was relentless, and Glam ran out of patience.

"Barton, as soon as Tamarka gets back, the two of you can take him down to the boat, cut his throat, and dump him in the river. He's outlived his usefulness."

"Now, wait a minute," the desperate Elf said. "Let's not be hasty. If I were to tell you where they took the king, would you be willing to give me protection against Ang?"

"Perhaps, but once we get you to Riverton Prison, it'll be up to them."

"I thought you were going to let me go?"

"That's before you became uncooperative. The best I can tell you is you'll get a fair trial."

"Yea, and once I'm let go, I'll be a dead man. No thanks."

"By then we should have Ang tracked down and killed."

Kain grimaced at the thought.

"You sound so damn sure of yourself, don't you. You don't know Ang. He won't stop until he tracks me down like a wild animal."

"I do know Ang. Better than you ever will, and I know his weaknesses as well. I know he uses people like you and the Grassmen to do his dirty work, while he seeks power and control over his own people. He is a disgrace to all of the Elven Kingdom."

"The great Elven Kingdom is no more," he bellowed. "It died when the Shudolin people took over. Our infamous kings fell when the empire did. There hasn't been an Elf other than Ang whose had the belly to reclaim it."

"He doesn't care about our race, only helping the Licarions destroy all of us. The Elves sought peace and alliance with the Wobloes and humans, not war."

"Ang knows the real Elven ways, not those of the persistent innovators who would change our history."

"Back to the matter at hand., and don't change the subject. Where are they taking the royal party? This is your last chance."

He shook his head in defeat.

"I guess I'm dead either way. His men are taking them to North Licarion City, at least that's what I've heard. He won't tell me himself. He trusts me, but not that much."

"Well, he's right not to trust you. You'd turn him in just to save your own skin. A true soldier would've faced death before he revealed any information."

"Who ever said I'm soldier material?"

"When Tamarka gets back, put a gag in his mouth, bring him to the boat, and keep a watch on him. Lilly and I will meet you down by the dock, once we pick up Bargo and the weapons. If you see Ang anywhere in sight, dispose of him."

""Hey! What about a little respect."

"Barton, make sure the gag is tight, we wouldn't want him screaming for help while his blood runs down the river."

Kain struggled, as Barton put the gag in his mouth. Glam walked out the door, and down the stairwell into the bar area, which was vacant, except for Gimgo, Belinda, and Lilly, who were all drinking tea.

"Do you have another cup for me?" Glam asked.

"Of course," Belinda said, as she walked over with a wet rag, and grabbed the tea kettle, which hung over the fire. She then grabbed a clay cup on the counter, poured the hot liquid into it, and handed it to Glam.

"Well, Barton and Tamarka are going to bring our prisoner down to the boat until we're ready to leave."

"It's a bit early," Lilly said. "Why not a little later when we're actually ready to go?"

"Because I want him to sweat a little."

"You're using him for bait, aren't you?" Gimgo asked.

"What about Barton and Tamarka?" Lilly questioned. "Doesn't that leave them in a vulnerable position?"

"Tamarka knows what to do if he shows up. And as for our friend Barton, I have no doubts he can handle himself." Glam said.

"One thing is really bothering me," Lilly said.

"And that is-"

"Why you allowed Bargo to come along in the first place, when you knew his father was against it."

"I see qualities in him I don't see in Elves or men; qualities only a Woblo would possess."

"Is that the only reason?"

"Of course. And the fact his father was a great Woblo, and would expect him to be nothing less."

"But by your own admission, you said he wasn't as skilled as his father."

"We all need to learn, Mrs. Tumberhill."

She gave him a squint of her left eye in disbelief, while she took another sip of her tea.

"I still say you're hiding something from us. You might as well tell me what it is, because eventually I'm going to find out anyway."

"Well," Glam said, as he placed his cup down. "I guess it doesn't matter now anyway, Ang already knows why we're here. You won't believe the real reason anyway, having to do with 'fairy tales."

"What are you babbling about?"

"It's a well known fact among the Woblos certain folk have

the ability to distinguish between various gemstones; such as rubies, sapphires, and diamonds. Information was brought to me stating Bargo possessed these abilities as well."

"Back to that blue stone again. I agree with what you're saying; he does have an interest, but by no means is he an expert. And I hardly doubt there is such a thing as a magical stone."

"It is said the Woblos were created with the use of Elven magic."

"I heard that as well, but I never gave any credence to it."

"Still, the non-believer, huh, Mrs. Tumberhill?"

"All I know is this whole affair has gone far enough. I think it's time to send Bargo home back to take care of his father's shop. The king is your problem."

"Don't forget, Bargo's cousin is among the party as well."

Lilly grew angry at his persistence at getting her involved with his own agenda.

"I don't believe you. You'll use any excuse to get what you want."

"I didn't get to be where I am if I didn't. Look, I know you don't agree with all of the mystical business, but the Royal Council does, and they're expecting me to retrieve the gem and the staff from the Licarions, if they have it, and to retrieve the king's party as well. You can either help me retrieve them, or leave with your Woblo, and go home. It doesn't matter to me, I can get new recruits in Riverton, if I have to, but none of them have the ability Bargo has. I need your help."

"Does Bargo know you need him for such a job?"

Well, no," Glam said, as he finished his cup of tea. "I was planning to tell him when we got to Riverton. In the meantime, can you keep it between us?"

"Well, I guess. But you'll tell him the minute we get to Riverton?"

"Of course." The Elf handed his cup back to Belinda. "You won't regret this. When this is all over, Bargo will be able to fix up his father's shop, buy a new shop, or whatever he wishes to do. We'll all be extremely rich men and women."

"I thought the pay was only 100 pieces of gold?"

"That's just the down payment, shall we say? The real payoff is when we raid the Licarion temple."

"You never said anything about raiding a temple. I won't steal anything."

"We're only stealing what was stolen from the Elven and Shudolin kingdoms in the first place. When we return it to the king, there will be a considerable reward."

"You can keep the reward, I'll just take the 100 gold pieces."

"You sound like your Woblo friend."

"Well, in Woblo Town, we're brought up to be content with what we have. We only buy what we need to survive, and to make us happy. Riches mean a community of friends who help one another."

"Are you saying I only care about money?"

"Take it for what you want it to mean."

"What's your interest in the Woblo anyway?"

"I promised his father I'd take care of him when he was gone. We have known each other since we were young. We used to play together."

"I see, so you're kind of like a big sister to him?"

"Yes, I am. And I don't like people taking advantage of him."

"I get your meaning, and I would never make him do what he doesn't want to do. You should know, I don't work like that. We better get the wagon down to the dock to unload, and see to getting the boat ready for departure. Thanks for your help, Gimgo."

"Don't mention it, my brother," the Elf answered.

"You take care, Belinda. Thanks for letting us stay."

"Your welcome," she said. "And good luck."

"Thanks," Glam said, as he and Lilly headed for the back door, where the wagon was parked. He glanced around the area, and noticed a note attached to the wagon with a drop of blood on it. He opened it, and read it aloud. "My Dear Friend Glam, I look forward to meeting again on the west side of Riverton. As you leave your precious Royal Council, I'll be planning the attack where I'll kill your king, take what's mine, and leave you to bleed on the battlefield. There will be no militia to save you, and I'll enjoy watching you slowly suffer. Yours truly, Ang."

"Well he was definitely here again," Lilly said. "And from the sounds of it, he's not so overly fond of you."

"Unless he left it last night. Either way, we need to be on the lookout. Just because he says he won't attack us right away, doesn't mean he won't. Besides, I'm not worried about his threats; he knows damn well I'm faster with the blade than he. Let's get the wagon down to the river, and then see how Bargo and Maurice are coming with our weapons."

After spending the afternoon loading the boat, they walked back to the Blacksmith shop. Tamarka sat at the boat for hours, and Ang didn't seem to fall for the bait of his subordinate, Kain. Deciding they were safe for the moment, Glam and Lilly entered the shop.

Bargo was finishing the order, and working on sharpening the calthrops. Their leader realized the swords were done, and picked one up in admiration.

"Beautiful job, Maurice," he said, and swung it back and forth.

"I can't take all the credit," the old Blacksmith said. "If it weren't for your Woblo friend here, I would have never finished it."

"There's something different about this batch." Glam ran his finger up the side of the blade.

"You can thank him for that too. He showed me a new technique. I guess it's never too late to learn new things. Glam, there's something I need to tell you."

"What is it?"

"I had a visit from an Elf in a hat last night."

"Kain. And?"

"And I kind of told him where you were going, and what you were going there for."

Glam placed his hand on the old man's shoulder, and came closer to his right ear.

"No matter, friend. He would have found out anyway. But don't worry, I've got him safely tied up down in the boat. He won't be going anywhere but the royal dungeon."

Bargo brought the last of the calthrops over, and placed them inside a bag. He smiled, as Lilly and Maurice returned the gesture.

"All done," he said, and handed the bag to Glam.

He took one of them out, and looked it over carefully.

"Fantastic job, Bargo. They're razor sharp. You made these

BARGO LYNDEN

all by yourself?"

"Yes. Sir."

"For someone who hates this line of work, you have amazing potential. These will work just fine."

"He doesn't give himself as much credit as he deserves," Lilly said. "When this is over, I wish he'd reconsider taking his father's shop."

"We'll see," Bargo said. "I still think I'd be just as good a soldier, if you'd just give me the chance to prove it."

"Like you said, Bargo," Glam said. "We'll see. Let's take the weapons down to the boat, it'll be dark soon. I want to get a head start; enough so we're not followed again. Maurice, thanks again. My payment will be sent by the usual courier from the Royal Council."

"Thank you for allowing me the pleasure of working with your bright young friend. Perhaps when I retire, I can pay you a visit in Woblo Town. It will be a pleasure to see where one of the greatest Blacksmiths used to work."

They shook hands to bid farewell, and headed down to the boat, looking behind them for any sign of Ang. Once they were there, Tamarka got the sail ready for their trip. Lilly helped Bargo load the weapons and the remaining loose items into the boat, then Glam untied the bow and aft lines. They pushed the vessel away from the dock, and the current pushed them away from the small town of Sanctin Creek.

The sun set behind them, and they floated down the waterway. Barton's arm was no longer in a sling, but he did have to be careful, for his shoulder was still rather sore. He looked through the supplies they bought, and found a bottle of Blackberry wine.

"Nice," he said, as he held it up in the diminishing sunlight.

"Crack it open, and pass it around," Glam said. "I think after what we've been through, we deserve a little celebrating."

Barton handed it to Lilly, as if to infer his shoulder left him too weak. She shook her head, and popped the cork with her knife. Barton reached over for the bottle.

"Ah-ah," she said, and smiled. "Ladies first."

She took a small sip, handed it to Barton, who handed to Glam, who also took a sip. Tamarka refused, due to sailing. Glam handed it to Bargo, and that's when Barton objected.

"You're going to let him drink? He's nothing but an animal."

"We're all friends here, with the exception of Mr. Kain," Glam stated. "Even Woblos. If you don't like it, don't drink."

"Ahh. I'll be glad when this is all over."

"It won't be over until the evil empire of Garlock is defeated."

"What are you talking about? That magic nonsense again?"

"Like I said before, it is no myth, he is real, and the evil is real. Bargo has seen it himself. Kain has seen it as well."

"I saw something, but now I think maybe I was just having a bad reaction to something I ate."

"Don't be so quick to dismiss the mind, Master Bargo. Ang has much instruction on the dark arts. It is said he learned his magic from Garlock himself."

"How's that possible?" Lilly asked. "If he's real, he's an ocean away."

"And Ang has been across the ocean," Glam reiterated.

"Suppose you're right," Barton said. "What can we do about it? None of us know magic."

"That's where you're wrong," Glam said, as he took a big sip of the bittersweet wine. "Bargo, there's something I have to tell you, and it's something you might be a little angry about."

"Yes?" Bargo questioned.

"I didn't bring you along just for your fighting ability, or even your Blacksmithing ability."

"Then why did you bring me along?"

"Because of your interest in stones."

"What? Why would you want me for that, I'm just a collector? I don't buy or sell them."

"But you have great knowledge about them. And that is where you can help me."

"Help you what?"

"Help me find the most valuable stone of all-the blue stone of Rebolin. The one which gives Garlock his destructive power over all mankind. With the Staff of Varlana, and the tine of Dimorter, he is unstoppable."

"I don't think I'll know what to look for, but if you say so,

BARGO LYNDEN

I'll help. Why didn't you tell me this earlier?"

"Maybe because someone told me that honesty was the best policy," he said, as he glanced at Lilly, who threw a blanket around herself to keep warm.

"It should be a good traveling night," Tamarka said. "Most of the river's fairly calm after this point."

"As long as we're in the presence of a beautiful woman and a bottle of wine," Barton said in glee. "It's a great night."

"Well, thanks for the compliment, old man," she said.

"My pleasure." Barton drank from a second bottle of wine being passed.

"Well, we don't have to worry about the jackline this time at least," Bargo laughed.

"Or Grassmen," Lilly said, as she put her arm around Bargo's shoulder.

"I propose a toast," Lilly said. "To fallen comrades."

"To fallen comrades," Barton said, as he raised his bottle. He glanced over at Bargo's banjo, which was lying in the pile of supplies near the back. "Are you ever going to play that thing, or did we bring it along just for show."

"I was hoping to earn a couple of dollars playing somewhere."

"Play for us. I'll give 5 gold pieces when we get paid if you play a song right now."

"Very well, what would you like to hear?"

"How about you make up something peppy, or a tune that pertains to our voyage?"

"Okay," Bargo said, a little nervous. Barton handed him the banjo, and proceeded to tune it. "It's a little out of tune from the bumping around, and getting wet." Bargo began to pluck the strings. "Let's see, what can I play?" He began his little tune, that sounded a bit like this:

> *"There once was a man who lived by the sea,*
> *Cunning, brave, intelligent was he,*
> *Killed so many fishmen they tried to take his soul,*
> *Barton was his name, and he wanted all their gold*
> *One day they tried to drown him under the deep blue,*
> *Until a girl named Lilly came to his rescue.*

94

He was so ashamed a woman had saved him,
That he fell back in the water to do it all again."

"You call that peppy?" Barton, asked, a bit annoyed Bargo made fun of him.

"You asked for it," Lilly laughed.

"Lilly?" her Woblo friend asked, changing the subject.

"Yes?"

"Do you think my father would have lived if I listened to him, and didn't come on this trip?"

"Do not feel responsible, young friend," she said. "You did what you had to do, and he did the same. When you have a son of your own, you will understand."

"I hope you're right. I can't help but feel if I only listened, he'd be alive."

"Sometimes we must listen to our heart, and not our mind. We must do what we feel is right, even if it hurts the ones we love. Your father knew this, and that's why he felt the way he did. You will be a great Woblo someday, Bargo Lynden, no matter what you do, please remember that."

Bargo thought about what she said the rest of the evening, until he began to doze off from the effect of the wine. Right now he didn't feel so great, but as far as legends go, they never know their worth until they know how many lives they save, and how much they are worth to others.

CHAPTER NINE:

IN THE PRESENCE OF THE ROYAL COUNCIL

They arrived in Riverton in the late afternoon the next day. It was a long, exhausting day on the river, but uneventful, except an occasional wave to a passerby boat on the waterway. Kain gave them no problems, bound and gagged, he was unable to weasel out of the knots Tamarka tied. Once they left the dock, the remainder of their journey would be on land, with the use of horses. They were expected at the Royal Chambers by 6:00 pm, as the prince specifically invited them to be guests of the palace, where they would be able to receive hot baths, and nice comfortable, private rooms.

They pulled into the large marina, which was full of small and large river and sea going vessels. There was some recent news that spices, gemstones, and gold were found in the far away lands, and more sailors were going there. Most of the expeditions were much farther south of Bereuka Island, to avoid the curses and strange events associated with it. It was said if you could get past the island, and the Glorcion city of Marino, there were untold riches waiting. Glorcs feared the ocean and water, in general, after a great flood created by the Elven god Rhiatu washed them out of the Shudolin. They were generally not a sea faring race.

The Licarions, on the other hand, were creatures of the sea, and also heard the stories of riches. The Shudolin Navy until now kept them under control, and contained them within Shudolin borders. Occasionally, there was news of a stray Licarion ship which went farther out to sea, but it was unlikely they were ever heard from again. The far away lands were said to be a dangerous and violent place, with savage and evil creatures created by Garlock, or already indigenous to the area.

A very tall, muscular man with curly blond hair greeted them on the shore, and tied their lines to the dock.

BARGO LYNDEN

Three Elves and another man with black hair, a beard, and mustache approached them as well, and extended his hand to Glam, while he exited the boat.

"Glad you made it back in one piece."

"Thanks, Christopher," Glam replied. "I'd like you to meet Lilly Tumberhill, Mr. Barton, and Bargo Lynden. You, of course, know Tamarka. I have a prisoner for you." Two of the Elves took Kain into their custody, and left towards the marina's exit.

"Rather motley recruits you have here. Bargo Lynden, huh? Are you related to Sgt. Barlow Lynden, or Lt. Jeremiah Lynden?"

"Barlow is my cousin, and Jeremiah was my father."

"He just recently passed away," Lilly stated.

"My condolences," Christopher said. "I hear he was a brave Woblo in the last war. I fear another one is coming soon, due to recent events. Come, I have a coach waiting for us just beyond the marina to take us to the palace. I'll send a courier to get your things, and Sal will watch the boat until it's unloaded."

The blond man named Sal began to unload the boat, as they walked towards the outside of the marina, and to where the coach wagon waited for them. The seven of them climbed into the large vehicle, as the driver directed the two horses in the front to proceed down the cobblestone path.

"Has Glam told you the nature of the problem we're facing?" Christopher asked the others.

"He's told us the king and Bargo's cousin were kidnapped by the Licarions," Lilly said. "We were followed and attacked by Grassmen, an Elf named Ang, and our prisoner, Kain, who were all looking for a blue stone that Bargo, because of his gem collecting ability, is supposed to know what and where it is."

"Yes, the Gem of Rebolin," Christopher said. "It's supposed to have mystical powers, but it's real value is the weapon it can create with the Staff of Varlana, and the Tip of Dimorter."

"Don't tell me the king believes in this nonsense as well?" Lilly asked.

"Mrs. Tumberhill, the presence of evil is no nonsense. You may not believe in magic, or evil spirits, but I've seen them with my own eyes."

"You're the one Glam talked about," Bargo surmised. "You've

been to Bereuka Island?"

"Indeed I have. And I can tell you, the stories are true; the sea serpents, the giant whirlpools, the Fishmen, all of it. I lost my whole crew of sixty men to that place."

"How come you survived?" Barton asked.

"It was the Staff of Varlana that saved me. As long as it was in my possession, the sorcerer's spells couldn't harm me."

"Where did you find it?" Bargo asked in fascination. These were legends he heard as a child, and now he was actually part of the folklore.

"I didn't, it was in his castle."

"How did you get out of there with it?"

"I trapped him inside his own lair. Once he reached the door, I used the staff to blockade the door. I chanted the ancient Elven words 'gala ti quella', meaning 'lock the evil within', which sealed him within his own walls. I then took the staff and left for home."

"Not to be skeptical," Lilly said. "But just how exactly did you get home across the ocean?"

"Our ship was no longer navigable, so I used one of the long boats, and made a short sail. It was a long and dangerous journey, but about halfway, I was lucky, and picked up by a Shudolin vessel."

"That's quite a story," Barton said to the man. "But if you have no proof, why should we believe you?"

"This is all the proof I need," Christopher said, as he pulled up his pant leg to reveal a burn on his leg in the shape of a webbed handprint. The others stared in disbelief at the wound. "This is where I was grabbed by one of the Fishmen. The burning seared skin of evil has stayed with me since."

"Assuming you're right, what can we do? I'm sure you have all kinds of royal guards, why were we specifically chosen?"

"Bargo was chosen for his astuteness in examining gemstones and minerals; you were chosen because you have a ruthless nature, never give up once provoked, and because you are an expert marksman. Lilly was chosen because she has the ability to negotiate, and is one of the best swordsmen' in the land. A mission of this complexity cannot be done with a mere militia. The prince will explain more when we have dinner tonight."

BARGO LYNDEN

When they pulled up in front of the palace, Bargo and Lilly were in awe at the beauty of the structure. They never saw a castle before, let alone one so elegant. They heard of stories to the North of the Great Elven Palace, located in Elf City, and run by the current king, Glaridia, who was part of the alliance against the Licarions. The Woblos were said to be the chosen magical race by the Elves, and were thus honored greatly.

Bargo never understood this part of the folklore because he never performed magic, and never knew anyone who could. The tale was largely dismissed in Woblo Town, and if there was magic within their small community, they would have at least encountered something by now. Elves were said to have invented magic, but there again if this was true, it was long forgotten by their kin folk. They were, however, excellent marksmen with a long bow, and could fight well with swords.

The Front doors of the palace were decorated with stained glass, and surrounded around its edges were rubies, diamonds, and gold. Several guards waited in two lines facing each other, as they exited the coach, and blew into three feet long horns that annoyed Bargo to no end, due to his sensitive hearing. He hurried by them, the others waved, and Christopher's Royal Guardsmen followed behind him. Once they entered the grand entrance hall, Christopher turned to the party.

"Glam is more than familiar with the palace, and can help you with all your accommodations," he stated. "He'll be your guide to the tour, but please understand, some areas are off limits even to the Royal Guard."

"Thanks, Chris," Glam said, as he put his right hand on his friend's shoulder.

"I have one more question for you, Sir?" Barton asked.

"Yes?"

"Why are we waiting two days before we set out to find the king? Won't he be dead by then?"

"That, my friend, is something you'll have to ask the prince."

Glam walked them through the great ball room, which was said to have held one thousand guests at one time, and many wedding receptions. Now seldom used except on a few special occasions, the king was considered to be still mourning over his wife's death, and didn't like to be in that part of the castle. After the ball room, the Elf showed them the master dining room, where they would be eating, the kitchens, and finally the outside garden. They were directed to each of their spacious rooms, which contained a bedroom with a king sized bed, a bathroom, and a balcony.

Bargo wasn't used to this kind of treatment, being a Woblo. It was nice to be honored, not ridiculed by the townspeople, and to be seen as an equal. That's all he ever wanted in life, especially from his own father. He felt the years of being around men and Elves hardened his father's heart to the ancient ways of the Wobloin race, and he preferred being around them more than his own kind. It was rather ironic Woblo Town was named after the race, but very few still lived there. Most of his kind remained rather secluded deep in the Forbian Forest, and refused to succumb to man's ways. It was said even though there was a representative for the Forbian Forest region, the Woblos still had their own king.

He walked out onto the balcony, mesmerized by the beautiful valley and river below. While he admired the view, he noticed Lilly was also out, all cleaned up, and in a beautiful red dress with frills around the neckline, down to her ankles and red slippers. Her blonde hair French braided to her waist, she wore a gold tiara on her head.

"I thought you were pretty the other day," he said. "Tonight you are the most beautiful woman I've ever seen."

"Bargo Lynden," she jested. "If I didn't know any better, I'd say you're taking a fancy to me. Well, just remember, I'm a married woman."

The Woblo laughed. "I know. It's just the past week and a half I feel a lot closer to you. Like a sister, of course."

"Of course. It's quite a sight, isn't it? The view, I mean."

"Yes, it is. I knew if I came on this journey, I'd see things I never saw before-Grassman, the river, the palace. It's just so overwhelming. My father spoke of such things before my mother died, before he became obsessed with his work."

"Maybe work was just a way for him to cope with your mother's death. There's nothing wrong keeping busy.""

"He used to be so happy. It's almost like he blamed me."

"Bargo, don't think like that. Your father never thought it was your fault. Your mother grew ill, and nobody could help her."

"But if I could've helped her through learning the ancient ways, maybe I could've cured her."

"There is no magic able to change the hands of fate."

"You don't believe in any of this, do you?"

"No, I don't. And frankly, I just prefer to get the king back, and call it a day."

"But what about the burn mark on the Head Guard's leg?"

"Coincidence. It could be from a Licarion who got too close to a fire."

They heard a loud knock from Lilly's door. "Sounds like dinnertime," Bargo said.

"Indeed. I hope you're hungry? Royalty has a habit of overindulgence."

"What do you mean?"

"You'll see when we get to the dining room." She smiled, and left the balcony to answer the request.

When they reached the royal dining room, they entered, and took their places around the twenty six chair mahogany table, overshadowed by a large, silver chandelier with lit candles in it. It was decorated with the best silver goblets and tableware, the napkins were the finest silk money could buy, and the china sparkled so one could see their reflection in it. There were various fruits, vegetables, breads, and cheeses on the table, as well as a nice browned, roast turkey, and wild boar. Bargo never saw so much food in his life; there was even more than the celebrations back in Woblo Town, and there were only half the people here. Now the Woblo knew what Lilly meant by "overindulgence."

They sat down, as one of the wenches served them all wine. Just when everyone was comfortable, two men came in, raised their horns, and blew into them. A man with long, braided gray hair behind his back stood in the doorway with his hands behind him.

"Please rise for his Royal Highness, the Prince of the Shudolin, Phillip Pendercost," he announced. The others watched Glam to see what the proper etiquette was; he clapped, and the others followed suit, until the prince sat at the head of the table.

His red cape waved, as he walked in an egotistical nature towards his seat, while his crown of gold and rubies glistened in the bright candlelight of the room. He was a young man, not much older than Bargo, with wavy and curly blonde hair, a mustache, and a beard. He wore a velvet colored shirt with gold cufflinks, light tan rather large pants, and dark tan leather boots. The man who announced him, his royal advisor, sat by his side, and the other subjects sat at the far end. He greeted his guests with a smile, as he clasped his hands together.

"Please, sit down," he said. "Good evening, my Friends. Welcome to my palace. As my guests, you are free to use any facilities you wish-the courtyard, the hot spring, or the ball and game room. Now, as for the feast, and the reason you were brought here. First, a short prayer, as we bow our heads." The guests followed his suit, and closed their eyes in silence. "Rhiatu, Oh great Lord of the Shudolin, please accept our thanks for this meal so elegantly prepared for us today, and help us get through the crisis which now awaits our great land."

"Amen," his advisor added, and stood for another announcement. "For those who are new to our procedures, let me introduce our illustrious council members to our guests. At the end of the table is the royal advisor to King Glaridia of the Elven Kingdom, Talandra, to the left of Mr. Barton is Duke Cyres, of Bacon Hills, and to the right of him is Duke Torika, of the Forbian Forest providence. You, of course, all know Christopher, Head Guard of the Shudolin Royal Guard, and Glam, Royal Guard of Investigative Affairs. I'm Vladimir Postof, Chief Advisor to the king."

"I, of course, am acting on behalf of my father, who is currently missing," the prince said.

"Which brings me to ask question of your Highness?" Barton asked.

"Yes, Mr. Barton, what is it?"

"Sire. I would like to know how he was kidnapped in the first place, and why we are waiting almost a week before we look for him? No offense to royalty, but wouldn't it have been easier to just send us looking for him in the first place?"

The prince seemed a little disturbed by his question, and

fiddled with his fork.

"Well, it's a bit of an embarrassment on why he was captured. He wanted to take an excursion near Licarion Territory to see what the current situation was. I warned him about the danger, as to the recent battles both on land and sea which occurred recently. Being as stubborn as he always was, he decided to take a horse and break from his own royal guard to investigate. I sent a militia division containing a group of twelve men after him. Sgt. Barlow Lynden was delivering a message to Bashworth, when he ran into the party, and they were all ambushed. He disappeared, half the men were attacked and killed, and the other half captured as well. As for why I haven't sent anyone after them yet, it is my affair, and my affair alone. I have my reasons why I waited, and will reveal them to the council when I'm ready."

"I always trust your good judgement in this matter," Talandra said. "King Glaridia has told me to offer any help you might need from the Elven Kingdom."

Barton wasn't satisfied with his answer, but when addressing royalty, he didn't want to seem disrespectful. He sensed the Prince hid something, and purposely held off the search for some reason. It was just a feeling, and he had no proof of any wrong doing yet.

"I meant no disrespect to you, Your Majesty," Barton said.

"None taken," he answered. "And please, Majesty is my father, and I am not my father. I summoned each of you for special skills you possess which will aid in the rescue of Mr. Lynden's cousin and my father, and will be extremely useful in our search for the Gem of Rebolin."

"Just what has the gem got to do with finding your father?" the skeptical Lilly asked, who was the only woman there.

"Let's just say the gem has certain properties."

"Which are?"

"Christopher will explain more when the time warrants it."

"I'd like to know now, if you don't mind."

"As a woman, you'd be wise to know your place and curb your tongue," Vladimir interrupted.

The prince waved his right hand, and shook his head.

"It's quite all right, Vlad. She has a right to be curious, and I'm inclined to give such a lovely lady an answer." Lilly smiled as if to thank him for the compliment. "All those who touch the gem have the power to connect with it, and to determine its whereabouts, if separated from it. Christopher has touched it, and thus knows where it is."

"No disrespect to the prince, but I have a hard time accepting this whole magical deal."

"That's all right," Christopher replied. "Most people are non believers of magic or sorcery. Mainly because they live their entire lives without any proof of it."

"And we've yet to see any proof."

"Sire, are we going to listen to this woman and her driveling tripe, or get on with the meeting?" Vladimir asked, annoyed.

"Relax, Vlad, she's our guest. Please forgive my father's advisor, he's a bit impatient, and lacks the manners required in the presence of a lady. I can see Mrs. Tumberhill has her doubts about the ancient legends and their relevance to the situation. But I can assure you, when this is over, I'll make it completely worth your while. You'll be the richest woman in the Shudolin, next to my mother, rest her soul."

"Just what makes you think I can find what you're looking for?" Bargo asked.

"Because, my small friend, I have faith in your gift," the prince said.

"Perhaps if you could tell me exactly what I'm looking for, I can be more of an assistance to you."

"Of course. It is a round, light blue stone similar to a sapphire crystal, and transparent. It's about four inches in circumference, and cold to the touch."

"Cold to the touch?"

"Yes, cold as ice, until placed on the Staff of Varlana."

"And then what happens?" Barton asked.

"It glows a bright blue to white color, and becomes white hot to touch."

"Perhaps a reaction between the metal and stone," Bargo suggested. "But that doesn't sound like magic."

"Please, Your Highness," Vladimir interrupted. "This has gone far enough. If they don't believe in what you're trying to accomplish here, then you should find other recruits for the job.

BARGO LYNDEN

"Just what are you trying to accomplish here, Your Highness?" asked the suspicious Barton.

"I'm not sure I like your tone," the prince said. "Like your insinuating of something criminal."

"No, Sir, not at all. Just trying to get to exactly why we're here."

"Gentlemen, Gentlemen," Glam said. "I've already explained to our guests, the stone is to be used to defeat the evil bestowed upon us. It will be instrumental in finding both Bargo's cousin and the king. They need to know as much information about it as possible in order to locate those who were kidnapped, including the location of the stone."

"If you know where it is, why don't you just go get it?" Lilly asked.

"Again," the prince said. "Your abilities are needed for such a task. Our men have tried, and failed. Christopher, please tell us where the stone is."

The man closed his eyes for a moment, then reopened them, and turned towards the king. "It is near Bacon at the moment, in a secluded cave, guarded by a creature of some kind, a cross between a Woblo and a Licarion," he said.

"Interesting," Glam stated.

"Are Barlow Lynden and my father still alive?" the prince asked.

"Yes, they are, but your father has lost some of his willpower to live. The Woblo is trying to help him to survive, but his will is diminishing. The Licarions are pushing them to continue to their capitol."

"He can tell all that from connection of the stone?" Barton asked. "This is just getting too weird for me. I'm done, give me the 100 gold pieces, and I'll go home." He stood up, ready to leave.

"Sit down, Mr. Barton," the prince barked. "You will listen to what we have to say, and then if you decide to separate yourself from our little venture, you'll be free to leave with 500 gold pieces, if that's your wish." Barton, embarrassed, reseated himself, and the let the council continue. "Christopher also can connect with anyone else who has touched the stone."

"So Bacon is our new destination?" Glam questioned.

"Yes," Christopher said. "But we'll have to be careful, because Ang and his army of Grassmen will be close by in the Bacon Hills area."

"Why do you believe that?" Duke Cyres asked. "I've received no reports of attacks on any my villages in the area."

"Ang knows better than to attack in Shudolin Territory, but in neutral territory, such as on the west side of the hills, he has the advantage. He'll be waiting for us there."

"You said we'll have to be careful," Lilly said. "Are you coming with us."

"He must go with you., as he is the only one with the link to the stone," the prince stated. "The Woblo already has the ability, but not a clue how to use it."

"What are you talking about?" Bargo asked.

"There is an ancient legend about a Woblo with the ability to connect with certain types of stones. His name was Shala. It is said he once was human, and because of the Elven king's jealousy of his gift, he cast a spell on him, and made him a combination of animals, such as a rabbit, eagle, and man. He was the father of the Wobloin race. It was said certain descendants of him would have the ability as well; and I believe our friend Bargo to be one of them. The Elven folklore says the next king was so remorseful about his predecessor, he declared the Woblo as the Elven race's chosen people, after themselves. Tell me, Mr. Lynden, do you look at a stone, metal or mineral and know exactly which one it is?"

"Yes, but that's because I've studied about them."

"And before you studied?"

Bargo thought about this for a minute, and couldn't remember when he first knew how to identify stones, but it was sometime in his childhood. "I can't remember."

"You have the ability for magic, my friend, and the ability to defeat the evil surrounding us."

"The Woblo?" Barton laughed. "You must be joking."

"Must this simpleton be a part of this expedition, Sire?" Vladimir asked. "His manner of voice is most unbecoming."

"I must agree with Vladimir," the prince said. "If you can't be more productive, I will have to ask you to leave us."

"A minute ago you wanted me to stay. Very well, please

continue, I promise I won't interrupt again."

"Thank you, Mr. Barton, it's much appreciated," the prince said.

"The magic the Woblo possesses cannot be learned, it must come from deep inside him," Christopher said. "He must have the ability to bring it to the surface."

And how will I do that?" Bargo asked.

"It must be an act of desperation, a sacrifice for another to summon the power within your soul. Once you locate the gem or the staff, you'll use them to channel the power," Talandra explained.

"Does Ang know about this?" Bargo asked.

"Of course, that's why he wants it," the prince said. "It's imperative we stop him before he reaches his destination."

"But halfway across the countryside?" Lilly said. "We'll never get there in time. Which makes me even more curious why we're waiting to stop him."

"He knows not of the gem's whereabouts," Christopher said.

"I'm a bit confused," Bargo said. "I thought you said anyone who found and touched the stone had the ability to connect with it. Why can't Ang connect with it?"

"Because it masks the power of evil," Christopher said. "That's not to say evil cannot be used to summon the weapon's power against us; it can, but evil doesn't have the ability to use the stone for the purpose of finding itself. It's kind of a safeguard against our enemies. Only those who have a true heart for others are able to find it, and use it properly. Anyone else will be destroyed by the power of the staff and gem itself. Those who use it for evil purposes will face the wrath of the great Elven God Rhiatu, and be consumed by the very evil they spread tenfold. Our Woblo friend may be the Shudolin's only hope.."

"Well," Lilly stated. "I still don't believe in all this magic business, but if you're willing to pay me handsomely for killing Licarions, I'm in."

"Spoken like a true soldier," the prince said. "What about you, Mr. Barton, are you willing to go the distance as well, and head for Licarion territory, or are you going to leave here with a mere 500 gold pieces?"

"Well, if you put it that way, I guess I'm in. I might as well make this whole fiasco worthwhile."

"Very well. I will arrange for you to leave the day after tomorrow, early in the morning. Tomorrow, you will rest. Now, as I have other affairs to attend to, enjoy your dinner, and have a pleasant evening."

The prince, the council, and his advisor left the room. After they left, Barton turned to Glam.

"He doesn't seem too concerned about his father's safety."

"He and his father have a stormy relationship at best. I rather think he enjoys having control, but I know despite his misgivings, he loves his father."

"You'd never know it by his attitude."

"Like he said, he has his reasons," Christopher replied. "You know royalty has its privileges."

"I know," Barton answered. "I'd just like to know why we're not acting on this affair sooner."

"It seems like we're not allowed to question his motives, only do what we're told," Lilly said. "Let's just hope you're right about Bargo, or we'll be facing a whole army of Licarions without any help."

"I don't see how he could be," Bargo said. "Me performing magic is the most ridiculous thing I ever heard, even though I do believe in the stories."

"There you go again, Bargo," Lilly said. "You are capable of all kinds of magic, and you don't even know it yet. The magic of courage, bravery, and the magic of self sacrifice."

"I hardly call those things magic."

"They are magic to someone who has never been a fighter or soldier. You do not need a staff or gem to defeat an enemy, only courage, determination, and endurance."

"But if there are such things, they would be a nice reassurance," Barton added.

They continued their dinner, and Glam and Tamarka both retired early. Bargo, Lilly, and Barton sat on the balcony, while the Woblo played his banjo. He refrained from singing this time, as not to offend the man again. The week dragged for them, and knowing their party was well protected in the castle, they figured on catching up with their rest. They all needed to be prepared for the long journey they were to undertake, and the impending evil curse upon them all if they should fail. Lilly, for one didn't accept failure, and wouldn't stop a task until she followed through. She knew if the stories of magic were true, Bargo was the key to their survival and salvation, and she believed in him, just as his father did.

CHAPTER 10: OLD FRIENDS AND SUSPICIOUS MINDS

The next day, the party was scheduled to go into town to meet with Bargo's other cousin, Lieutenant Joeseph Garkee, of the Royal Navy, the only Woblo in the fleet to achieve officer status. Bargo was five years his senior, but made him quite proud, as being one of the youngest as well. He was staying over at a pub called appropriately "The Dark Days Ahead," which was next to the marina where his ship was stationed. Glam heard he was going to be there from Joeseph, back when they were in Dragginbuck.

Barton decided to stay behind, to nurse his arm for another day. He could move it quite well now, but still had some pain in his shoulder. His other reason for staying behind was to investigate if the prince was being honest with them or not. He had a strange feeling they were being lied to, and wanted to discover the truth once and for all. If he was caught, however, he'd be executed, and this was why he had to do it alone, without his friend's involvement.

Tamarka, and Christopher attended to their royal business, while they dropped Bargo and Lilly off at the pub. They left two guards outside the door of the pub, while they went in. The pub was crowded, and there were many races there including Elves, Woblos, and men. They went to the bar, and ordered two ales, as they looked around the pub. There were many sailors there on leave, as well as longshoremen, all enjoying their short time on land. A young man in his thirties approached them, and tapped on Bargo's shoulder. He turned to face the six feet, two inch man with curly black hair and a shaven face.

"Are you Bargo Lynden?"

"Yes." He was a little nervous, due to his height, over two feet taller than him.

"Your cousin is back in the corner of the pub, sitting at a table."

BARGO LYNDEN

"Thanks."

They walked to the back, until they came to a table where a brown Woblo sat, his stern look of having braved the sea first hand, as well as fought a few battles. For a young sailor, he was well seasoned at the art of war on the water. When he greeted his cousin, he rose to his feet, and extended his hand.

"Welcome, my Cousin Bargo. Please sit down. Joeseph told me you'd be in town. He tells me that you've decided to join our cause against the Licarions?"

"Yes, but I'm afraid it cost my father his life."

"Yes, I heard about it, and I'm truly sorry," he said, and took a sip of his ale. " I just heard he tried to protect you."

"If it weren't for me, he wouldn't have had to. I'm such an idiot."

"Bargo," Lilly interrupted. "Don't you dare call yourself that."

"Do you think you're only one who hasn't lost someone at the hand of the Licarions? I have seen many of my friends stabbed, pierced, burned, or hung. Do you think with you it would any different? This war is worse than any of us imagined, with the Licarions gaining control of the waterways. The area by Old Mongo used to belong to the kingdom, until Ang and his marauders took it over. They've never traveled that far north before."

"What about the militia?" 'Lilly asked.

"What militia? Most of the militia has been depleted inland. And the Elves aren't willing to leave their kingdom vulnerable."

"That's funny. The prince seemed to think he had everything under control. He was going to send a militia troop with us through Bacon Hills."

"He would." His tone smacked of sarcasm.

"What do you mean?" Bargo asked.

"Despite what he says, he's not fond of his father at all. In fact, he loathes him. He wants you to believe everything's fine, while everything's falling apart around him, and when his father does return, he'll blame the whole thing on him for leaving."

"How do you know all this?" Lilly asked.

"I have my sources too. Enough business. So tell me, Bargo, how's Aunt Catherine in Woblo Town?"

"She's fine. She's about the only local family I have left."

"I remember she used to make the best rhubarb pies. I can still remember smelling them three blocks away, and every kid on the block would hate those kind of pies, but they loved the smell just the same."

"That was a long time ago. When Mother was still alive."

"Bargo must look to the future, not the past. Isn't that right?" Lilly asked, as she tried to put him in a more cheerful mood.

"Yes," Bargo said. "How long will you be staying?"

"A day or two. Then we have orders to head towards the Licarion Islands. The fighting is extremely tense there. I was supposed to go with you, but things changed. Where is your mission taking you?"

"To Bacon and Jarod."

"That's awfully close to enemy lines. Be careful."

"He has the expertise of Glam and Christopher of the Royal Guard to protect him, as well as Mr. Barton and myself."

"Barton? Horatio Barton?"

"His name is Horatio?' Lilly asked, as Bargo laughed loudly.

"The man I know is Horatio. Describe him for me."

"An older gentleman with a scar on the left side of his cheek, has grayish hair, about five feet ten inches," Lilly said. "He has a tendency to be annoying."

"Sounds like him. How come he isn't with you now?"

"He said he was resting his sprained arm before we left on our quest."

"If I know him, he's doing more than that. Well, tell him I said hi when you see him, okay?"

"I will do so," Bargo said. "After I ridicule him for his name."

"You will do no such thing, Bargo Lynden," Lilly scolded. "Let's keep this our secret. If the time is right we should mention it, we'll mention it together, agreed?"

"Yes, Ma'am."

"Well, it's good to see you again, Bargo," Joe said. "I hope you're successful in your assignment, and everything goes well with the shop, even if you do decide to sell it. I always admired your father for leaving this disaster called a military. It wasn't this bad before the king left."

"How long ago was that?" Lilly asked.

"Three weeks, maybe four."

The two of them looked at one another in disbelief, and then back at the Woblo.

"He really isn't in any hurry at all to find his father, is he?" Lilly asked.

"He wants the kingdom for himself."

"But he seemed so nice. He even flattered me with compliments."

"Just manipulation to get what he wants. I've been with the navy about five years, and I've seen enough to know when someone is trying to manipulate the system to get what he wants."

"Do you have any proof?"

"I'm afraid not, but I do have this." He reached inside his pocket, and pulled out half of a small, four inch squared stone tablet with Elven writing on it. He handed it to his cousin. "I found it near the beaches of the Licarion Islands."

"That doesn't make sense. Why would there be an artifact with Elven writing on it so far south?"

"This is a mystery I'm afraid I can't answer. I do know when I visited the palace over a month ago with some recruits, I saw the other half in the king's trophy room."

"In his trophy room?" Bargo asked. "Perhaps it has some significance to the gem and staff?"

"Gem? Staff?"

"Fairy tales," Lilly said. "Do you know what it says?"

"I have no idea, I never learned to read Elven."

"Do you mind if we borrow it for a while?"

"You can have it if you want. I just kept it for a souvenir."

"Thanks, Joeseph. I have a feeling it will be of some importance to us, I'm just not sure how yet."

"Well, good luck on your venture. I'll try to get to Woblo Town as soon as this mess is over with. I have some business to attend to and some money to collect, so if you'll excuse me?"

"Of course, Joe," Bargo said. "We'll see you soon."

They finished their drinks, he gave his cousin a hug, and then the two of them met the guards outside the pub. The Royal Guard then escorted them back to the palace.

During this time, Barton left his room to get a peek around. He heard the prince would be extra busy, which gave him the opportunity to do a little investigating. He ventured just down the hall, and tried to gain access to the royal wing upstairs from their quarters, but found it over guarded, and impossible to navigate. He went downstairs, and took a look around, first in the ball room. He didn't believe there was anything in there worthwhile, so he continued on. A guard took an interest in him, so rather than avoid him, he approached him in the large front room, next to where the trophy room was.

"Excuse me, Sir," he said. "Would it be possible for me to view the trophy room? I have an interest in ancient artifacts and the such."

"Of course," the guard said. "But I'll have to be present while you view it. No one is permitted in there without supervision. The king has always been very suspicious someone might try to steal something."

"That's fine. You can trust me."

He unlocked the door, and Barton followed him, eyeing over the several animal horns on the wall, as well as a variety of vases, weapons, scrolls, and pottery. One mount on the wall contained an object which caught his eye right away; a long, staff made of pure gold-the Staff of Varlana. There was a small stone tablet which was broken in half which also peaked his curiosity.

"This small stone tablet on the shelf," Barton asked. "Do you know anything about it?"

"It was given to the previous king long ago by the Elven king. It's been here as long as anyone remembers."

"What happened to the other half of it?"

"I have no idea. Is there anything else you would like to know?"

"Yes, this staff here, what can you tell me about it?"

"The king does not permit us to discuss it."

"Why's that? Is not the Staff of Varlana public knowledge?"

"I did not say it was the Staff of Varlana. I merely said I won't discuss it."

"Whatever your wish. Hey, can you tell me how to get to the royal wing? I have a meeting with the prince later."

"That is also off limits to our guests. If he is expecting you, he'll summon one of the guards to retrieve you, wherever you are on the grounds."

"Thanks, I'll go to my room and wait there."

After Barton realized he would get no where with this guard, he walked up the stairway, and back to his room. Frustrated, he paced a few minutes to think of a way he could get into the royal wing, and into the throne room, or even perhaps the council chambers. He wasn't exactly sure what to look for, except for some form of implication the prince was somehow responsible for his father's disappearance.

He walked out on the balcony, looked towards the moat below, and spotted several of the guards walk the floors below and in the front of the palace. There were at least one hundred of them, who periodically checked above them, behind them, and sometimes even below them. The situation seemed hopeless, until Barton noticed the vines growing over the castle, and how they connected on the different sections of the outside walls.

He was never much for climbing, but did do a little in his youth. Nervous, but determined, he grabbed the vine and tugged it to make sure it would hold him. When he saw the coast was clear, he climbed off the balcony, and onto the building, navigating the vines upwards about fifty feet, until he came to the next balcony. He looked down once or twice, which scared him to no end, but told himself he'd be safe, as long as he stayed focused.

When he reached the next balcony, he climbed onto to it, pressed himself against the wall, and peered around its corner to look into the council chamber. At the moment it was empty, so he thought he'd go in to explore the room. Before he could do so, the doors opened, and the prince entered with his advisor. He remained motionless, while they had their secret conversation, unaware they were being spied on.

"Vladimir, did you take care of our problem yet?" the prince asked.

"It's in the process, Sire. As soon as we find your father, and he reveals the whereabouts of the last three Licarion base camps, we'll discover the location of the stone, and I'll have someone finish the job."

"These three spies Glam enlisted. They seem like they could be trouble."

"I can have them eliminated as well, if that's what you wish?"

"Not just yet. Why don't you send for Kain; I'd like to talk to him first. We'll take care of the Elves, the woman, and Barton once they reach the other side of Bacon Hills. They'll have no militia protection there."

"What about the Woblo?"

"We need him. He's the key to the weapon's power."

"And Ang?"

"We need him as well; at least for a while. I haven't decided whether he has a place in our new kingdom or not yet."

"He won't like it if you doublecross him."

"What makes you think I'm scared of him?"

"Sir, he has the power. Even if he's just a servant for the sorcerer."

"And we have the staff, and as long as we have the staff, we have the real power. Just make sure my father's dead before they find the stone. Now go get Kain."

"Yes, Sire."

The advisor left the room, and the prince thought he was alone. He sat down in a chair at the table, and waited for Vladimir to bring his prisoner up. Barton was about to sneeze from the smell of the ivy leaves, and covered his nose. He made a soft noise, but still loud enough for the prince to hear. He got up and walked to the balcony, while Barton hung over the side. The guard on the floor above him heard the leaves rustle, and looked below. He crawled, hanging on with both his hands and feet, until he was upside down, and under the balcony. His muscles tensed up with fear, but once he realized the prince went back inside, he crawled back on the balcony. and looked above to make sure the guard left.

Back in his position, he heard the door open and shut again. The prince directed his prisoner in, and offered him a seat. The guard unlocked his shackles, and the prince sat down across from him.

"Mr. Kain," he said. "As you know, I'm a fairly reasonable man. I'm willing to offer you a full pardon for a little information."

"What kind of information?"

BARGO LYNDEN

"The location of Ang and his Grassmen."

"I don't know what you're talking about."

"Don't play coy with me. I know you're his right hand man, and you will help me, or you'll die a slow, agonizing death."

"What's in it for me if I agree to your terms?"

"Your life spared, and about 500 gold pieces."

"He said something about heading towards Bacon Hills, and onto Bacon."

"Why Bacon?"

"I don't know, something about a blue stone he was looking for."

"He knew it was in Bacon?"

"That's what he said."

"Very well, I will spare your life, but you have to do something for me. I want you to find Ang and stay with him. We will have a troop of men in the Bacon Hills. I'll see to it personally they follow you the whole way. Once you find him, send us a signal."

"What kind of signal?"

"I'm sure you'll think of something. Do you have any requests before I turn you loose?"

"Yes, my hat returned to me, if you don't mind."

"Of course, Mr. Kain. Have a good day."

When he and the guards left the room, the prince turned back to his advisor.

"Do you think he'll tell Ang he saw us?"

"No, Sire. If I know Mr. Kain, he reacts to the highest bidder, and Ang isn't paying him 500 gold pieces. He'll be loyal, as long as there's money involved."

"Nonetheless, I want him followed as well; to make sure he follows through."

"Yes, Sire."

"It will be a new day in the Shudolin Kingdom, where we'll crush the Licarion Army first, then gain the trust of the Elves. Once I have the power of the staff, the Elves and the rest of the Shudolin will bow to me alone. Come, we have much to do."

When they left the room, Barton entered the council chambers to have a look around. He found a piece of paper which interested him to a great degree. It was a drawing of the tablet, but was whole, and missing the writing on the left half of it. Whoever drew it was trying to decipher it, but without the other half, this was impossible.

Not able to find any other evidence, he grabbed it, left the room, and climbed the ivy vines back to his own room, making sure no one saw him. Just about this time, there was a knock at his door. Out of breath, he walked over to it, and was greeted by the prince himself.

"Are you all right, Mr. Barton, you seem a little pale, and out winded?"

"Yes, just struggling with my arm." He rubbed it, as it was even more sore from climbing.

"It seems one of my men saw or heard someone moving around the outside of the palace. You haven't seen anyone, have you?"

"No, I haven't."

"If you do, you will let me know, won't you? If there's one thing I can't stand, it's spies. You aren't a spy are you, Mr. Barton?"

"Only for the Shudolin."

"I hope that is the case, Mr. Barton. I would hate to have to do anything I might regret, if you take my meaning?"

"Yes, your Majesty, I mean Highness."

"Have a good day, Mr. Barton."

"Good day, Prince."

While the prince left the room, Lilly and Bargo returned, and Barton waved for them to come in. He shut the door behind him, and faced his friends in anticipation.

"I've got some information for you," he said.

"And we've got something to show you and Glam, whenever he gets back," Lilly said.

"I know what the prince's plan is?"

"What in the Shudolin are you talking about?"

"I overheard him and his advisor talking. They're planning to kill the king, then us, and then Ang as well."

"And how did you happen to just overhear him?"

"I climbed up the side of the building to the royal floor."

"You could have gotten killed," Bargo told him. "That was a

foolish thing to do."

"But it paid off. Look what I found." He pulled out the sketch and showed it to the two of them. Bargo folded it, then pulled the stone tablet fragment from his pocket, and placed it next to the other half of the drawing, revealing the entire text. "Hey, where did you get the other half ?"

"My cousin gave it to me," Bargo answered.

"What does it mean?"

"I don't know, but Glam will," Lilly said. "Bargo's cousin seemed to think the prince was less than savory as well. Does he know you have the drawing?"

"Not yet, but I do believe he's a little suspicious," Barton said. "I think we should get out of here while we can. There's no way we're ever going to collect on this deal anyway. He wants us eliminated; everyone but Bargo that is."

"Why does he want Bargo?"

"For the same reason Ang wants him. He has the power to use the gemstone and staff."

"As soon as Glam comes back, we have to come up with a plan. Joeseph Garkee thought the prince wants to take the kingdom for himself, and have his father murdered."

"That ties in with what I overheard. I'd say we have sufficient evidence to turn over to the Royal Council."

"Yes," Glam said, as he and Tamarka entered the room. "But who will be the ones to hear it? The council cannot approve a request for removal of a king or prince without authorization by the royal advisor, and from what you say, Barton, he's in league with the prince."

"Can't the Elven king take his place?" Bargo asked.

"His power is limited here," Glam said. "Unless you can prove to the council Vladimir is conspiring against the king, you won't be able to remove either one from power. And everyone around here knows he and the king have been close friends for years."

"Then why is he conspiring to kill him?"

"Simple," Lilly said. "Greed, power, and promise of security."

"Exactly," Glam remarked.

Lilly handed the Elf the broken tablet and the drawing to evaluate.

"I found the drawing in the room above us. The actual part is in the trophy room on the first floor," Barton said. "And Bargo's cousin, Joeseph Garkee gave us the tablet."

"He said to say hi," Bargo said. "To you and Barton."

"Yes, I know him," Glam stated. "He and I were stationed together at Fort Shendlekend. He's a good sailor, and remarkable Woblo. You can tell you're related. As for the writing, it's an old Elven language seldom used anymore, and judging from this half of the stone, I would say at least 1000 years old. Unfortunately, it's a bit under my expertise, but Chris will be able to read it in the morning. We need to return the drawing so the prince will believe we know nothing of his plot. Tamarka, copy down the other half of the writing on a separate piece of paper, and then Barton can return it back where he got it."

"But that means I have to go back up the side of the castle again."

"That's the price you pay for not minding your own business," Glam laughed. "Cheer up, when this is all over, I may consider hiring you as one of my own spies."

"Thanks. But if it means risking my neck to return a dumb piece of paper, you can count me out."

"That dumb piece of paper may have given us a very important clue as to where the gemstone is."

"He also has the Staff of Varlana in the trophy room as well. They denied it, but judging from what you described, it has to be it."

"There's only one problem. If the prince has the staff, once we get the stone, he could use it against us. We have to get it away from him somehow."

"But if we steal it tonight, he'll know we took it," Tamarka said.

"Yes, that does present a problem," Glam said. "I think for the moment, we should follow his lead. Once we get to Bacon and find the stone, we can figure it out from there."

"He said he was sending a troop behind us to keep an eye on our progress," Barton said. "And there's one more thing-Kain's with them."

"What? That fool?" the angered Elf said. "He'd make a deal

with a demon if it could keep him out of jail. Does Ang know?"

"I'm not sure. But Vladimir said they were going to pay Kain considerably more money to let them know of his whereabouts."

"Blood money. If Ang discovers Kain's doublecrossed him, he'll gut him for sure. Well, you better get going, and be careful. At least at night, you'll be harder to see."

"And so will the side of the wall."

"You'll do fine. You've been fumbling in the dark for years, and I think you're used to it by now."

CHAPTER ELEVEN: THE TRUTH REVEALED

Later that evening, Barton climbed the ivy again to the royal council chamber. Fortunately, no guards saw him, and the room was dark. He fumbled his way through, as he felt objects around the room, trying to be careful not to trip over something. He placed the drawing on the table, and headed for the balcony. The door opened behind him, he panicked, and hid behind a large cabinet. The prince came in the room, and saw the drawing moved from the spot where he left it. He looked about the room for proof of a visitor, but decided he was alone. Feeling satisfied the wind moved it, he dismissed it, and left the room.

"That was close," Barton said aloud. He then slipped out the back, climbed down the ivy, and back to his room.

The next morning, the prince arranged for them to have eleven horses; two for the wagon, and nine for the group. Three of Christopher's men were to go along, as well as a regiment from Fort Shendlekend, who were to meet them on the other side of Bacon Hills. Glam was doubtful of this, however, after now knowing the prince's involvement in his father's disappearance.

They left the palace early in the morning, and headed down the road that would take them to Baconsworth, and eventually over to Bacon and Jarod. They knew at some point they would be ambushed, but guessed this wouldn't happen until they found the stone. When they were sure they weren't being followed, Glam stopped to address his party.

"They'll think we're going to cross the hills at Baconsworth, using the north access route," he said. "But that won't be the case. We'll cross at Morka, and go right across the hills. Ang won't be so easy to deceive, however, because he knows me too well. So once we leave Morka, stay sharp. Christopher, did you get a chance to decipher the writing on the stone tablet?"

"Yes. It says: those who have true belief of the power of the of the Orac Valatu will be the one who unlocks its power. The ultimate sacrifice of one's soul will be the only thing that will protect one from the evil stone which will consume you."

"The Orac Valatu?" Bargo asked.

"I was puzzled by that too," confessed the cunning linguist. "Until I did a little reading into some old texts, and found out what it was. The Orac Valatu is an old Elven term for "the chosen one.""

"Could that be Bargo?" Lilly asked.

"I cannot give you a definite answer. But I can tell you this. The stone tablet is connected to the Staff of Varlana and the Gem of Rebolin; there's no doubt about it."

"Which explains why the Prince has the other half of it." Barton said.

"Ah, yes, but he doesn't know the whole text. We do," Glam said. "Are you sure you can trust your men, Chris?"

"Yes. They are loyal to me, and me alone. They answer to the king, not his ungrateful son."

"I hope you're right," Barton said. "I wouldn't want to have to kill the only ones protecting us."

"You flatter yourself, Mr. Barton. As good a marksman and swordsman as you are, you're no match for these men."

"Let's hope it doesn't come to that point," Glam said. "We're all on the same side here, and we have to work together. Until I hear otherwise, we'll assume there are no spies among us."

"I hate to be a stickler for details," Barton said. "But just how are we going to collect our portion of payment if the king is murdered?"

"You will be paid, Mr. Barton," Christopher assured him. "Even if I have to do it myself."

They continued down the path towards Sanoth, a small village south of Riverton which was on the sea, where three generations of two families lived. They knew Glam and Christopher well, and were more than happy to trade supplies and lodgings for the night for some pelts they brought from the king's palace. After Sanoth, they continued on the South Pass towards the hills. They circumvented Morka, to avoid drawing too much attention there, and continued into the hills from there to a small homestead, where an old friend of Glam's lived.

His property rested on a steep hill which overlooked the valley and river on its back side, with a large green field in front covering at least a mile. The 20' by 20'house was made from sod and stone, and had a wooden stable located next to it with room for twelve horses. When they approached the structure, they could smell beef stew permeating in the air, and watched as the bright sun set behind them. Glam knocked on the wooden door, and was greeted by an older gentleman in his seventies, who walked with a cane and a limp. He smiled at his old friend and gave him a tight hug.

"Glam, my friend. So good to see you. Come in, all of you. What brings you around these parts?"

"A mission to protect the Shudolin, as usual. William, I would like you to meet my friends, Bargo Lynden, Lilly Tumberhill, Mr. Barton, and Tamarka. Christopher, Daniel, Reginald and Thomas are with the Royal Guard."

"Please to meet all of you. Make yourselves at home. I've got some great stew. I've got room in here for three of you, but the rest will have to sleep in the stable. I'm sorry."

"Lilly, Christopher, and I will sleep in here. Tamarka, why don't you and Chris take care of the horses. I'll be out in a minute. I have something to discuss with you."

"Anything we need to know about?" Lilly asked.

"Not at this time. I just need to discuss our plan from here. Once we've reached a decision, we'll fill you in. I promise."

The two Elves and Christopher met out by the stable, while the others ate dinner. Glam approached Tamarka, who fed the horses some hay, and lit his pipe.

"Do you think Bargo will be able to fulfill the prophecy, once we find the stone?" he asked.

"I don't know," Glam stated. "I'm beginning to wonder if we haven't made a mistake trusting in him."

"But he is the one who is able to use the magic properly once shown how. Is he aware of your powers?"

"My powers are limited to parlor tricks and crystal balls, and will do nothing against the Licarion Empire or Garlock. We need one of the chosen, and I don't believe Bargo is it. Does he know what the rest of the encryption meant, the part you failed to tell him?

125

BARGO LYNDEN

"What part you failed to mention?" the eavesdropping Woblo asked. "I'm sorry, but I came out to get my banjo."

"Bargo, it's really of no consequence at this point." Glam said.

"You seem to think because I'm a common, every day Woblo, and some kind of freak, I won't be capable of following through. What did he fail to mention?"

"The other part of the Elven writing states the Woblo who possesses the staff and gem will also have the power to change all his kind back to humans, if they wish."

Bargo thought about this for a moment; what it would be like to be the same as everyone else, and free of the insensitive remarks said by others who saw him as different. Then he also thought of all the pride and heritage his relatives brought him up upon, and what it meant to his race.

"I used to think you believed in me, Glam. Now I'm not so sure."

"Bargo-"

"Leave me alone!" Lilly, who was now also outside, tried to place her arm around him, but he shrugged it away. "I'll show you what a Woblo's capable of."

"You shouldn't feed such nonsense in his head," she said. "Isn't it enough he's mocked for who he is, without telling him some fable he can change everything through magic?"

"I only state what has already been written," Christopher said. "It's up to him whether he believes or not."

"It would help if people believed in him once in a while as well," Lilly barked, and ran into the house.

"Something tells me this is going to be a long night," Glam said.

While they rested for the evening, there was talk of Glam's earlier days, when he fought in the infantry with William. He was stationed as a corporal for the Shudolin Militia, and William was a fellow soldier who fought beside him near Bashworth.

"Did you know Bargo's father, Sgt. Jeremiah Lynden?" Lilly asked the old man.

"No, I'm afraid not, but I have heard of him," William said. "I met Glam when we were at battle near Bashworth. I was about to be stabbed by a Licarion, and Glam jumped in and saved me.

We've been friends ever since, and whenever he's in the area, my home is his home, as well as his friends' home."

"Well, we appreciate it," Glam said. "We'll be leaving first thing in the morning. Do you have some blankets for our stable guests?"

"Of course," he said. "I wish there was more room in here for all of you, but it's just the right size for me, and a guest or two."

"That's quite all right," Barton said. "We're used to roughing it, aren't we, Bargo?" The Woblo, who was still sulking about the argument earlier, nodded. "Come on, Bargo let's turn in."

"Okay," he said, as Lilly came over to him.

"Don't take what they said to heart," she told him. "You are the bravest Woblo I've ever known."

"Thanks. At least you appreciate that."

Barton, Tamarka, and Christopher's men went out to the stable to situate themselves for the evening. The smell of the horse manure was something Bargo had a hard time getting used to, but where they were sleeping, there wasn't any.

As they sat down on their makeshift beds, Barton lit his pipe, took a puff, and turned to his Woblo friend. "You know, Bargo," he said. "When I first met you, I felt the same as other people, and questioned why we were allowing an animal come with us."

"Yes, I remember."

"I'm truly sorry for that; it was mean and unfair. But after I got to know you, I realized you're the same as anyone else, despite your size and appearance. It's been a pleasure to know you, and call you a friend."

"Why thank you, Barton. I never expected you to say such a statement. It's a real comfort hearing that."

"And I also want you know, if you ever run into trouble, I've got your back."

"Thanks. Well, good night."

"Good night, Bargo," Barton said, as he tapped out his pipe on the ground, stomped on it, then threw the blanket over himself.

The next morning, they packed the wagon with some more supplies, and prepared the horses to leave. William came out to see them off, and pulled Glam aside.

"Before you leave, I'd like to show you a little something I picked up in Bashworth last week," he said.

He walked in between the house and the stable, where something was covered by a quilt. He lifted the quilt, revealing a device of some kind. It was a long, wooden box supported by four wooden wheels, and hollow in the middle, which allowed a long arm with a weight to move freely back and forth. There was a tension rope which pulled the arm all the way back, and locked by a trip lever. There was a cloth sack at the end, used to launch projectiles.

"What is it?" Glam asked.

"I like to call it a "rock thrower."

"It's a very nice weapon, William, but impractical for our purpose, I'm afraid. Thanks for the thought anyway."

"If you change your mind, it'll be here for you. Goodbye, friend, it's been nice seeing you again."

"William, take care, my dear friend."

They left the homestead, and headed up the hill to the west, traveling down the South Pass, which led around the river and valley. They had to follow the direction of the waterway, but stay to higher ground. Hidden from Glam's view, the Elf sensed they were already being followed by Ang and his men once they left Sanoth. Two hours passed, when he heard commotion coming from the direction of William's home. He turned to his party in haste.

"Tamarka, take the others and pass through that crest to the west. Chris, come with me."

"What's wrong?" Barton asked.

"Just go to the other side, I'll catch up."

Glam and Christopher darted on their horses as fast as they could back to William's house. They found William fending off Ang and the Grassmen with the catapult. Glam and Christopher approached the front of the homestead and drew their swords, fighting off the invaders, who tried to charge the land. An arrow plunged into Christopher's chest, as he fell off his horse, and against the side of the stable. Glam dismounted, and ran to his friend, for he feared for his safety.

"Are you all right, Chris?"

"I'll be all right. Once I reach the afterlife. Get out of here, while you have the chance."

"Don't talk that way, you're going to make it."

"Good bye, old friend," he said, as he gripped his hand tight. "It's been a pleasure to serve with you."

"As it is for me."

He closed his eyes for the last time, and Glam turned to William, who loaded another rock onto his device, when a dark figure came from behind him, and lunged a knife into his back.

"Kain!" Glam yelled, as he threw a star of death at him. The elusive Kain dodged it, as it stuck in the wall behind him, and he disappeared around the house. Glam ran around the back to chase him, but mounted his horse when he was attacked by three Grassmen. He fought them off with his sword, slicing the arm off one, and stabbing the other two with the end of the weapon. After he realized he was outnumbered, he took evasive action, disappeared up the path, and away from the land, only to look back at the smoke coming from that direction. He raced the horse up the hill to catch up with his friends. Once he reached them, they could tell by the expression on his face things didn't go well.

"Where's Christopher?" Tamarka asked.

"In paradise now, as well as William," he answered. "Kain stabbed him."

Bargo, after hearing this, was a bit remorseful of the way he treated Glam earlier.

"I'm sorry," he said.

"He knew the risks involved," Glam said. "He died like the great soldier he was."

"Now what?" Barton asked. "He was our only connection with the stone."

"Well, he seemed to think it was near Jarod. We'll start there. But we have to keep moving; Ang is not far behind."

They continued up the hill, navigated the tough terrain, and followed the river valley below. As his horse trotted along, Glam noticed something and stopped. He dismounted the animal, and picked up a dry fish bone.

"What would a fish bone being doing this high up?" Tamarka asked.

"Licarions," Glam said. He also noticed some tracks in the

dirt which were still fresh. There was no rain the night before, and it was a sunny day. "Look, tracks. I notice the human and Licarion tracks, but I don't know what the others are."

"Woblo tracks," Bargo said. "They've been through here."

"The tracks lead to the south," Glam said. "We'll keep moving in that direction. We only have a few hours of daylight, so we better find a place to camp for the night."

"We're really sorry about Chris," Lilly told him."

"No matter," Glam reiterated. "We've all lost people to wars. I lost my parents when I was young, and many friends since that."

"You're an orphan just like me," Bargo stated.

"Yes, I am," Glam said. "And us orphans have to stick together, right?"

"Yes," Bargo said, as he saw Glam tried to make a mends with him. "You're absolutely right."

By nightfall, they found a comfortable spot on a hill in a clearing of about 300 feet. It was at the top, and surrounded by trees on the south and west sides. They weren't too concerned about the east side, for it overlooked the valley, and the south side of trees was far enough away to see anyone coming. Once they set up for the night, Glam turned to his party.

"Tamarka, you and Barton take the first half of the night on the south side. Daniel, Thomas and Reginald can take the west side. The rest of us will take our turn later."

They followed his orders, as Bargo and Lilly started a small fire to keep warm. They didn't want anything larger, for it would attract attention and give away their location. After dinner, Bargo was eager to play his banjo, but Glam advised him against it.

"Just because we don't hear them doesn't mean they're not out there. I'm afraid the odds are against after this point."

"What are you saying?" Barton asked. "That we should run?"

"We are outnumbered. We should wait at least until the prince's men arrive. At least then we'll have a fighting chance."

"Are you going to let them get away with killing your friends? I say we fight now."

"As much as I'd like to, to do so would not only be foolish, but suicidal. Bargo is the key, once we find the stone, it is our only defense. When we're ready to attack, I'll give the order to do so."

"I thought you didn't believe I was the chosen one?" Bargo asked, surprised he changed his tone.

"I was wrong," Glam said. "I should've listened to you. We'll be safe once we retrieve your cousin, the stone, and get back to Riverton."

"Do you ever regret living this kind of life?"

"Many times. I had a woman once I loved very much."

"What happened?" Lilly asked.

"She didn't want a man who was always away fighting battles, and I wasn't ready to settle down."

"What about Ang? What's his story?" Barton asked.

"He and I were close friends once, but the power of evil consumed him. He was a member of the Royal Guard as I, and at one time we fought along side of each other. Greed and power made him the monster he is today, working hand in hand with the Licarions to destroy the Shudolin."

"Why is after you? For the stone?" Lilly asked.

"That, and we have an old score to settle."

"What score?" Barton asked.

"I'd rather not talk about it. It was a long time ago, and it's time it was put to rest, as Bargo should as well."

""Bargo's doing just fine," Lilly said. "He just needs a little respect."

"And that he shall get," Glam announced. "I wouldn't be surprised if the king gave him a medal when this is all over."

"I don't need a medal, just my father back," Bargo said.

"A medal won't bring him back, but it would at least get you the respect you deserve," Barton said. "We all owe you that much."

"Enough of these melancholy thoughts," Glam said. "Tomorrow is a new day, with a new plan."

"We'll need a miracle to get through this trip," Barton said. Bargo thought about the legend of the gem and the staff, and how it pertained to him. After he overheard Glam, he remembered the stories told when he was younger about how Woblos were once men, and it made him think of Lilly and him. He told her he loved her like a sister, but the truth was he had deep feelings for her, and even though she knew her husband was a good man who treated her right, he couldn't help but feel she would be better off with him. He wished he was human in this respect, because maybe she would feel the same way about him. Barton was right about one thing, however. They did need a miracle to defeat Ang and his Grassmen, and the Bargo just hoped he was the miracle they were all looking for.

CHAPTER TWELVE: THE SOUTH PASS

The next morning, Vladimir's men arrived on William's land, only to find ashes and rubble. They approached the land with caution, as smoke still billowed through the air. The commander approached the top of the hill, dismounted his horse, and walked towards the homestead. His second in command, Jonathon found Christopher's charred body lying next to where the stable was. Next to him lay half of a small stone tablet, which Vladimir put in his pocket, for he knew it was the second half to the one in the trophy room. Sorrowed by his death, he said a prayer, stood up, and realized there was also the body of William a few feet away.

"Who would do such a thing to an old man?" Jonathon asked.

"Ang and his Grassmen, that's who," Vladimir answered. "And from the looks of it, he wasn't here long ago. We haven't received a signal from Kain yet, however."

"Do you think he's remained loyal to him?"

"No, he'll contact us. The only thing he's loyal to is gold. It looks like they crossed the west passage over there to get around the river. Let's head that way."

"Yes, Sir."

Vladimir knew with Christopher dead, the connection to the stone was lost, but was grateful he found the other half of the tablet. The prince, a fond collector of artifacts, would be pleased he found it. He was shocked Christopher had it in his possession, and wondered where he might have got it from, considering the prince looked for it for years .

He was struggling with the decision to follow through with this endeavor, and reconsidering his position. Although the prince wanted him to kill his father and the others, he felt when the time came, he couldn't actually bring himself to do it. He hoped Ang would take care of this part of the mission himself, and save him the trouble.

BARGO LYNDEN

Although there were differences between him the king, they were friends for years. He just found it very hard to accept his lackadaisical approach to the Licarions, and felt he lacked the courage to take a head on attack. The prince was much more aggressive, however, and Vladimir agreed more with his principles than his father's, but he sometimes doubted his sanity as well. His obsession with the staff and gem made him worry he might be consumed by evil the way Ang was.

When they reached the top of the western crest, alongside of the path, he found a bloody cloth, which looked like part of the king's jacket. He dismounted, and looked it over carefully. "The Licarions have been through here. Horses as well. Let's move on, shall we?"

Further to the south, Glam and the others were still following the river valley, and found it difficult to navigate with the wagon. The foliage was thick through the forest, but there were also moments where the ground was level and more open. They knew Ang was at least a couple hours behind them, and this drove them on for as long as the sun would allow them to travel. While they started up the south pass, a treacherous road which took them closer toward the valley, Bargo remembered something.

"Glam, Christopher never returned the stone tablet to me."

"Don't worry." His horse galloped next to him. "Even if they are able to decipher the writing, the prince or Ang won't be able to do anything without the stone or the staff."

"Glam, I'm sorry about what I said the other night."

"Forget it. We've got more important things to worry about. Once we get near Jarod, we'll be near Licarion Territory, and won't get any help from militias."

He walked his horse ahead, as Bargo slowed down to talk with Lilly.

"What a gorgeous afternoon," she said to him. "If the rest of the trip's weather is like the past two days have been, we should get there in no time."

"Lilly, there's something I need to ask you," Bargo said, as he came closer to her horse.

"What is it, Bargo?"

"If I was different, say a human, how would you feel about

me?"

"That's a strange question to ask me now. I guess I wouldn't feel any different."

"Would you still think of me as a brother?"

"I already think of you as a brother."

"I guess what I mean is, do you think of me as an animal, or a pet?"

"Of course not, I've told you that before. You're my friend, no matter what."

"Could I ever be more than a friend to you?'"

"Why would you ask such a question? I have a husband I love very much."

"What if something happened to him? How would you feel then?"

"I would be heartbroken. You're silly, Mr. Bargo Lynden, talking about what ifs? You are what you are, and I am what I am. There's nothing that's ever going to change that, despite what these crazy Elves tell you."

"Try to keep up with the rest of us, you two," Glam commanded, as he came to a rock cliff which overlooked the path. "Be careful through here. There may be some loose rocks above us."

They watched the cliff, and kept closer to the valley's edge, but careful they didn't lose their footing. They passed the cliff, and went up a path in the woods, which led to another large clearing with good tactical advantage. The plateau allowed them to see for a good mile away, and was completely surrounded by trees, which were all below the clearing, enabling them to see from all directions. Glam stopped, dismounted, and stared out at the landscape and the river valley below them.

"We'll set up camp here for the night," he said. "Same watch schedule as last night. If you hear anything, let us know. Tamarka, why don't you double back about a half mile to see if we're being followed? We'll have to camp light tonight, and no cooking. We'll keep a warm fire, but a small one."

"Do you expect Ang to attack tonight?" Barton asked.

"No, he'll probably just keep an eye on us until we get past Bacon Hill, then he'll attack. But it doesn't hurt to be careful."

"I still say we should attack them before they come after us."

"When I say we can vote on it, I'll let you know. Right now, I'm in charge, and I say we keep moving."

"Why do you have to be that way?" Lilly asked Barton, who took a puff off his pipe.

"What way?"

"So annoying."

"I guess it's just my way. You're awful quiet, there, Woblo. What's up?"

"Just thinking I guess," Bargo said.

"Well, think about setting up some bedding for the night, and getting wood for the fire," Glam told them. "We've only got an hour left before sundown."

They gathered wood for the small fire, and the four of them gathered around it, while the other four kept watch. The first part of the night was uneventful, as they talked of their plans once the journey came to an end.

"So Bargo, are you planning to continue what your father left for you?" Lilly asked.

"I haven't decided yet," he said. "On one hand, I would because he would want me to do so. On the other hand, I would like to sell it. I just don't know. That is, if we even make it back."

"You'll make it back," Glam said. "Don't you worry about that. I know when this is over, I've got much bigger plans."

"Such as?" Barton asked.

"I was thinking maybe I'd take Christopher's job."

"Working for the prince?" Lilly asked.

"When this is all over, if we succeed, he will no longer be the prince. He has no other family I'm aware of. Glaridia will most likely have to take over both kingdoms."

"Didn't his advisor agree with most of what the prince said at the council meeting?" Barton asked.

"That's because he was deceived by Phillip's rhetoric. Glaridia will listen to me, but only if I can prove to him the prince is corrupt. What about you, Barton, what do you plan to do when this is over?"

"Take a long, hot bath, open a bottle of the finest wine, find me one of the finest women, and have the best time of my life."

"Typical," Lilly said.

"Well, what do you plan to do?"

"Never have to plow another field again. And buy some of the finest dresses money can buy, and buy my husband some of the finest coats money can buy. Then I might even buy a brand new house, with large pillars in the front, a garden, and a swimming hole in the back."

"Sounds boring."

"Boring to you, but heaven to me after the last year's harvest. He just started planting last week, and he's busting his back right now for me to make up for it."

"Things will work out, they always do," Glam told her.

Just then they heard a tussle in the leaves, as Tamarka and Daniel dragged a disgruntled Kain from the bushes, and dropped him into the clearing. Glam and Barton got up from the fire, and came over to them.

"Look who I found lurking in the shadows," Tamarka said.

"Mr. Kain," Glam said. "It's a pleasure to see you again. Shouldn't you be in prison, or did you make a deal with the prince?"

"I don't know what you're talking about. I escaped by tunneling out of the rat hole."

"I find that one a bit hard to swallow. Tell me, why are you really here?"

"He's here to give us away to Ang," Barton snapped.

"Ang wants to make a parlay. He wants to trade the Woblo for the rest of your lives," Kain said.

"Why does he have a sudden interest in the Woblo? I thought he was after me?"

"He has his reasons. He's says you have two hours to comply, or he'll kill you all, and take him anyway."

Glam walked over and removed Kain's hat from his head, throwing it to Tamarka.

"Hey, that's my lucky hat."

"Your luck just ran out, Friend. Tell Ang we're not interested in deals. If he wants a war, tell him to bring it on, because we'll be ready."

"Now you're talking," Barton said. "I don't know why you

don't just kill him now. He killed two of your best friends, for crying out loud! You can't just let him go."

Glam backhanded Barton, and knocked him to the ground.

"I won't tolerate any more of your insubordination on this journey," Glam told him. "You are a soldier first, and not to let personal feelings affect your decisions. Is that clear?"

"Yes, Sir," Barton said, as Tamarka helped him to his feet.

Kain smiled and straightened his tie, as Barton stared at him in anger.

"You know it was a pleasure to watch your friend suffer," he told Glam.

"Get moving, before I change my mind," Glam commanded.

Kain hopped back on his horse, and disappeared into the darkness. Tamarka turned towards his commander. "Now you've done it. We'll have to fight them now."

"Reginald and Barton, come with me, I have a job for you. I saw some ivy vines back near the trail, just before the rock cliff. I have an idea."

Glam threw some rope in his saddle bag and jumped on his horse, as the others followed him on their animals. They could see fairly well due to the light of the hunter's moon. Their commander sent Reginald to gather and tie the vines together, making a thirty feet rope. The young man with dark brown hair and brown eyes in his thirties then returned to the top of the cliff, where Barton and Glam were.

"Gather some rocks together and put them in a pile about two feet high," he ordered. They followed his command, and Glam placed the end of the vine on top of the pile. "Now, let's make another pile on top."

After he pulled it to make sure it was secure, he tied a rope around a tree, and then to his waist. He propelled himself down the face of the cliff, holding the vine in his free hand. When he reached the bottom, he pulled the vine across the trail, and tied it to a root near the valley's edge. He threw some of the calthrops from his pack on the path, covered the vine with dirt and stones, and signaled Barton to pull him up. Once he reached the top, he handed the rope to the man.

"Go back and tell the others to get down here," Glam said.

"Have Tamarka, Daniel, and Thomas come down here to the spot just before the clearing. Barton, you get back up to the top of the trail, just above the cliff. Have Lilly and Bargo stay back with the wagon. Reginald and I will stay here."

Barton nodded, and left, as Glam turned to the member of the Royal Guard.

"Don't you think it's kind of funny Kain knew right where to find us?"

"He's probably been following us all along."

"Just out of curiosity, how many years have you been with Christopher?"

"About three, maybe three and a half."

"Where did you receive your training again?"

"Sir, I don't see what this has to do with the situation at hand."

"Just answer the question."

"Fort Parkwood, in the 44th infantry division."

"Under the direction of General Caldwell?"

"Yes, but I don't see-"

"General Caldwell never commanded the 44th."

Reginald pulled his knife out and tried to stab him, but Glam grabbed his arm, which made him drop the knife. The man kicked him in the groin, causing him to drop to the ground. Glam was punched across his jaw, and fell to the ground on his back. His assailant grabbed the weapon, and pushed it toward his throat. Glam shifted his weight, which caused him to roll over so he was on top. He knocked the knife from his hand, and punched him in the face until he was dazed. The Elf rose to his feet, as his aggressor reluctantly did the same, and prepared to throw his knife. Glam turned around, and flung his knife into his chest first, which caused a fatal blow to his heart. A little out of breath, he stepped over his immobilized, lifeless body, and prepared to wait for Ang and his Grassmen.

The next two hours dragged, while they watched the sun rise over the crest of the eastern side of the valley. Barton positioned himself just above the tree line on the part of the path which passed the rock cliff. The others were back farther in case the two of them ran into difficulty, and if all else failed, protect Bargo and Lilly from harm's way. The Royal Guard took a vow to protect all under their direction, even to the death, if necessary.

Christopher was a firm believer in this, especially with the king, who he stood behind and protected for years. It was hard to believe someone he personally screened himself betrayed his trust, and dishonored the king. Glam's advantage was his speed with a knife over his foe, and was lucky he caught on to him first.

Then there was Kain; a sneaky, dishonest, self preserved leech which sold himself to the highest bidder. That's why he wasn't too concerned about having to kill him. Once Ang found out what he'd done, he would get his just reward, and Glam's job would be done for him.

He peered into his periscope, and saw the one eyed Elf, who followed with the Grassmen on foot. They carried their usual spears, swords, and bows, but were traveling at a slower, more cautious pace. It was obvious the double crossing fiend Kain tipped them off, but interestingly, was nowhere to be found.

Glam readied his sword, and grabbed the rope, which was still tied to the tree. Once they were closer, he waited until the trap was triggered. Ang passed over the vine with no effect, as did the Grassman behind him. It was the second beast who tripped over the vine, and stepped on a calthrop, which caused the rocks and logs to fall from the cliff above.

The Elf propelled himself to the bottom, strangling one of the Grassmen with the rope, and stabbing another who lunged at him. Ang quickly dismounted, and drew his sword, as it was met with a clang from Glam's.

"We meet again, my friend," the evil Elf said, as he swung high for his head. Glam ducked, and knocked him off his feet by kicking him in the left leg. He fell on his back, dazed, but still coherent. "You will pay for reluctance to take my offer."

"Don't you realize Kain has betrayed you?"

"What are you talking about?" Two Grassmen went to grab Glam, but Barton fired arrows into them to assist his commander, while Ang rose to his feet.

"He's made a deal with the prince. Ask him about it."

While Ang was distracted by the succession of arrows, their Elf commander climbed quick back up the rope and back to his horse, which he mounted. Barton continued to shoot arrows at them until Glam was at a safe distance. He fought them off with his sword, as they merged upon him, and he mounted his horse to escape. He sliced the arm of one and the head of another, and galloped down the forest path.

The others, realizing it was a losing battle, did the same, and headed up toward the clearing, followed close behind by the Grassmen, and a trailing Ang, still in shock about Kain's bargain. Glam led them out of there, while Barton and Bargo hitched the horse to the wagon.

"Up the South pass," he said. "And don't stop until I say so."

They followed behind them, as Daniel and Tamarka doubled back to hold off the Grassmen. Lilly grabbed Bargo's arm, and threw him on the back of her horse, right behind Barton and the wagon. The path was extremely bumpy, and at one point the wagon began to tip to the left, and went over the side, falling into the ravine; Barton, the horse, supplies, weapons, blankets, pans to cook on, and even Bargo's banjo. Lilly and him could only watch in horror, as the wooden vehicle smashed into tiny pieces, tumbled down the hill, and scattered on the rocks below.

"Barton!" Bargo yelled, as Lilly forced her horse to come to a halt. They edged their way to the side, only to see the scraggly Barton still hanging onto a branch with his good arm. Glam doubled back, threw a rope to him, and he climbed back up.

"Glad you're still with us," Glam said.

"For a minute there I was starting to wonder. Except now I'm without a horse."

"Take Reginald's," he said, as he gave the reigns of other horse with him. "He won't be needing it."

"What happened?'

"He made a fatal error in judgement that cost him his life. He trusted the wrong people."

"What about the wagon?" Lilly asked. "It had all our supplies in it."

"And my banjo," Bargo cried. "My father gave it to me when I was 18."

"At this point, we'll have to rough it," Glam said. "When we get back, Bargo, you can buy a brand new one."

"What about Kain? Do you think he'll stay loyal to Ang, or

change his mind, and work for the prince?" Barton asked.

"Kain is a fool, and acts without thinking. Only fools and dead men change their minds; dead men can't, and fools won't."

CHAPTER THIRTEEN: BATTLE AT BACON HILL

Vladimir and his party reached the rock cliff by midday, and stopped at the fallen rocks and debris partially blocking their way.

"Looks like our friend Glam set a trap for them. He's a resourceful fellow when he needs to be. Well, they won't be hard to track, just follow the bodies."

"Looks like they're heading down on the South Pass, Sir," Jonathon said.

"Yes. Let's continue, shall we?"

They ventured through the forest, and on to the clearing, where Glam and the other stayed the night before. Upon entering the field, they found the hat lying on the ground.

"A clue, Sir?"

"No, I don't think so. He was awfully fond of his hat, and I don't think he'd just leave it. Ang must have took care of him."

He used his sword to grab it, and placed it next to him on his saddle.

"Sir," another man said. "Could this be a signal?"

There was some logs tied together in an "x" fashion pointing towards the path to their south.

"Yes. That must be it. Let's head that way."

They continued down the path, past where the wagon crashed, totally unaware of its existence. The path got narrow, as they traveled along the side of the ravine and the river below. With their heavy armor, they had to be particularly careful of top heaviness and balance. They were well trained from an early age to wear, fight, and ride in it. Their weapons were no less professional, made from the finest metals, and sharp enough to slice a walnut with one strike.

There was some commotion just ahead on the path, and a dark, bumbling, beaver pelt suited figure rolled clumsily down the hill, and landed on the path in front of them.

"Mr. Kain," Vladimir said. "So glad you decided not to back out of our offer. Did you locate Mr. Ang for us?"

"Yes. He's ten miles ahead of you, near the river bed."

"Good. Now you can lead us to him."

"I'll take the 500 gold coins and go, if you don't mind. I have a little lady waiting in Bashworth for me." Vladimir pulled out his hat, dangling it on his sword in front of his face. He went to grab for it, as he lifted it higher, and out of his reach. "Hey! That's my hat."

"If you want it back, you'll lead us to Ang."

"That wasn't part of our agreement."

"Very well, you can take 100 gold pieces and go, if that's what you wish."

"You said 500."

"I'll give 500, but only if you take us to Ang."

"Do you know what he'll do to me if he finds out I betrayed him?"

"That s your problem, not mine."

"You're all heart. Do you have a horse I could ride, at least?"

"Who ever said anything about riding a horse."

"You've got to be kidding," the annoyed Elf said, as he grabbed his hat, and struggled down the path.

During this time, Glam and the others were a great distance from Ang and his party, mostly from the disorganization of the Grassmen during the attack. They were aggressive, but not very smart creatures on the whole, and were slow at following orders. After the attack, they scattered, and it took a couple of hours for Ang to round up the fifteen fighters he had left.

The others used the time to their advantage, and were close to one of the toughest parts of their journey, the scaling of Bacon Hill. It was covered with thick vegetation and thorny bushes, which very difficult to navigate. It was decided Tamarka and Daniel would take the team of horses, using a cross path to the west to circumnavigate the hill, and meet up with them in Bacon. Glam placed his hand on his friend's shoulder.

"This is where we part ways. Be careful, we're getting close to Licarion Territory, and the tracks still say they came through here. We'll continue to follow them."

"You be careful yourself," Tamarka said. "The prince's men may be waiting on the other end."

"Something tells me they're following us as well. They aren't going to attack until we reach Jarod and have the stone. Good luck."

"You too."

"Just when I thought it couldn't get any worse," Barton said. "Why didn't we just take the same road as the other two?"

"Because that's what they would expect us to do," Glam replied.

"Well, if that's true, wouldn't they also get to Bacon before us?" Lilly asked, also vehement about having to traverse through the thick and thorny brush.

"If they did, we wouldn't be there anyway, and they'd have to backtrack."

"I hope you're right," Barton said.

"It's not your job to determine if I'm right or not, is it? I'm getting tired of your negative attitude, Mr. Horatio Barton. You will follow my orders, or you can go home with nothing but hurt pride."

"Looks like the secret's out," joked Lilly.

"What secret?" Barton asked.

"Your first name," Bargo said, as he giggled.

"What's wrong with my name?" Barton grew a little irritated when the two of them laughed at him.

"Nothing," Lilly said. "It's just that it doesn't really fit you. I always pictured you as a John, or Jim, or something like that."

"Well, now you know why I just prefer Barton."

"Can we just get on with this, please?" Glam asked, as he eyed the hill which lay in front of them.

"How are we going to cut through that brush?" Lilly asked. "No offense to Bargo, but I don't believe even the finest steel can cut through those thickets."

"We have axes, and Bargo's sword is sharper than anything I've ever known," Glam said. "Come, we're wasting time on folklore, when we should be climbing."

The morning was treacherous at best; they were punctured by thorns repeatedly, slipped several times due to oncoming rain, and to make matters worse, it began to thunder and lightning. There was no cover on the 5,000 feet hill, and no mercy on their weary souls, as the pouring rain drenched the only clothing they had. Vladimir or Ang's party were nowhere in sight, which was a good thing, considering they only had about twenty arrows left among them.

Once they got to Bacon, they would have to replenish the supplies they lost over the river embankment. Some items were irreplaceable, however, such as Bargo's banjo, and the beautiful blue and red dresses Lilly brought with her. Their time in the fortress town would be limited due to the king's disappearance, and the haste of the situation. The most important items to be picked up were food, water, and weapons, and they could no longer afford luxuries such as musical instruments or fancy apparel.

Bargo's fur grew wet and heavy, and the cold rain didn't help to comfort him. He longed for his soft bed at home, and a nice book by the fireplace, along with a hot bowl of lamb stew. He missed using the forge each morning, as strange as it sounded, and would've gladly decided now to take over the shop, if he could only go home. He had enough of this adventure; enough of being chased, enough of being told he was their only hope, and enough of living dangerously.

When they reached two thirds way to the top, the skies cleared, and they were covered with mud and dried blood from the thorns. Barton turned towards Glam, tapped him on the shoulder, and pointed to the north.

"Ang," Glam said, as he pulled out his periscope, and looked in the direction of the tyrant's party. "Looks like he's working with a very small army now."

"Can he see us?" Lilly asked.

"No, we're too well hidden. Looks like they're just sitting there now by the river. As if he's waiting for something."

"Do you think he's waiting for Vladimir and his men?" Bargo asked.

"No, I don't think he even knows they're following him. Either that, or he doesn't care. Let's keep moving, and try to put as much distance from him as we can, while they're resting."

During the time they ascended toward the top of Bacon Hill,

Vladimir and his men advanced to the ridge just above Ang and the Grassmen. Jonathon and the advisor stared down from their horses at the valley below them, and out of his view. Kain, whose feet throbbed in pain from walking the entire distance, showed up behind them.

"Looks like you were right, Mr. Kain," he said, as he threw the bag of gold down to him. "We'll handle it from here. You're free to go."

"No tricks? You're not going to stab me, or shoot me with an arrow when I leave, are you?"

"Now why would I do that? I have no quarrel with you. Ang, on the other hand..."

"I thought you were going to offer me protection against him?"

"He won't be giving you anymore trouble. We'll see to that, I can assure you."

"You don't know him like I do. You think you're safe because you outnumber him. Well, you're wrong. He'll cut up your men into little pieces, and then he'll come after you."

"Not before he cuts you up first. I've given you the money. Be on your own way now."

"You traitorous welcher. I knew I shouldn't have trusted you."

"I could bring you back to the prison?. For your own protection?"

"I guess I'll be on my way after all," the Elf said, as he reconsidered.

"Go back up the South Pass," the king's advisor told him. "We'll keep an eye on Ang." When Kain left them, he turned back to his second in command.

"Are we going to just let him go?" Jonathon asked. "What if he goes down and tells Ang we're coming?"

"I don't believe he will, considering the options he has. He's the least of our worries. I want ten men to go ahead and come down the embankment, where it gets closer to the river. Have ten more go back a mile, and come down near the river as well. The two of us will stay here, and shoot with our crossbows from above. We'll surround them, and attack before they ever see us coming."

"Sir, do you think the stories are true about him having the mystical powers they speak of?" Jonathon asked, as the other men followed his orders.

"Who, the Woblo?"

"No, Ang."

"Nonsense. The stories about him being immortal are just stories. Elves have never been such, and die like everyone else. Let's get this over with, and retrieve the Woblo from the others."

"What will Glam think when he's faced by a hostile militia?"

"He'll think we're there to assist him, but he'll be wrong. We'll finish them off as well, and find the king and the stone. And don't let the other men know what our real intentions are, got it?"

"They will get suspicious if we don't return with the king, Sir."

"Then we make sure we don't return with him. Just make sure it's done by a Licarion hand, and not ours."

"We just can't let him get killed."

"We won't, but we'll make sure we try our best not to save him."

"If the men find out you're responsible, they're not going to like it. Many of them are loyal to the king."

"That's why I'm leaving you in charge of that."

"Sir?"

"You heard me. You'll make arrangements for his demise."

"Sir, I'm not a murderer."

"If you want to live, you're whatever I say you are. Understand?"

"Yes, Sir," he reluctantly said.

The first patrol came down the embankment, catching Ang and his men by surprise. The ten horses approached, as the men fired their crossbows at the green creatures, who scattered and assumed fight positions. They grabbed their knives, bows, and axes, then launched a retaliatory attack on the patrol, as one of the larger ones jumped onto a rider, and brought him and the horse to the ground. The Grassman stabbed him just below his mail and breastplate, and then threw his knife at another knight, who blocked it with his longsword, and beheaded him.

During the commotion, Ang noticed he was being watched by Vladimir from the cliff above, the same direction arrows were also coming from. "Up there, shoot," he told the Grassmen next to him, who fired, and hit Jonathon in the arm, just below his arm plate. He fell off his horse in pain, and Vladimir bolted up the South Pass towards the attack.

Five more Grassmen attacked the remainder of the first patrol, systematically killing them, either by knife, bow, or sword, and even with their own body armor. The other nine creatures were killed by the second patrol, who approached from the north, as their swords clashed together in a barrage of metal. Several of the green beasts were decapitated from the longswords, which had a better reach than the shorter ones Ang's men used. Ang stood in confusion and anxiety, as the six of them found themselves surrounded by fifteen knights.

By this time, Vladimir arrived, and Ang found himself at a loss of words. He gestured his men to stand down, but keep their weapons handy, while he spoke with the advisor.

"Hello, Ang."

"Vladimir," he answered, as he smiled. "To what honor do I have the pleasure of feeding you to my men?"

"You're in no position to be coy with me. Tell your men to drop their weapons. Admit it, you've lost this fight."

"Why were we even attacked? We're just passing through the area."

"You have the nerve to ask me that? After what you did to that old man back there, and Christopher."

"You have no proof."

"I'm not stupid. It is well known you have associations with the Licarions, as well as the Grassmen here, and there is of course, Mr. Kain."

"What has he told you?"

"Enough for you to want him eliminated."

"Yes, right after we eliminate you. Attack!"

The Grassmen wielded their swords, killing three more men who dismounted from their horses. The remainder of the knights fought them until they were either dead or wounded to different degrees, until Ang and Vladimir faced off. When the advisor was ready to swing his sword, one of the other men lunged his longsword into Ang's back.

"No," Vladimir yelled to the man. Ang fell onto the rocks,

face first next to the river, while water ran around him.

"I guess he wasn't immortal after all," the knight told his superior. Vladimir shook his head in disgust.

The remaining patrol of five tread onward, and left a trail of body parts after the malee. Blood ran into the river, and flowed towards the north, in the direction of the tributary to the Swift River. They found a set of horse tracks which they continued to follow up the river, in hopes they would catch up with Glam and the Woblo.

Once they reached the top of Bacon Hill, Bargo and the others watched the attack from the hill, in both anticipation and fear of the outcome. Once Barton saw Ang lying in the river, he turned to Glam, in disbelief.

"I thought you said he can't be killed with an ordinary sword?"

"Believe me, he's not dead."

"Well, he's not moving either," Lilly added.

"Not now, but he will be," Glam said. "It's time to go. The prince's men will be waiting on the other side, unless we can stay ahead of them."

"I hope the other side isn't as bad as the north side," Barton said.

"Actually no, it's just a bunch of large cliffs," Glam answered.

"Cliffs?" Bargo asked, as he thought about how this trip could possibly get any worse. He'd already faced Grassmen at least three times; been set up by the prince, lost his father, as well as his banjo, and now felt he also lost Lilly because of what he said earlier in the day. He began to wonder if this whole trip was worth 100 gold pieces, or 1000 for that matter.

Barton felt this way as well, fighting a war that wasn't his fight. If he wanted to be a soldier, he would have joined the militia. Horatio was always a mercenary, working only for himself, and not for king and country. It was an insult to him to believe he should get involved in something which didn't concern him. He didn't feel threatened by anyone, especially some animal who lived in caverns and only came out at night, and could handle himself. Magic wasn't something he cared about or believed in, and he began to think this whole fiasco was a wild goose chase, looking for something which didn't even exist. He did, however, view the staff with his own eyes, and hear the prince with his own ears, and wasn't about to turn the kingdom over to a homicidal lunatic who ordered to have his own father killed to gain the throne.

CHAPTER FOURTEEN: ENEMY TERRITORY

After everyone left the river basin, a Elven figure with a hat approached a body lying face down in the water. Recognizing the black cloak, he carefully rolled it over, revealing the empty face of Ang, his good eye open. He listened to his chest, but heard no heartbeat, so he laid him back down face up, and scurried away into the woods. After he left, the one eyed elf began to breathe slow, and his wound healed itself; its skin blending back together, causing the sword injury to disappear. He then sat up, looked around, and realized he was by himself. He picked up his sword next to him, placed it back in its sheath, dusted off the loose mud from his clothing, adjusted his cape, and walked to the south.

He knew Kain turned him over in the river, and also betrayed him. The only option at this point was to meet up with the Licarion patrol just ahead of them near Bacon. He knew they were taking King Phillip to meet King Glamara in North Licarion City, and he wanted to make sure he delivered him, the stone, and the Woblo personally.

Things were not going as planned, and he never suffered such a blow as he had on this quest. He lost an entire army because of the Shudolin's knights and mercenaries, and now he wanted revenge against all of them, and recognition for his fervent effort.

By this time sundown crept in, and Vladimir's men prepared to set up camp for the night. While they were cooking dinner, they noticed a familiar face approaching them. Vladimir rose to his feet, removed his helmet, and handed it to Jonathon.

"Mr. Kain. What are you doing here? I thought I told you to go north."

"I decided I was safer with you."

"Ang is dead, and you need to move on. I'll give you twenty seconds to leave in the direction you came, and then I'll have Jonathon put an arrow between your eyes." His second in command pulled back his bow, and pointed it at the frazzled Kain.

"He's not dead."

"Are you going to feed me that rubbish as well?".

"Your man stabbed him all right, but he will heal, and he'll come back to kill everyone of you."

"You're mad. Jonathon get ready to fire."

"No need to get hostile. But don't say I didn't warn you."

Kain turned around and walked back up the road, until he was no longer in sight. They heard some commotion behind the bushes, and a short scream in his direction. Vladimir and his men advanced with their small troop, and found the Elf dead on the ground with a knife in his back.

"Looks like Ang took his disloyalty rather personal," the advisor said. "Forget about camping here tonight. We have to get moving. Pack up and stay sharp, he may be anywhere."

The party left the area, and as one of the men trailed behind, a ruthless Ang pulled him off the horse, ripped off his breastplate, stabbed him five times, and then stole his horse. He followed them down the path and into the darkness, while the prince's patrol was unaware he watched their every move.

By this time, Bargo and the others set up camp on the top of the hill, for it was the safest place to be at the time, protected by cliffs on one side and thick brush everywhere else. They decided to have a fire that night, so Thomas and Barton took first watch, and Lilly and Glam agreed to take the second. When they saw what happened below, they knew Ang wouldn't attempt to meet them alone, and Vladimir was waiting for a chance to grab the stone once they found it. They sat around the flames, and discussed their plans once they reached Bacon.

"Tomorrow morning we'll scale the cliffs," Glam told them. "We're at least five hours ahead of them. That should give us enough time. Tamarka and Daniel will be waiting at the South face with our horses. It is most likely the Licarions took an alternate route than us, probably through the cavern system underneath us. We'll have to be careful; they could be right below us."

"Their tracks led to up to the base of the hill," Thomas said. "After that, there was nothing."

"They will not go into Bacon, probably around it. If we don't stop them here, they'll enter enemy territory, and then it will be impossible to save him."

"I'm scared," Bargo said. "I've never climbed a day in my life until today."

"You're not afraid of heights, are you?" Barton asked him.

"No, just afraid of dying."

"You'll do fine," Lilly said. "You can climb down on my back."

"Can you carry that much weight?" Barton asked.

"I can carry him just fine, thank you," she said. "When are you going to start treating me like the soldier I am, and not just as a woman?"

"Sorry, just trying to help you out."

"Well, Horatio, when I need the help I'll let you know."

"Please don't call me that."

"Why? Because it makes you feel like less of a man?"

"I'll show you what kind of man I am, you little brat," he said, as he went to grab her. Glam punched him again, much harder this time, and knocked him to the ground. He got up, and returned the favor, as he and the Elf began to tussle to the ground. Thomas, Lilly, and Bargo grabbed them, and pulled the two apart from their confrontation.

"Barton, I've had enough," he said in anger. "Grab your gear and get out of here now. As of this moment, you're no longer a part of this expedition."

"That's fine with me," the man said, and began to follow his orders. "You won't last a day without my help, and don't expect the prince's men to back you up either."

"He's right," Bargo interrupted. "Right now we need all the help we can get. We all need to learn to put our differences aside and work together."

"For a small creature, you can be very wise," Lilly said.

Glam gave a look of disgust at Barton, but he had to concur with the others.

"Very well," Glam said, reluctant. "But from now on, keep your mouth shut, or you'll get smacked again, got it?"

"Yes, Sir," Barton said, as he rubbed his jaw in pain.

"You and Thomas get to your posts. We'll see you in about

three hours."

The next morning, Glam adjusted a harness around Lilly's waist first, and tied Bargo to her back.

"When you get to the end of the rope, tie and anchor some rope to a ledge," Glam said, and handed her the three by three inch wide strand of hemp rope, and ten metal spikes, about four inches each. She placed the rope around her shoulder, the spikes in her pack, and prepared to scale down the face of the mountain. "I'll be right beside you on a separate rope."

"We weren't trained for this," Lilly said.

"You'll do just fine," he said, as he adjusted the harness around his waist as well. "Just follow my lead."

After he tied the rope to a nearby tree, Glam helped her over the edge of cliff, which overlooked the open fields below them, and was divided by the South Pass dirt road. To their southwest, they could faintly see the town of Bacon. There wasn't any sign of Tamarka and Daniel yet, but that didn't mean they hadn't found a place to temporarily hide until they showed up. There were several cave openings below them, and anyone of them could have been hiding Licarions, or Ang himself.

Lilly propelled the two of them down fifty feet, and watched as Glam anchored the next rope to the ledge with a spike, which he pounded with a small metal hammer. She copied his motion, which was difficult with Bargo on her back, but with a little help from her friend, she was able to perform the task. He held the spike, while she hit it, and hey propelled another fifty feet.

Thomas and Barton were behind them using separate ropes. Most of the ropes they brought were draped on the horses themselves, which was fortunate, considering they lost the wagon. Barton, who was the last one down, propelled himself to the next ledge, when there was a sudden tug on his line, and a snap. He found himself struggling to grab anything, as he free fell at least forty of 1500 feet of the cliff face. If it wasn't for a fortunate grab by Glam, he would have met his demise for sure. The force also tugged Glam to hang from his rope, but Thomas pulled out a spike quick, and anchored Barton's rope. They looked above to a vengeful one eyed Elf surrounded by Licarions, who drew their longbows, and prepared to fire.

"Down, quickly!" Glam yelled, as the others followed their orders. "Into the cave below us."

Each one of them swung the rope enough to make a rough landing in the ten feet wide, five feet high cave. Upon entering, they heard the hissing sound of the reptilian Licarions throughout the cavern, and Ang's voice as well.

"We won't be safe here for long. They know these caverns well, and they'll be on us shortly."

"Go ahead, Sir," Thomas said. "I'll hold them off as long as I can."

"No, we go together."

"You'll never make it without me staying behind. I'll lure them to come after me, and allow you to scale the rest of the rock face."

"You truly are worthy of the Royal Guard title." He placed his hand on his shoulder. "Be careful, and try to return safely."

"I will, Sir." He pulled out his sword, and turned his back to them.

They propelled back out using the only two ropes left, but it was enough to get them near the bottom. While scaling down, several Licarions ran across the field about a half mile away, which was unusual, being daytime. Glam took out his periscope, and saw them push a brown woblo, and drag the king, who was extremely weak. They hit the bottom, as Tamarka and Daniel came around the South Pass from the north direction. Ang also emerged from the cavern, and pushed their friend Thomas down 500 feet of the cliff face, and to his death. The Licarions shot arrows at the two Elves and their horses, who tried to get to their friends.

"The king!" Glam yelled to them. "Over there."

Glam sent the two other Elves toward the Licarions, as they pushed the king to walk. The others jumped onto the field, and hid behind some trees and rocks to get a tactical position against Ang and his lizard men in the cave, who sent a barrage of arrows at them.

When they saw the two Elves upon them and had drawn their bows, they dropped the king on the ground, where he lay motionless. The creatures picked up Barlow, and disappeared into the nearby woods, just north of the town of Bacon. The other Licarions in the caves propelled from the cliff, and launched arrows as they hit the ground. The two Elves dismounted to attend to the king, who was up further near the road.

Just when they thought they were outnumbered, Vladimir and his knights trotted up the road. They attacked the reptilians head on, as the creatures found themselves cornered and trapped. Ang himself disappeared into the darkness of the caverns, once he found his forces on the ground were either killed or chased away. When the encounter came to an end, the two Elves rejoined their friends, and left the king where he was.

"Vladimir?" Glam asked, as he hid the knowledge he knew of his plan. "I don't know what you're doing here, but I am glad to see you."

"The prince felt you needed a little added protection, so here we are. What about the king? How is he?"

"Unfortunately, he's dead," Tamarka said. "The trip and abuse was too much for him. I'm sorry."

"If he hadn't been such a foolish man, he'd still be alive," Vladimir suggested.

"You don't seem too concerned, and neither did the prince," Barton replied.

"We haven't seen eye to eye for a while. His reluctance to listen to me cost him his life."

"And Barlow?" asked the anxious Woblo.

"I'm afraid they still have him," Tamarka said.

"Do you think they have mistaken him for Bargo?" Lilly asked.

"That's entirely possible," Glam said.

"We have to go after them," Bargo insisted.

"We will, we will," Vladimir said. "After we find the stone."

"Now, wait just a damn minute," Lilly said, angered by his selfishness. "We have to find his cousin so the same thing doesn't happen to him."

"I agree," Barton said. "The precious stone can wait."

"Do I sense malcontent and mutiny among the ranks?" Vladimir remarked. "Glam, I thought you were going to pull these people together, and accomplish what we came here to do?"

"I thought we came to save the king, but I guess I was wrong. They're not going to succeed without some cooperation from you.

We head south tomorrow, towards North Licarion City."

"After we find the stone."

"We head south, if we find the stone on the way, we do."

"Very well, if you insist."

"Let's just hope Ang doesn't follow us all the way there."

"He won't, he was killed at Bacon Hill."

"We just saw him in the cave on the cliff," Barton said. "Very much alive."

"Impossible," Vladimir said. "I saw him die with my own eyes."

"I told you he was immortal," Jonathon announced.

"Not totally immortal," Glam said. "He can be killed by the right person, and the right method."

"Which is?" Vladimir asked.

"I don't know. But I aim to find out."

"I thought you could kill him with-" Bargo started to say, but his shirt was tugged by Lilly.

"How?" the advisor asked.

"The Woblo heard something about Elven folklore, but it was wrong," Glam lied. "Forgive his ignorance."

"Well, at any rate, we need to move on to Bacon and Jarod," Vladimir stated. "After that, we'll head on to North Licarion City."

Although they knew they were handing themselves over to the enemy at the moment, it was still safer than being captured by Ang and the Licarions. It was tempting for them to argue the point of why the king's death was of little significance to the advisor, but they didn't want to give away their knowledge of the prince's dastardly plan either. Now he was out of the way, the prince had control of the kingdom, and would be planning an all out attack on the Licarions the minute he received word of his death. Vladimir immediately dispatched a rider to head back up the south pass towards Riverton to deliver the message. Glam wished there was a way to intercept him, but he knew any attempt would arise suspicion from Vladimir.

For the moment, they had to go along with his plan. Glam was hoping when they did find the stone, they would be able to negotiate with him to spare their lives. He knew Vladimir pretty well; that he could be a liar, a cheat, and a piece of scum, but one thing he wasn't was a cold blooded killer. He hoped his weakness for compassion would work to their advantage.

They mounted their horses, and continued down the road which led to Bacon, about ten miles away. It was near midday, and they looked forward to getting cleaned up, having warm beds again, and some relaxation. Even if Ang did try to get them there, they were well protected by the town's militia.

Bacon was the last town in the area before enemy territory, and the last place they would have a safe place to stay. There were few militia patrols out here, and the fortress town protected itself against the mostly nocturnal Licarions. Their enemies kept to the south, due to the warmer and drier climate in the region, as contrast to the Shudolin and Elven regions, which were lush with coniferous rain forests. Humans out here fought to survive, and had built a strong town against a constant barrage of attacks. There was a huge wood wall around it, lookouts from four different points, and patrol guards at all times.

The lookout from the north side saw the party approaching, as the sun set, and opened the gate for them. Every night here was an eventful night, where there was news of death or injuries on either side. Vladimir led them in, as Glam and the others trailed behind. Bargo kept looking back, worried whether Ang was waiting for night to make another attempt to kidnap him. He was also troubled about what would happen if he did successfully obtain the stone.

They were led inside, watched closely by the townspeople, who were surprised to see the king's advisor among them. They knew who Glam was, for he'd been through these parts many times, and was a frequent guest to Bacon, but everyone else but him and the advisor were strangers to them. Glam approached the man who called himself Mayor, Marcus Templeton, who was a stout, grayish haired man with a large scar on the left side of his face. He walked with a limp of his right leg, and the look of a man who'd seen incredible hardship. The Elf dismounted, and extended his right hand to his old friend.

"Marcus. How's life been here in the wilderness?"

"Rough at best. We've exhausted most of our resources here in the past year. We can only be able to hold them off for so long. We could sure use some help from the Royal Militia." Vladimir snubbed the remark, as he dismounted his horse as well, and fiddled with his saddle bags. "Well?"

The advisor turned to him, nonchalantly.

"I sent you thirty men last year, and most of them ended up dead. The prince doesn't have the time or resources to protect a town in the middle of nowhere."

"Not very hospitable, is he?" Marcus asked his Elven friend.

"No, but he is in charge," Glam answered.

"He's correct," the advisor said. "And while I'm in charge, you will follow my orders only."

"Now, wait a minute," Marcus said. "I respect the king's authority, but this is my town, and only I know how to run it."

"The way you've almost ran it into the ground? Jonathon, I want four guards posted on the front and back gates, and seven on the west and east wings. If anything outside the gates moves, kill it."

"You have no idea what you're getting yourself into. These reptilian devils have ways of infiltrating the fortress you'd never guess; they've even dug underground and underneath the village. I have fifty men on the wall each night, and every night I lose at least two men."

"Well, if they show up on this side of the gate, they'll be easier to kill. In the meantime, our men need some nourishment, sleep, and fresh horses for the morning."

"Yes, of course," Marcus said, still not pleased with the overstepping of his authority.

"The Licarions had a Woblo hostage near here about two hours ago," Glam said to him. "Have you noticed them coming this way yet?"

"My men haven't reported anything," Marcus said. "They may have gone into the forest, to the east of the village. The mountains aren't far from there, about ten miles south."

"Any sign of Ang?"

"If we see anything, we'll let you know," Vladimir said to him. "Why don't you all have some dinner and drink? I will handle things up here."

"Why does that worry me?" Barton mumbled, so only Bargo and Lilly would hear him.

BARGO LYNDEN

"Tomorrow, we'll replenish our supplies, and start towards Jarod," the advisor said. "They won't get far, I assure you."

Back at the foot of Bacon Hill, the dark shadow of nightfall fell upon the open field, just north of the village, and a cloaked figure emerged from the caves with his small army of reptilian soldiers onto the open field near the road. He held his torch over the cold body of the king, furious his subordinates beat him to death. He turned to the head Licarion, named Surac.

"What in the Garlock's name happened here?" he asked him, and placed his hand on his smooth, leathery shoulder.

"Human give us trouble," he sneered. "We make him listen to us."

"He's no use to me now. You killed him, you idiot. Glamara wanted him alive. I wanted him alive."

"So sorry. We still have Woblo."

"The wrong one. Who's idea was it to beat him to death, anyway, yours?"

"No, Sir. It just happen as we bring him."

"Who was the last one to bring him?"

"That was me. When I lift him, no breath come out."

"Just like this," Ang said, as he thrust his dagger into the reptile's stomach, and he fell to the ground. The others stared at him, approached, and surrounded him. "Listen to me, all of you. Glamara has given me the authority to complete this quest, and if anyone, and I mean anyone, interferes with my orders, they will be killed. If any of you try to kill me, you will be the ones killed. Do not underestimate me; he has chosen me for a reason. If you doubt my word, come towards me with your sword drawn, and your fate will be in my hands."

The group dispersed, except for two of Surac's close friends. They charged Ang head on, with their short swords drawn into the air. Ang was quick in his executions, slicing one's head clear off, and stabbing the other in the heart. The others succumbed to his command without an incident.

"Hear me, oh followers of the king of all evil, Garlock," he announced. "We will find the Woblo and the stone, and force him to use it to unleash its magical power. We will march upon this town and burn every inch of it to the ground, and kill every man, woman, and child in it. After we find the stone, we'll then march upon Riverton with our massive army and take what is rightfully ours-the Staff of Varlana. Once Glamara receives both, he will destroy the Shudolin once and for all, and return it to the Licarions and Grassmen. March on, comrades, march on, and destroy the town of Bacon once and for all!"

The creatures shouted a victorious scream in the night, as they raised their swords, and ran toward the village. Ang followed behind on his horse, and a smile ran across his face, excited he would finally be able to get his just revenge on Vladimir, Glam, and his friends.

CHAPTER FIFTEEN: A GRAVE MISTAKE

Glam and the party sat down that night in the local tavern, dined on smoked venison, and drank Mulberry wine. Although they felt somewhat safe in the fortress town, they couldn't help but feel Ang was out there waiting for them the minute they left town. Glam felt the king's advisor took his authority from him, but figured with the death of Christopher, and his plan to kill them in the end anyway, it was just a matter of time before things went sour.

While they kept entertained, Bargo felt anxious, and in his mind could sense danger. How could everybody be so at ease when his cousin was still missing? It made him feel once again that the humans and Elves thought very little of their Woblo brothers and sisters. He sipped his wine at a snail's pace, partly because of anxiety, and partly because he just wasn't in a mood to drink. Lilly was also on his mind; a love he knew he'd never have, and a dream shattered by the reality of her home life. He knew her husband well, and that he was a good man, but he also loved her more than life itself. Before he felt their courtship was an impossibility, but now he had a means to achieve such a dream, and his mind raced in all different directions.

She acted differently since Bargo told her about how he felt. She didn't seem as quick to put her arm around him to keep him warm, and talked to him very little about his father's shop anymore, or being a Blacksmith. He knew she was disturbed by the insinuation they could ever be a normal couple, knowing what he was.

Lilly was equally as quiet. Barton pissed her off the day before, and Glam focused on keeping an eye on Vladimir's men, while looking like he wasn't doing so. She drank her three glasses of wine quick, and retired early for the evening. Barton continued on, until he could barely stand, as he drank with Tamarka and

BARGO LYNDEN

Daniel. Bargo shook his head at his carelessness, as he knew all too well the Licarions could attack at any moment. He left as well, and retired early in the small room they provided for him in the west wing of the fortress.

It was late in the evening when Glam finally relaxed a bit, and finally succumbed to a little ale at the pub. By this time the men drank their share, and were resting for the night. While he swallowed a taste, Vladimir walked up to him, and placed his hand on his shoulder.

"It won't be long now," he told him. "We'll have the stone, the staff, and finally crush these Licarion scum once and for all."

"Just where is the staff?"

"We have already found the staff, and it is on route to Riverton."

"How convenient."

"What is that supposed to mean?"

"Nothing," Glam said, as he took another swallow. "All I meant is that it makes things easier for the kingdom. What about the Woblo's cousin?"

"What about him?"

"Just when do you plan to look for him, after the Licarions have stripped our skin from our bodies?"

"Like I said before. We'll look for him, after we find the stone."

"You know damn well he'll be dead by then, and that will be on your conscience."

"Save the sentimentalities to someone who cares, Glam. The prince has given me a job to do, and I'm here to see it gets done. If you had done your job, you would have stopped Ang and the Grassmen before they killed the royal security guardmaster."

"Unlike you, he was my friend," Glam reminded him. "And I only drink with my friends. If you feel you're my friend, you'll have a drink. Otherwise, we've got nothing more to discuss. Now, if you'll excuse me, I have to relieve myself of my worries, and my ale."

He left toward the public latrine, and Vladimir noticed he was alone, except for the pub owner, who was busy cleaning up. Without being seen, he took out a small canvas bag of crushed

166

poppies chopped into a fine powder, and dumped them into Glam's drink. He then left the pub, and smiled at the bartender. "Good evening," he said, as he left.

Glam came back, finished his ale, and headed to his room to get some rest. He needed all the energy he could spare to get out of Bacon, and lose the prince's men by the time they got to Jarod. His room was right next to Barton's and Elves' rooms. Lilly was given her own room, on the other side of Bargo, and was already fast asleep.

The hour grew late, close to midnight, when Vladimir went up to the north guardhouse to get a report. Jonathon was up there, along with two of Marcus' men. Vladimir climbed into it from the ladder, and stood next to his subordinate.

"You are relieved for the moment," he told the two other men, who nodded, and climbed down the ladder. When they left, he placed his hand on his subordinate's shoulder. "I drugged Glam, he should be out for hours. Get two men downstairs to the west wing, and grab the Woblo. Take him out the back, and wait for me outside the gate. Do what you have to, but be careful not to wake the others."

"Sir, what about the Licarions, and what Mayor Marcus said?"

"They are weak here. Only true warriors like us can deal with these despicable creatures. We'll grab the Woblo, and make him find the stone."

"Sir, they have us at a disadvantage. We are miles from any militias, and we have been depleted of our own men. To make an attempt like the one you're suggesting is foolish."

"Are you questioning my authority?"

"No, Sir, merely stating a fact."

"Just do what I tell you, keep sharp, and you'll be fine."

Jonathon exited the guardhouse, as two new men came up the ladder. Vladimir started to leave himself, when there was a loud blast from a horn in the distance from the north.

"What was that?" he asked one of the men.

"A Licarion battle cry," the man said. "They're calling for help." All of the sudden there were a least ten different horns in the distance from all directions. "This is not good."

Vladimir looked worried himself when he saw the look on

their faces. One of the men rang a large bell, and the advisor climbed quick down the ladder and into the darkness. Forty men raced in all directions to make sure every part of the fortress was protected, drew their bows with napham soaked arrows, and waited for the nocturnal reptilian creatures to appear out of the night.

When they did, they realized they were tremendously overmatched. From the north side alone there were hundreds of them, running towards the fortress, holding torches in one hand, and swords in the other.

"Fire!" the watchtower guardsman yelled, and twenty men launched the flaming projectiles into the crowd of Licarions, killing just a few of them. It wasn't long before they overtook the gate, and set the fortress on fire.

On the first floor of the fortress, in the west wing, the others awoke to a flurry of commotion. Lilly was the first to awake from the permeating stench of burning wood and flesh. She smelled it once before, when the Licarions invaded their area, and killed some of the townspeople. She put on her armor quick, sheathed her weapons, and headed for the door. Once she opened it, she was faced by one of the beasts, who she stabbed with her stiletto dagger. He fell to the floor, and she opened Bargo's room, only to find it vacant. Tamarka, Daniel, and Barton came into the hallway, and faced the young woman.

"Is Bargo with you?" she asked.

"No, not with us," Tamarka said. "Let's check Glam's room."

"What the heck is going on?" Barton asked.

"Sounds like we're under attack," the Elf answered, as they could hear footsteps in both directions. "Quick, into Glam's room!"

They entered their leader's room to find him almost unconscious. Tamarka slapped him a couple of times in the face, but he was unresponsive.

"Wake up," he said to him to no avail.

"Where's Bargo?" Lilly asked again.

"I don't know, but we have to get out of here now.'

He gestured for Barton and Daniel to carry their incapacitated leader, and pressed a stone panel on the wall, revealing a stairway that led down to an underground passageway. They scrambled into it just in time, for when the panel closed, several Licarions bust into the empty room.

During this time, Vladimir, Jonathon, and a handful of his men dragged the bound and gagged Woblo out of the back gate. They could see several dark figures coming from the south and east. They mounted their horses quick, and headed southwest away from the town, only to be faced with hundreds of the creatures, who came down from the hills to block their way.

They reversed directions several times, dodging them through the nearby forests and hills, until they finally found themselves surrounded. They came to a dead stop, the creatures encircled them, and then rested their swords and spears with the points to the ground. They watched in horror, as the village of Bacon burned to the north.

"Why don't they just kill us?" Jonathon asked. "What are they waiting for?"

"Not what, who. They're waiting for Ang," his commander answered.

There was nearly a half hour wait until Ang finally arrived. The Licarions cleared a pathway, as he trotted casually on his brown horse, until he was face to face with Vladimir. He pushed his dark cloak to the side, and spat on the ground.

"Hello, Vladimir. It seems the tables have turned, and now I am in charge."

"For now. But the prince shall have his revenge soon."

Ang laughed, as several of the Licarions snickered as well.

"The prince? He's as weak as his father was, and will die just as easily. Give me the Woblo, tell me where the staff and stone are, and I might let you live."

Bargo struggled to get away, but found the tied ropes impossible to slip out of. The advisor approached Ang, realizing he was in a tough position.

"And if I don't?"

"I would hate to even think about what your prince will say when they find your body scattered all over the countryside."

"You leave me in a grave position," he said in a despairing tone.

"Exactly," Ang said, as he waved his hand, and arrows flew and killed the only three men Vladimir had left besides Jonathon.

BARGO LYNDEN

"You said you'd let us live?" Jonathon cried in fear.

"I said I might let you live. You should know I'm a man of my word."

Vladimir went to draw his sword, but was subdued by the vicious reptilians who knocked him off the horse, and used their claws, knives, and spears to finish him off. They did no less to his underling, leaving the poor Woblo to witness the whole incident. When it was all over, Ang approached his prize, and smiled, his one blue eye staring an evil glance.

"So you are the brave Woblo who will lead us to victory?" he asked. "Once you find the stone, we will work together to destroy the humans." Bargo tried to speak, but the gag made it hard. Ang untied it for him. "You were saying?"

"I said there's no way I'll help you. Why should I? You killed my father."

"I didn't kill your father. His lack of common sense killed him. Why should you care for humans anyway? They've done nothing but make fun of you, and treat you like a common farm animal."

"They are better to me than you are." He was frightened, but he also felt he'd had enough of this oppressor. He thought about the special sword, and if he could get one good shot at his heart, he could end this.

"Talmok, take his sword from his sheath, and give it to me," Ang ordered, almost as if he knew his thoughts. The subordinate followed his order, and Ang placed the weapon in his extra sheath. "You will help me, Mr. Bargo Lynden, or your cousin Barlow will die."

"You know where he is?"

"Of course, I do. On his way to North Licarion City, as you will soon be."

"Let him go, he's done nothing to you."

"After you help me."

"I don't believe you."

"That, of course, is you're right. But if you don't help, he'll die, because I'll surely keep my word when it comes to killing him."

"Well, then, I guess I have no choice. Shall we start towards to Jarod?"

"You are a wise woblo not to test me. Such a small creature

170

is no match to an army of real soldiers. Your friends were not so lucky."

"What about my friends?"

"They are merely cinders now. Cinders in a burnt out shell of a town, and a newly conquered territory."

Little did he know, but they were actually safely tucked in a secret room off of the passageway, underneath what was left of the fortress. Hidden from the Licarions, they stayed there for hours until the invaders long departed. It also took that amount of time for Glam to finally gain his bearings, after the opiate derivative wore off. He sat up in the makeshift bed and rubbed his face.

"What happened? Last thing I remember I was drinking an ale and talking with Vladimir."

"Apparently, he dosed you with something," Tamarka said.

"Bargo's missing," Lilly told him.

"He must have taken him," Glam said, as he tried to stand, but was still a little dizzy. Lilly sat him back down.

"You have to rest a little longer."

"There is no time to rest. We have to get to Jarod."

"Why didn't Vladimir kill us like he was told to do?" Barton asked.

"Perhaps he felt with Bargo he didn't need to, or maybe he had a change in heart," Glam said.

"Just wait ten more minutes," Tamarka said. "Then we'll have a look around."

They gathered their meager supply of food, weapons, and water, and prepared to surface from the underground hideout. It was sunrise when they opened the stone door, which took three of them to push, and emerged to the charred remains of the fortress town. The few survivors left were either dying, or so injured they would never recover. Glam turned towards his friends with grim news.

"I'm afraid at this point we're on our own. I'm just sorry I didn't catch on to Vladimir's plan. I'm usually much more observant about these things."

"Perhaps you were preoccupied," Barton said. "We all get that way sometimes."

"What about these tracks?" Daniel asked. "Where do we

start? There's so many."

"Look for the horse tracks," Glam said. "That's where we'll find Vladimir."

"If Ang didn't get to him first," Tamarka said.

"If he did, may Rhiatu help Bargo," their leader stated. "I really don't know what to do at this point."

"What do you mean?" Lilly asked, frustrated. "We go after Bargo and Barlow."

"To do so without help would be a suicide mission."

"Then we get help."

"The nearest place to get help is Bashworth, a three day ride," Tamarka said. "And don't count on the navy, because most of them are near the Licarion Islands. The Licarions have depleted most of our land militia units. We're really on our own here."

"Then somebody needs to go to Bashworth," Lilly said.

"Out of the question," Glam said.

"We can't just wait here," Lilly said. "You're not going to give up on Bargo. We've come this far because of him, we can't stop looking."

"We have no choice but to go back to Riverton, and tell them we failed."

"That doesn't sound like the Glam I know," Tamarka said. "Don't worry, I'll go."

"I'll go with Tamarka as well," Daniel said. "The four of you can continue to Jarod."

"I can't spare you, we'll need you in case we're attacked on the way back."

"You'll have to round up some horses," Glam said. "The fire chased them into the countryside. Try to find enough for all of us. We'll look around here, and see what's salvageable."

"Do you think they'll come back?" Barton asked.

"Why? They have no reason to. As far as they know, we're all dead, which may work to your advantage," Tamarka said.

"But we're at a disadvantage as far as numbers," Glam added. "If we're to save them, we have to be discrete and quick."

Tamarka and Daniel were able to collect five horses, and Glam found a little extra fruit to take with them. They packed some saddle bags on the animals, and then their leader hugged his two closest friends.

"Take care, and be careful," Glam told him. "And don't let word of this get back to the prince. If he finds out, he'll have us killed. We're expendable to him. Try to intercept his messenger if you can."

"Yes, Sir," Tamarka said.

The two Elves said goodbye, and started north on the South Pass. When they were finally out of sight, Barton turned towards the others.

"Now what?" he asked.

"We find the Woblos," Glam said, reluctant. "I wish I could say it won't be difficult. It's three of us against an army."

"Well, I know what I said about things before," Barton said. "But I've grown fond of that furry little guy, and I feel I can call him friend. He needs our help more than ever."

"I agree," Lilly said. "We have to do whatever is necessary to get his cousin and him back."

"But how?" Barton asked.

"That, my friends," Glam said. "Is a good question. One I hope to have answered by this evening."

They rode their horses, heading south with the sun now high in the sky, which illuminated the green, lush valley around them. They looked back at the town of Bacon, and couldn't help but feel a sense of failure and defeat. Glam saw this coming, and knew unless Bargo found the gem, it would just be the beginning of a long, dragged out war. The last time war was upon the land, thousands died, and cities were destroyed. He just hoped Ang wouldn't get to the prince as well, and steal the staff from his trophy room. If he followed through with his plans, it would mean the end of all races; Elves, humans, and Woblos. That was a risk he wasn't willing to take, and would do anything to prevent, even giving his own life.

CHAPTER SIXTEEN: THE GEM OF REBOLIN

By sundown, Ang and his army were near Jarod. This was a very small village, where the humans sided with the Licarions in order to save their own skins. They kept them abreast of what was going on in Riverton, and helped them take down any small parties nearby which might have supplies they needed.

The Licarions, like the Grassmen, were marauders who would kill, burn, and steal anything in their paths. The difference was the Licarions created several cities, and a real civilization, whereas the Grassmen were more like nomads who lived off the land. Most of the reptilian civilization was built underground in the Dagar Mountains, a range which started near Jarod, and extended south past South Licarion city. The gem stone was somewhere in between the 500 mile radius, which explained why its location was so elusive.

They stopped for the night to celebrate their victory, with a huge bonfire and lots of Strawberry wine. Bargo, tied to a tree, sat on the ground in fear. While Ang's company celebrated, he conversed with their prisoner.

"Tomorrow you can help us find the stone," he said.

"What makes you think I know where it is?" Bargo asked.

"Because you have a connection with it."

"How could I? I never touched it."

"You don't have to touch it, but then you already knew that, didn't you?"

"You're mistaken. There is no way I am what you think I am. I'm not some magical beast who can solve yours or Prince Phillip's problems. In fact, I've never performed any magic in my whole life. I'm just an ordinary Blacksmith."

"I'm well aware of who and what you are, Mr. Lynden. And I know you had your doubts about magic before you started this journey, but I can assure you everything is true. You are indeed

175

the one we're looking for, and are capable of the power to have everything you want in life; money, fame, and prestige?"

"What makes you think I want any of those things?"

"Because you're tired of being treated like half a man, an outcast, and a freak. Wouldn't it be nice to be admired, respected, and treated like everyone else?"

"Sure. But Lilly's told me I don't need magic for that."

"Ah yes, and then there's Lilly. Wouldn't you like to have her love you as the man you really are, not some caricature in an animal's body?"

"Yes, I mean no. I don't know. I'm confused right now. Besides, Glam told me you're just trying to use the stone for evil purposes."

"Glam has no idea of the staff and gem's real powers. Why don't you let me train you in how to use them properly?"

"I don't think so. I think Glam was right, and I shouldn't trust you."

"Well, I'm sorry you feel that way. Tomorrow, we'll be heading into the mountains near Jarod, and into the cavern systems. Remember, if you disobey me, I'll have your cousin killed, and then I'll make sure you join him-very slowly."

"Don't worry, I won't give you any trouble. I'm not dumb enough to cross you."

"I'm glad to hear that. We'll be leaving in the morning. Until then, have a pleasant night's rest."

He left him tied to the tree, as he watched the fire start to burn down to embers. By this time, most of the Licarions dissipated, and moved back on to other parts of their kingdom. Ang kept a small regiment of one hundred to travel with him into the cavern system, where the gem was thought to be. While the night raged on, Bargo stared at the fire, mesmerized by the dancing flames over the coals. He thought he was hallucinating, when he saw the two red eyes glowing in the fire, and heard the voice again.

"Bargo Lynden," it said. "You must say nothing and listen to me. Your power can help you out of this situation, but you must do exactly what I tell you to do. Repeat these ancient Elven words, and your kidnappers will sleep, allowing enough time for you to free yourself. They are as follows: Fiari Ul dutu Karaf."

"Who are you?" Bargo mumbled. "And don't tell me your name's not important."

"I am your destiny. I am your dreams, your hopes, and your fears."

"You speak in riddles. Make some sense, will you?"

"It will be revealed to you when the time is right. First, you must say the words."

"Fori Uldoto Karaf."

"No, Fiari Ul dutu Karaf."

A Licarion, who heard Bargo speak aloud, looked over towards the prisoner, and then approached him.

"Who you talking to?" he asked, as he pointed his spear at him.

"No one," he said. "Myself, I guess."

"Well, quiet down. Or I'll gag you again."

He turned his back, and Bargo shouted the words again, this time correctly. He wouldn't have believed it if he hadn't seen for himself, but the whole group of them, as well as Ang, collapsed into a deep sleep, as if under a magical spell. Glam was right about his special power, but couldn't understand how he was able to do this without the stone. His only theory was the voice he heard from the fire was a magical spirit of some kind helping him.

He managed to get the ropes loose enough so he could cut them from a sharp edge on the tree. When he was free, he started to run away, but realized Ang still had his sword. He carefully approached the Elf, still not completely convinced he wouldn't wake up, and grabbed the sword from his sheath. He looked down at his foe, held the sword close to his chest, and decided whether to kill him or not. Glam told him when this time came, he shouldn't hesitate, and plunge the sword deep within his heart, but he found himself unable to kill a helpless Elf, even someone as cruel as Ang. He put the sword back in his sheath, mounted a horse, and headed quickly for the nearest mountain.

When he found one of the many cavern entrances, he figured he'd be on foot from here, so he slapped the horse on its behind, sending it on its way to whereabouts unknown. It must have had something to do with the fire, but he was beginning to feel a closeness to the stone, almost as if he sensed it was nearby. He couldn't understand this; he never had this type of power before, and it felt like a built in compass.

He was tired, and comfortable he had a ten hour head start, so he figured it was a good time to get a couple hours of sleep. He knew they'd taken Barlow to North Licarion City, and after he found the stone, that would be his next destination. He sensed his friends were still alive, and hoped he was able to find them before he reached the underground civilization, but also knew there were no guarantees.

While he slept, he began to dream of himself sitting on a throne, as a man, holding the staff with the gem on its end. Next to him was his queen, Lilly, and he was surrounded by Elves, Woblos, and men who were his subjects. There were riches all around him; diamonds, rubies, sapphires, gold, and silver, and sitting at a table counting the money, was no other than Ang. He stopped for a moment, looked up, and squinted with his one good eye. He smiled at Bargo, laughed, and picked up a handful of money. Then his one good eye turned bright red, and his teeth grew razor sharp. Bargo awoke with a fright, and when alert, he heard the sound of footsteps. He heard a voice in the distance, and ducked down the cavern passageway.

"I think I see him this way," the voice said. "Strangest thing I ever saw."

Bargo ran down the tunnel, until he came to a decline in it. It was steep, and he tried to be careful, but found it too slippery to anchor his feet on. He slid uncontrollably down it, until he fell into an underground spring. He lifted himself out of the water, which was about two and half feet deep, and started to walk to where it was dry. The only light in the cavern was an opening near the top, which provided a small ray of sunbeams to penetrate the chamber.

He knew navigating the tunnels without a torch would be difficult. He used what little visibility available to reach land, and felt his way into another passage. He noticed a lit torch on the wall just a little ways ahead of him, and stepped slowly toward it to investigate, assuming it might be Licarions. He drew his sword, as he inched near the light.

He entered an large empty chamber, perhaps one hundred feet long and thirty feet wide, covered with diamonds, gold, silver, rubies, and sapphires, just like in his dream earlier. There were two other passageways, which led in other directions, and they were both well lit. He eyed the room to see if anything resembled the blue stone he was looking for, but nothing looked familiar. He was tempted to pull out his magnifying glass, but he could tell they were authentic even without examination. There were four torches burning in the room, which lit it well enough to see the gold glitter and the silver shine. He never saw so many jewels in his life, even when he visited the palace. Could he have experienced a premonition in the form a dream?

He wondered why it was left unattended, but guessed the two Licarions he heard outside guarded it, and would soon return. Sure enough, he heard footsteps again coming down the passageway. He hid around the corner and to the left, as one of them stopped at the entranceway.

"Licar, cala raco," he hissed in his native tongue, which was unfamiliar to the Woblo, but meant "unbelievable, or in my dreams." The two of them came in to look at the massive amount of precious chattels, shocked.

Although he was very scared, Bargo took advantage of the opportunity and turned quick, lunging the Elven sword into the stomach of the one closest to him. He fell to the ground, as the other creature drew his sword, ready to do battle. The clang of the weapons echoed throughout the hall, as the two of them defended themselves.

Suddenly, there was a loud noise, and a tremble throughout the cavern. The Licarion scurried the way he came in fear, and left Bargo alone in the chamber. He watched the fifteen feet wide, ten feet high entrance, as a large ten feet black scorpion entered the room. He thought he was terrified minutes before, but Glam never mentioned anything like this. He backed up towards the way he came slow, and with his sword drawn.

The creature's stinger flew at him with a force strong enough to shatter the rocks above him, but luckily missed its intended target. He swung the blade at the beast, slicing part of its right pincer off. This just infuriated the creature, and it grabbed him around his waist with its left claw, slamming him against the cavern wall. It drew its stinger back again, ready to finish him off, when the Woblo stabbed it in the head. It loosened its claw, and dropped him, just as the stinger slammed into the area where he was. On the ground and under the beast, he thrust his sword into its belly, and mortally wounded it. He rolled it out of his way, as it slowly writhed in pain, until it died.

Amazed he was able to perform such a feat, and horrified to face such a monster, he sat down and took a breath. He could swear he sensed something approaching, and it wasn't a Licarion. He ran back into the cavern, and watched from around the corner, as a small and pathetic creature entered the chamber.

Bargo could faintly see the resemblance, remembering the story Christopher and Glam told him, about a creature who was half Woblo-half Licarion who guarded the stone. His ears were shorter than Bargo's, malformed, and he was hairless. Its pale, greenish complexion was scaly, had two horns on its head, short wings, and a sharp beak, similar to his. His eyes were red like fire, much like the ones he saw in Kain and Ang before. They were different, however, as they were always that color, and didn't glow. His body was thin and leathery, with webbed feet, and razor sharp claws on his fingers. The Woblo didn't want to have to tangle with him, but to find the stone, he was afraid it was inevitable.

When the creature saw the scorpion was dead, he was enraged. Bargo figured it must have been some kind of sentinel, protecting his treasure. He saw the Licarion lying dead, and figured it must have been him, and didn't even acknowledge the Woblo, who watched him from around the corner. He walked out of the chamber, and Bargo once again took a deep breath.

He figured his next move was to get by the beast without being seen, and locating the stone while doing it. He knew it wasn't in the main chamber, so he fathomed it must be in another chamber somewhere else. It would be a bigger problem, of course, if there were any more of the giant scorpions guarding it.

He felt very alone, scared, and wished his friends would come soon, if they even knew where to look. Ang had a major head start on them, and there were so many tracks to follow, they might follow the wrong ones. He knew the traitorous Elf commander was also a good tracker, and may already be close on his tale as well.

He grabbed a torch off the wall, and followed the creature as it left the first chamber, and disappeared into another passageway on the right. He went into a smaller area with a stone table which was also lit with torches, and had a crystallized blue stone on it. The stone gave off a powerful white light, and its brightness could be seen in the outside tunnel, where Bargo was hiding. He edged back, careful not to be seen, and kept his sword ready in case he needed it.

He watched the creature, as he picked up two three inch scorpions by their stingers, and placed them next to the stone on the floor of the cavern. When he did this, a white, encircled light appeared around the table, and they grew until they were as big as the other one was. Bargo figured he better get out of there before he was attacked, and ran towards the way he came.

He'd seen some strange things the past few days, but he knew now they were real, even if they were unbelievable. Glam was right about everything; the power of the staff and gem, the magical powers he possessed but didn't know how to use, and the evil it drew in the wrong hands. He ran, as he could hear the beasts scamper towards him, and the creature yelling in the dark. "Kill him! Find the intruder thief, and kill him."

Bargo ran into the underground spring, and tried to climb the slippery wall he entered from. The scorpions waited at the dry part of the tunnel, unwilling to climb into the water. He was unable to climb it, and found himself at a stalemate with the creatures; they were unable to reach him, and he couldn't escape. He sank down into the water, and held the torch, as the Woblo-like creature walked in between his pets, his red eyes now glowing in the darkness.

"Well, well, what have we here?" he asked. "Looks like a distant cousin, perhaps? What's its name?"

"Bargo. Bargo Lynden. And if you come any closer, I'll be forced to defend myself."

"A feisty cousin, no less. Perhaps after me stone?"

"I got lost from my party. I've told you my name, now tell me yours."

"They call myself Jickle Siceleon. The keeper of the stone."

"Who's they?"

"All those who pass through here, or die here. As you soon

will. Who is your party?"

"I travel with three Elves, a man, and a woman. Maybe you have seen them?"

"I see no one. And trust no one."

"I'm just trying to get back to my friends. Perhaps you can help me out, and I'll be on my way."

"Have you taken any of my other treasures, perhaps?" Even though he felt the Woblo was harmless, he still was suspicious.

"No, not at all. You can search me if you like."

"No, I believe you. I will help you out, but if you return, I will not be so merciful."

"Thank you. I won't be back, I promise."

With that, he waded over to Bargo on the other side, and the slippery incline. Bargo put his sword back in his sheath as a sign of good faith, and Jickle kneeled down in front of him.

"Step on my back and climb out," the creature told him.

While he was bent over, Bargo grabbed a rock and smashed it over his head, knocking him unconscious. He fell into the water, and Bargo lifted his head out enough so he wouldn't drown. He turned towards the two scorpions, who moved back and forth frantically at the dry end, and climbed the ceiling. It was at this point he wished for a bow; even if he was a horrible shot, he would at least have stood a chance.

The beasts knew they couldn't get him in the water, so they tried to reach him from the walls, but were unsuccessful. Bargo surmised how to get in the tunnel, and with them on the ceiling, he felt now was the time. He ran towards the tunnel, and one of the scorpions quickly responded, he held him off with the torch. The scorpion swung his stinger, and as it hit his chest, he fell against the wall, certain he was going to die. Fortunately, the mail armor he wore underneath saved him, and he swung down with his sword, decapitating its stinger.

He then rose to his feet, and swung his blade, as the other scorpion arrived to assist his fellow sentinel. The first one lost one of his pincers, and found a torch directly between its eyes. It writhed in pain, ran into the water, and finally drowned in the spring.

Now faced against the other one, Bargo used his torch to keep the beast at bay, and waved his sword into its legs, which knocked it off balance. He pounced onto its back, cut off his stinger with the blade, and used his dagger to stab it in the back, until it no longer moved.

He ran down the tunnel and into the chamber where the gem was. When he entered the room, he was in awe at the sight of the beautiful stone. Being a collector, he was mystified at such a perfectly round specimen. He approached the stone, scared as well as fascinated, and took out his magnifying glass to examine it. He picked it up, and could feel a sensation shoot through him like he never felt before; a feeling of euphoria, and power to do anything. He put in his saddle bag, which doused its light, and searched for a way out.

He figured he couldn't get out the way he got in, so he decided to follow the cave system, in hopes he'd find another way out. He also figured without the stone, Jickle was no longer an immediate threat. He left the creature's lair, and followed a tunnel headed away from the area.

He knew he left many riches in the cavern, and Ang would probably find them and call them his own. He prayed the Elf would show the creature the same mercy he did, but knew in his heart this would not be the case, due to his homicidal nature. The main thing was he possessed the gem now, and no one could harm him; at least not after he learned to use it properly.

He continued down the tunnel, until he came to an opening, which overlooked a cliff which dropped to seemingly nowhere. He was careful to move along the edge, into another tunnel lined with the lit torches, and special Licarion writing on the walls. It was at this point he realized he left the Shudolin, and entered into enemy territory.

CHAPTER SEVENTEEN: DARK TIMES AHEAD

Glam and the others arrived at the spot were Bargo escaped, surrounded by several horse tracks, and the sign of a struggle. The prince's men were scattered about, all dead, and some in pieces. Glam rolled over the advisor's corpse, and shook his head in despair. He noticed the other half of the stone tablet fell from his clothing, brushed it off, and put it in his pocket.

"Poor Vladimir, he underestimated his opponent. This is not good. Ang has Bargo."

"Where's he taking him?" Lilly asked in anxiety.

"To find the stone, and then to North Licarion City."

"And little or no chance of finding him," Barton said.

"We can't just give up, we've come so far," Lilly said. "We have to find him."

"We don't even no where to start," Barton said.

"We don't know where, but we know what," Glam said. "Christopher mentioned something at the banquet about a creature protecting the stone in a cave near here. That's where we'll start."

"But there must be at least one thousand different caves up in those mountains. How do we know which one is the right one?"

"We'll have to search them one by one. But we'll have to be careful. We're in Licarion Territory now."

"Any idea where they've taken Barlow?" Lilly asked.

"My guess is by now he too is in North Licarion City. A prisoner of Glamara, the Licarion king. I don't think he'll be too happy when he finds out the king is dead, however."

They continued, and found the remains of the large bonfire which burned the night before, and the cut ropes tied around the tree. Glam picked them, and looking them over carefully.

"The ropes were sliced."

"Why does that surprise you?" Barton asked.

"Because Ang tied them around the tree. Why would he cut

them loose?"

"Perhaps he was in a hurry?"

"Or perhaps Bargo might have escaped," Lilly suggested.

"Let's not jump to conclusions," Glam said.

"You don't believe he's capable of escaping on his own, do you?"

"Let's not start that again. All I meant is we can't make generalizations without any proof."

"Well, isn't a cut rope proof?" Barton asked.

"Yes, but of what, I'm not sure yet. We'll follow the tracks to the southeast into the mountains. They said the gem is near Jarod, in a cave, about ten miles from here."

"What do you think they'll do to him?" Lilly questioned, both frightened and feeling guilty about her argument with him before.

"If he finds the stone before they do, nothing. The power of the stone will protect him, as long as he protects it."

"What if he doesn't?"

"Then it's up to the great Rhiatu to save him. If he gives the stone to them freely, its power to him will be gone."

"What if he doesn't, and they take it?" Barton asked.

"They would have to take it by him not protecting it. Say, if he was to lose it, or drop it, its power would again be gone, and the evil forces would take over. We can't let that happen."

"But isn't the gem useless without the staff?" Barton asked.

"Not entirely."

"Another thing you've hid from us?" Lilly asked.

"Please understand, the things I tell you are merely the folklore of our ancestors, and not always accurate. The stone has certain properties that allow some sympathetic magic."

"Such as?"

"Manipulation of objects or living beings."

"What kind of manipulation?" Barton asked.

"Moving an object without touching it, using an object as a weapon, enlarging or shrinking an object, things like that."

"I hope he knows the right thing to do," Lilly said.

"Now who's being negative," Glam said, as he mounted his horse. "I'm sure he will. He's a bright young Woblo who has a lot of his father in him. I can see it."

"I just hope he's not as foolishly brave as his father was. I would hate to lose him too."

"I'm worried for him as well," Barton said.

"He's never been alone like this ever before."

"He'll be fine," Glam said. "He has the Elven sword of courage, and Rhiatu looking down upon him."

"And about ten thousand Licarions as well," Barton added.

"We better get going, we've got a tough road ahead."

While they followed the meager clues left behind, Ang and his party started into the mountains to look for the Woblo, when they came upon a cavern with a drop to it. The Elf commander gestured for his Licarion party to follow him, as he dropped a rope into it, and tied it to a dead tree outside of the cave. He pulled it tight to make sure it was taut, and climbed in. He gestured for five of the reptilians to follow him in as well. He dropped thirty feet to the bottom, splashing into the water. He made a makeshift torch from his sword and a piece of cloth ripped from his shirt cuff, wrapped it around his weapon, and then lit it with a match.

He saw the two dead scorpions, and walked over to the dry area on the other side of the chamber. He walked down the passageway, as his subordinates followed him, staring at the dead beasts. He entered the chamber which held the treasures, and was amazed at the find. Beside them he saw the pitiful Jickle crouched down and crying. He saw he was being watched, and turned to the Elf, who spotted the dead Licarion on the floor of the cavern.

"You can't have it," he insisted. "It's mine, you hear me? Not yours."

"It was yours," Ang said, as he gestured the Licarions to grab him. "Kill him."

"Wait, I'll split it with you if you let me live."

"No deal, we'll take it, and kill you anyway."

"Please, please, don't kill me. I have information for you."

"What could you tell me that I don't already know?"

"You are looking for a Woblo, perhaps?" he asked, as he was picked up by two Licarions and brought to his feet.

"Why do you think that?"

"I saw him. He was here, this morning. He took it from me."

"What's did he take? Maybe a blue stone with magical

powers?"

"Yes, that's it. He took it from me. I can show you which way to go."

"Jalat, tie him up, and we'll take him with us. If he tries to escape, gut him. Glatar, go get some more of your people to come back, and start carrying some of the loot back to the king. Kill anyone who isn't a Licarion who comes near it. If any one of your 'men' steal any of it, they're to be executed immediately as well. Understand?"

"Yes, Sire," Glatar and Jalat said in unison, and followed his orders.

Four hours passed, as Bargo found himself deep within the cavern system, and his torch just about burned out. He remembered the gem gave off a white light, but was reluctant to pull it out, for fear he'd lose it. He opened the saddle bag, left it inside, but allowed the light to permeate outside so he could see at least. He tried to keep to some of the less used caverns, and find a way back to the outside world.

Occasionally, he heard voices of Licarions speaking in their own tongue, but they were far off. He carried the Elven sword close to his side, and kept a sharp eye on where he stepped. He wondered how he could use the stone against those who tried to take it, such as Ang. He saw Jickle use it to make the arachnids bigger, but wasn't sure how it could help him in his situation. He thought maybe Glam might know the answer to exactly what powers it generated, but had no idea where he was right now, or even if he'd ever see him again. He was truly alone, and scared his prize might fall into enemy hands without his friends' help.

He was sure by now Ang found Jickle's lair, and the treasures inside, and either killed him already, or questioned if he'd seen Bargo. The Woblo hoped his friends didn't run into him in their search, since the prince's men were all killed, and they were outnumbered.

He came to the end of a passageway which overlooked a large cavern and a stone complex within the canyon below, and similar to a small city. He saw Licarions move in every direction of its streets, and thousands of lit torches scattered throughout its domain. The stone city was carved within the rock of the mountain and the entrance faced out towards the valley. He backed up so he wouldn't be seen, and suddenly bumped into something in the dark. He turned to face two Licarions, holding spears. He covered the gem to hide it, but they already caught a glimpse of it.

"What we got here?" one asked, and pointed the spear in the Woblo's face.

"A spy for Shudolin no doubt," the other said. "And he got something in the bag."

"No, I don't," Bargo lied. "Just some supplies, that's all."

"What kind supplies?" the first one asked, as he reached for the bag. Bargo pulled it away, but found the spear inches from his eye. "Hand over."

Bargo was ready to do just that, but he tactfully dumped the stone into his hand instead, and stuck it in his jacket pocket, hidden from their sight. The Licarion looked through the bag, and handed it to his friend.

"The only thing here is flask of water, three matches, some kind of glass, and some old biscuits," the second one said.

"Well, what you doing here anyway?" the first one asked.

"I was traveling from Bacon to Bashworth, lost direction, and ended up in here," Bargo answered.

"You want us believe you lost?"

"Yes, I'm afraid so. If you could just show me the way out, I'll be heading home."

"The only place you going is grave," the first one said, as he pulled his spear back to stab him.

Not knowing what else to do, he pulled out the gem. The two creatures tried to stab him; but their spears lifted out of their arms, and into the passageway. The reptilians tried to grab him, and found themselves cowering in pain from the heat the gem gave off. After Bargo realized he also alerted half of the inhabitants below from the brightness and commotion, he threw it back in his sack, and ran back down the passageway.

He could hear the screams and howls of the creatures, as they came through the passageways to chase the woblo. He found himself faced by several, so he pulled out the gem again, and blinded them as well. He went into a tunnel on his right, with an ascending stairway to it, which he climbed for at least a quarter of

BARGO LYNDEN

a mile, until it led to the outside.

Once he emerged from the cavern, he could see the main entrance of the city, and a good distance of a mile from the mountain. There was a small regiment outside of another cavern entrance about the same distance, which he guessed was where Jickle's lair was. He also saw a larger unit to the left of the cavern, sharpening their spears and arrows near some trees. He could hear the beasts in the cavern still scurrying about, so he hid behind some rocks. When they exited the cave, they were unable to find him, so they returned the way they came.

While the Woblo tried to stay hidden, he looked to the north, and saw a very small party heading across an open field, unaware of the danger ahead of them. There were three horses with riders; at first he didn't think it was Glam because there were only three instead of five people, but after a few minutes he realized the truth that Tamarka and Daniel were no longer with them. He knew he had to warn them, but without a horse, if he ran out, the enemy would see him for sure. He needed to create a diversion of some kind, but he wasn't sure how to do it.

He looked at the rocks above the ridge, and saw there were some loose ones. He felt if he could move the spears, he might be able to move the rocks as well. He pulled the stone out, concentrated on the ridge, but found himself unable to perform the task. He figured he needed to be closer, and climb to the top of the ridge. He figured by the time he reached the top, his friends would be halfway across the field, which was scattered with several oak trees, and within sight of their aggressors.

It took him about forty five minutes to reach the ridge just above Jickle's lair. He could see Glam and the others approaching, their horses at a full gallop, and swords drawn. He pulled out the gem, raised it in the air, and concentrated, as the rocks just beneath him on the ledge began to loosen and break, creating an avalanche. He felt the earth move beneath him, and found it hard to stand up without falling. He lost his balance, and as he did, the gem fell to the ground close to the ledge and began to shake. Bargo reached for and grabbed it just before dropping it over the cliff, and turned to face the first Licarion he met before.

"Now you die for treachery, Woblo," he said, as he jabbed

down with his spear.

Bargo rolled quick, dropped the gem back in his sack, and rose to his feet. He lifted his sword, as the Licarion descended his downward, and blocked his attempts to slice him. The Woblo thrust low, chopped into his right leg, and gave him a deep gash. The creature screamed in pain, and pulled out his dagger, now armed with two weapons. Before Bargo could swing back again, an arrow went through the reptile's back, fatally wounding him, and he dropped to the ground.

The Woblo looked down at his friends, who emerged from the dust and debris, charging into the crowd of frenzied Licarions. Glam killed three of the beasts with his short sword, as they tried to pull him off his horse, and onto the rocky hill. Lilly was no worse for wear, when two tried to attack her, and she jumped from her horse onto one of the creatures, plunging her dagger into his chest. Another came from behind, so she sliced his sword arm right off before he even knew it. Barton's hands full with three of them, he fought them off just as quick. When it was over, and the smoke settled, Glam looked up towards his friend.

"Use the power of the gem. If you hold it, and concentrate, you will be able to levitate, and bring yourself down."

"Are you out of your cotton picking mind?" Barton asked. "Are you saying he can fly?"

"Only if he believes and concentrates. If not, he'll fail, and he will die."

"Isn't their an easier way?" Lilly asked. "Couldn't he climb down another part of the ridge?"

"He could, and is welcome to do so," Glam said. "But it will not teach him to use his gift."

"I can't," Bargo cried from above. "I'm scared."

"Have faith in yourself, young lad, " Glam yelled. "You have the courage within your soul."

"I won't let you do this," Lilly said. "This is insane."

"I'm in charge here, Mrs. Tumberhill, you have no choice."

"I'm beginning to think Barton is right, and this whole trip is just a waste of time."

"Silence! Bargo will be all right, if he does exactly what I tell him to do. Bargo, take a deep breath, concentrate, hold the gem above you, and repeat these words-Fira giola aratu. Then step off the ledge, and you'll slowly float back down."

Bargo followed his instruction and stepped off the ledge, at first wobbling from his own self doubt, and then levitating above them. Barton and Lilly stared in disbelief, now knowing from what they saw, there was no doubt in their mind the magic Glam spoke of was real. He glided to the ground, and as his feet touched the rocks below him, the light from the gem dimmed, until the stone turned back to its original bluish color.

"If I hadn't seen it with my own eyes I wouldn't have believed it," Barton said.

"I still don't believe it," the skeptical Lilly stated.

"Even after what just happened?"

"He must have used ropes of some kind."

"Invisible ropes?" Glam asked. "Bargo, did I influence you in any way by using ropes, or vines of some kind?"

"No, Sir," the Woblo said, still astonished by everything he just did. "It's magic, Lilly, real honest to goodness magic."

"But it's only good if you use for its intended purpose-to fight off evil."

"So just what is he supposed to be able to do with this stone?" Lilly asked.

"As you can see, he can levitate or fly if necessary, he can manipulate objects, such as the avalanche our friends experienced earlier, and with the staff, he would have unlimited power. The urge for its misuse is strong, however, and Bargo, being vulnerable to his father's death, will not help matters."

"I haven't had the urge to use it like you say," Bargo said.

"Not yet," Glam warned him. "But you will, just as things get the most dire, and the most desperate."

"You sound like you have the ability to see what is about to come," Lilly joked.

"Do not jest about things you can't possibly understand. I do have the ability, I just choose when and where to use it."

"Why didn't you use it when his father died?"

"What his father chose to do was unpredictable, and unavoidable, and very tragic. Do not think I lack compassion for you, my small friend. Your father was a brave Woblo, and a good friend to others. I was proud to have met him."

"It's all right, Lilly," Bargo said. "I'll do whatever's necessary to get through this."

"Well, if that's settled, we better get a move on," Glam said. "We'll enter through this cavern ahead. It will take us in the back way. They're probably keeping Barlow in one of the work camps in the caverns."

"I wouldn't go that way."

Barton got suspicious of the animal, and approached him.

"What are you hiding, Fella?"

"Nothing, I just wouldn't go that way."

"What's the matter, Bargo?" Lilly asked. "You're as white as ghost."

"That's where you found the gem, isn't it?" Glam asked.

"Yes, Sir."

"What was down there that terrified you so?" Barton asked.

"I'd rather not say."

"Well, whatever's down there, you'll be safe with us," Glam said.

"You said that before, and I ended up kidnapped, first by Phillip, and then by Ang."

"I promise not to take my eyes off you this time. Besides, as you have discovered, if used right, the gem can protect you."

"I realize that, but it doesn't stop me from being scared out of my wits. I am after all, only four feet tall, and you have no idea what was down there."

"With the courage of a man ten feet tall," Lilly added.

"She absolutely right; now is the time to face your fears," Glam said. "We've got a monumental task ahead of us, and we need everyone to have a clear head. Now, Barton, tie the horses over in those bushes over there, and then we'll all have a look inside."

He completed the task, and the small troop approached the cavern. Glam found the rope Ang tied to the branch earlier, and turned to his Woblo friend.

"Is this yours?"

"No."

"It's seems we're not the only ones interested in this cave. I can see why you're afraid. Be alert, there may be Licarions down here."

"There's also water, although I wouldn't recommend drinking it.

He lit a torch, and started down the rope, and into the underground spring. He waved his torch, as he found the two large dead scorpions, and the lit hallway at the other end.

"Come on down, but hold your breath; it reeks of death down here."

Barton followed him down, as Bargo stayed up with Lilly, and began to shake uncontrollably. Lilly held him tight against her chest, and consoled him.

"It will be all right," she told him. "You've no reason to fear the unknown, with the power of Rhiatu behind you."

"I thought you didn't believe in magic?" he asked.

"No, but I do believe in faith, and in some way the power of our god is involved. Now, come on, it's getting dark, and the Licarions will see us."

"Okay," he said, and shimmied down the rope, splashing into the water below. Barton pulled him up, as he helped Lilly down as well.

"It looks like Ang and his men took care of the beasts protecting the gem," Barton said. "This is where you found it, isn't it?"

"Yes, but it wasn't Ang's men who killed them," the Woblo said, as he stuttered.

"You?" Barton asked in astonishment.

"I knew you had a warrior in you," Lilly said, triumphant of his achievement. "No wonder you were scared."

"Well, let's not stay here admiring his trophies; let's get a move on," Glam said.

They waded through the water, and into the chamber, where the dead Licarion and jewels were. Barton turned to the treasure, overwhelmed. Glam stared at the Licarion corpse, and then at Bargo.

"I supposed you took care of him as well?"

"Yes," he answered, not really proud of having committed his first kill.

"Look at all this," Barton said in glee. "There's enough here for us all to share."

"We won't take one gold nugget, ruby, emerald, or diamond from this cave," Glam stated.

"And why not?" Lilly asked. "I thought we were here to raid their temple as well?"

"This is not the same treasure as the temple. It's blood money, and cursed with evil. Leave it."

"Isn't that stolen as well?" Barton asked.

"Yes, but this treasure belongs to evil, and has a spell upon it, and will bring nothing but death and misfortune. Did you find the gem in this room, Bargo?"

"Actually it was in another room."

"Show us where."

Bargo left the chamber, the others followed, and Barton lingered behind so he could pocket a few pieces of gold and silver for himself. He stuffed two pockets full, and quickly followed the others into a smaller chamber with the stone altar in it.

"This is where Jickle had it," Bargo said.

"Jickle?" Glam asked.

"The keeper of the stone. The half Woblo-half Licarion you spoke of."

"Ah, yes. What did he use it for?"

"He placed it on the altar, waved his hand, and the scorpions grew bigger."

Glam looked the altar over, and then held his hand out to the Woblo.

"Bargo, could you give me the stone, please?" He was reluctant to give it up after everything he heard about the gem, and how it could change those who touched it. He didn't want Glam to use it for evil purposes either, and he was afraid his hatred for Ang would get the better of him. "Bargo, trust me, I'll give it right back."

He took it out of his saddle bag, and handed it to him, and Glam felt a bit dizzy after he touched the stone. It began to glow white when he placed it on the altar.

"Taluk cara Alteiu," he said in Elven, which meant 'show the city,' and an image appeared on the wall in front of them, which displayed the passageway to North Licarion City. He took the gem off, and handed it back to his Woblo friend, who immediately put it back in his bag. "Looks like we head that way."

He pointed to one of the three passageways from the small chamber room. He held the torch high, as the others followed, unprepared for the terror they were about to face. Bargo opened his bag so his gem would provide light as well, but Glam shut it to discourage him from using it for this purpose. Upon leaving, Barton looked back at the hallway from whence they came, still mumbling about the treasure they left behind, and allowing its evil power to permeate into his soul.

CHAPTER EIGHTEEN: PRISONERS OF THE KING

They traveled deep within the bowels of the mountainous cavern system, and tried to stay hidden from the outgoing patrols. Bargo explained to his friends that Ang knew he had the stone, and was looking for him, so they found a small, but hidden cave within the passage, where they sought refuge to devise a plan.

"Our friends are mostly nocturnal," Glam said. "So it would be best to make our move in the morning. We have to be quick and effective if we want to rescue our young Woblo's cousin."

"What difference does the time of day make down here?" Barton asked.

"Even though it's dark, Licarions sleep like we sleep, only doing it in the day time. There will only be a few patrols around."

"How are we even going to get close to the prison?" Bargo asked. "There are doors forged from iron down there."

"If I'm right, that shouldn't be a problem with the stone." He held his right index finger up for silence, as they heard several Licarions go by them. He then turned back to his friends. "We'll have to stay here for the night."

"In here?" Barton asked, as he tried to find room in the eight feet by five feet cave crevice. He couldn't imagine sleeping in such an uncomfortable, cold, damp place.

"I'm afraid so. And no using the gem for light, Bargo. If they see it, we're all dead."

"Yes, Sir. I'm beginning to wish I never found it."

"Well, now that you did, we can use it to our advantage. I'd advise you all to get some sleep. We'll need all the energy we can get in the morning."

"But you still haven't told us how we're going to do this? I tend to agree with the others. It's extremely well guarded."

"Shame on you, Bargo, are you beginning to doubt me as well? Have I ever not come up with some kind of plan as of yet."

"No, Sir."

"Well then, here's what we're going to do. We're going to enter through the back way, and Bargo is going to say the magical words, which will place the Licarions in a deep sleep. Then we'll go in, move those doors with the power of the gem, and release Barlow."

"How did you know I made them sleep? I didn't tell anybody about that."

"I just know the power of the gem."

"I can't remember what I said. I saw the eyes in the fire, and they told me what to do."

"The eyes in the fire," Lilly said, disgusted.

"Yes, the eyes in the fire, and they are real," the Woblo insisted.

"Think hard tonight, and they'll come back to you," Glam said. "Okay, enough chatter for this evening."

The hours passed, and they tried to sleep in the small, confined space. They were uncomfortable, but content, until a large, ten inch centipede crawled down onto Lilly's shoulder, she screamed, and threw it to the ground. Barton stepped on it quick, Bargo let out a squeal as well, and the stone fell onto the ground, illuminating the small cavern. Glam woke up at the commotion, and scolded them.

"Fools," he whispered. "Do you want them to find us?"

"Too late," Barton said, as they heard the hissing sound throughout the cavern.

Bargo grabbed the stone, threw it back in his saddle bag, and followed Glam, as he emerged from the crevice. The others followed behind, as they saw several of their enemy running towards them with torches and spears.

"That way!" Glam yelled, as they ran down a cavern to their right. Once they entered, they heard Licarions coming from the direction in front of them.

"We're trapped," Bargo cried.

"Now would be a good time to pull that stone out," Barton suggested.

"No," Glam barked. "That's what Ang wants him to do. Come, down this other passage."

There was a small cave, just barely big enough for them to fit

fit through. They scurried down into it, and fell the thirty feet decline of the cave, and into a larger cavern. Glam and Barton grabbed the others, as they almost fell off the cliff of the ravine within it. They saw more Licarions head towards them on one of the ledges.

"Get to the city, and remain hidden until morning. I'll hold them off here to give you time, and meet up with you later."

"But, Glam, you'll be killed," Lilly told him. "I'll stay with you and fight."

"No, they'll need you down there. Now, go."

They followed his orders, as the Elf drew his sword to face his aggressors. They approached him, and as the others disappeared into the darkness, Glam battled the reptilian creatures, sending them over the cliff one by one, until he was overcome by the mob. They would've killed him, but a voice from behind stopped them.

"No," Ang said. "Glamara wants him alive. Besides, he could be of some use bringing his friends to us. They won't get far, I assure you., and they won't leave here without their friend."

Deep within the cavern tunnels, the others ran, and in every direction they heard the sound of Licarions scampering, or saw their shadows from the glowing torches. At one point they were separated, when Bargo lagged behind, and was blocked from the others.

"Bargo," Lilly yelled back, as three of the beasts blocked her path. She fought them off with her blade against their spears, and quickly stabbed two of them. She twirled around to fight the other one, who also drew his sword. The sound of steel clanged throughout the cavern, until she found herself surrounded by the creatures. Barton was further up the cavern, also fighting for his life, until he was captured as well.

By this time, Bargo slipped back into a cavern where there were less Licarions, and he was less obvious. While he walked down it, a smaller Licarion almost ran into him with his sword. The creature pointed his blade at him, as the frightened woblo backed up against the wall.

"I kill you here, Birdface," he said. "But me master wants you alive."

Bargo was unable to grab his sword, but had his hand next to his saddle bag and the gem. While the creature toyed with him, he reached inside, putting his hand tightly on the stone. He pulled it out, and the Licarion fell to his knees in pain, dropping his sword. Bargo ran as fast as he could into the darkness.

He came to the end of the tunnel, which again overlooked North Licarion City, and saw several of them carry his friends towards the metropolis' back gate. He slipped back into the tunnel in fear and despair, at a loss on what to do to save them. He sat down on the cavern floor and cried, as the tunnels became quiet, because it was the first time on this journey he found himself totally alone.

The other four were brought into the royal council chambers of the city, which was a large stone hall with pillars throughout, with large statues of reptiles on each side of the throne, representing the Licarion god Vilatu. They were led to it, and introduced to Glamara, the king of the Licarions.

"Bow in his Highnesses' presence," Ang said, as he pushed Glam to the floor. "Soon he will be your king."

"He'll never be my king," the Elf answered, on his knees, and lifted himself up. "My king is Glaridia, and my god is Rhiatu."

"Your Elven king is weak, and his magic is useless against the power of Garlock."

"Do not fret, Ang," Glamara hissed. "Glaridia has no power in Shudolin with prince in charge."

"I knew it," Barton said. "I knew he was working for them."

"Not exactly," the Licarion king answered. " He just do dirty work for us. He make it easy to help deliver all you to me, and stone as well."

"They don't have the stone," Ang replied. "The Woblo does."

"Then why you still here talking to me?"

"He won't leave without his friends, so I suggest a trade. His friends' lives for the stone, and himself."

"He wouldn't trade before, what makes you think he will now?"

"Because he doesn't have the belly for these matters like his friends here. He's weak, and vulnerable."

"That's what you think," Glam said. "He has learned to use the power of the stone, and resist your persuasion."

"Impossible," Glamara barked. "No way he could've learned so quick."

"Unless he is the Woblo in the prophecy, like I've said before," Ang said.

"Even so, once we get stone, I no longer need him. The stone be mine, and power be mine."

"The stone belongs to Garlock. We must return it to him."

"Yes, of course. After I use to destroy the Shudolin, like he asks us."

"The corruption of the stone has already poisoned your souls," Glam told them. "You will all destroy each other in the end."

One guard pushed him back into Barton, who fell over, and as he did, his bobbles fell from his pockets onto the floor.

"What we have here, a thief?" Glamara asked. "Where you get those treasures?"

"From a cave we found a ways back," Ang said.

"And you hide from me why?"

"I just didn't have time to tell you. The creature below was guarding it."

"Ah, the Garbolin."

"Garbolin?" Glam asked.

"Is an ancient Licarion legend about Licarion and Woblo who fall in love, and have child together."

"We have heard the legend as well, but it has no basis in proof. It's just a legend."

"No matter, if you steal in my kingdom, you lose hand," Glamara warned them.

"Not today," Ang said. "I've got other plans for him. Take all he has on him, and let him be for now."

"Very well, Ang, if it is your wish. Not in the mood for judicial procedures today anyway. I notice you have woman amongst you? Is customary for Shudolin to let women do fighting for them?"

"I am the best woman fighter this side of the Swift River," Lilly protested. "Choose your weapon, and I'll match you with it, and kill you as well."

"I may take you up on that," the king laughed. "Tell me, how you with heavy weapon, like mace?"

"Wouldn't you like to find out?"

"Your Highness, haven't we got more important issues at hand than to squabble with these commoners?" Ang asked.

"'You quite right," Glamara said. "Send troop out to find Woblo, and tell him we have his friends, and want to make deal."

"I'd like to first try to get him on my own, Sire," Ang said. "I think I may be able to reason with him."

"Very well. Take others to prison and guard them well. If anyone else comes, especially Woblo, kill them all."

"Yes, Sire," Ang said, as they pushed their prisoners towards the large, iron doors and down the passageway.

Ang and the king's men placed them into their cells, and then the evil Elf faced his rival again, inches from the bars. "It will be a pleasure to watch you finally die a long and torturous death," he told him.

"Bargo will never give in to your demands," Glam said. "I told him not to give up the stone for anything."

"He will. You may think because you believe he is the chosen one, he will have the courage to defeat the Licarions and myself, but you're wrong. He lacks the power within himself to complete such a task."

"We will see. And then I'll be the one to see your death once and for all." The Elf laughed, and shook his head, as he walked away, and up the steps to the next floor.

Lilly turned to Glam, who sat down on the cell floor.

"Where is this temple you spoke of earlier, and how do you expect us to rob it when we're all captured, and they get the gem from Bargo?"

"I just came from there," Glam said. "And there was no treasure."

"You lied?" Barton asked.

"The prince lied. I'm afraid we've been duped. I just hope Bargo makes the right decisions."

Bargo indeed thought long and hard about the words the fire told him to say, but he couldn't remember what they were. He usually had a pretty good memory, but the Elven language wasn't something he spent a lot of time studying. How was he ever to use the stone properly, if he couldn't learn the language which directed it? Glam was so secretive about it he even failed to instruct him on the true abilities of its properties, which made him believe maybe their Elven commander had his own motives for the rare rock.

"Fora Ulto durmid," he said, as he tried to remember, but knew he got it incorrect. "Fira giola aratu." He began to float in the air, banged his head on the cavern ceiling, and then fell to the ground. He sat there and rubbed his head in pain, as he tried to remember, and thought about the voice in the fire again. He wondered who the voice was, and why he kept hearing it. Could it be the voice of Rhiatu himself? That would explain a lot of things; but a god just didn't talk to anyone, only prophets, and he laughed at the thought of himself even being one. He wasn't even all that religious, and seldom went to the Rhiartutan festivals, which were held once a month. He was a simple Woblo, who led a simple life, and followed the ways of Rhiatu without all the ramifications involved,. Now he was asked to find a stone; which he did, use its power to save his friends, which he still had yet to do, and become something he was not, which was a wizard.

Hope of such things wasn't of any consequence at the moment, while he sat in a side cavern, waiting to be found and captured, or hurt any Licarions who tried to attempt such a feat. Much to his surprise, however, it wasn't a Licarion's voice he heard in the silence, but an Elf's.

"Bargo, are you there?" he asked. "It's me, Ang. I've come to talk to you."

If there was one thing his father taught him about the enemy, it was to never trust him to make the same mistake twice, and Ang was no different. He ignored his call to speak with him, as he heard the Elf's voice echo in the distance of the cavern system.

"I want to make a deal with you," he continued. "If you bring me the stone, I'll let all of your friends go, including your cousin, and yourself. What will say to that?" Ang listened for several minutes, and Bargo heard his steps echo through the caverns, as he came closer to his location. "Very well, if that is your decision, I have no choice but to kill all of them, and you as well, and take the stone from your bloody corpse."

The Woblo waited until he started to leave, and looked out to see the light of his torch fade into the darkness. He followed behind him in stealth, using the rocks for cover, and walked down a series of three sets of steps, which led to a tunnel beneath the city. There were no Licarions with him, and he twirled his sword around like an eccentric man with his cane. He placed it into its sheath, and unlocked the door at the bottom, while Bargo watched from the top.

The Woblo reached the bottom, and wondered if there was some possible way he could use the stone to break the key lock. He pulled the gem from the bag, and pointed it at the lock, but nothing happened. "Open the lock," he ordered, as if he were to get any result, but of course, there was none. As he stared at the two torches, he heard the voice again.

"Otul Liathra," the voice told him, and he repeated the words, which caused the stone to glow bright white, and so strong it made him look the other way. In a matter of seconds, it dimmed, and he looked back, now staring at a broken lock.

He slipped inside the iron door, and looked down the nearest corridor in both directions to make sure he wasn't seen. He proceeded down it, until he came to another iron door with a keyhole. He repeated the words, which opened that lock as well. He descended down a stone spiral stairway which led into a prison wing, where one guard sat outside a cell with one occupant inside. The guard couldn't see him, for he was at the edge of the stairway, which was hidden from view.

He took a small, loose pebble from the wall, and threw it away from the cell, near the end. The reptilian creature got up to see what was going on, and when he did, Bargo jumped onto his neck and twisted it hard to break it, as he fell to the floor. He faced the cell, as its occupant rose, expressing hope and relief.

"Bargo!" the prisoner yelled, as he grabbed his cousin's hand tight through the bars. His brown and white fur was soiled from dried blood, dirt, and grime from the prison cell.

"Hello, Barlow. Bet you never thought it would be me to rescue you?"

"How did you ever get here without getting killed?"

"It's a long story. And when I got time, I'll tell you. Now stand back, while I break your lock."

He pulled the gem from his pocket, and said the magic words.

Barlow stared in disbelief until the light blinded him, and he looked away, while the beam broke the lock. He walked out and hugged his cousin, but was interrupted by a snarling voice. He saw two red eyes glow from the cell next to him, as Bargo held the gem in front of them. A long, scaly, green hand reached its way from the cage, its claws wiggling to reach for the stone, and a beak slammed against the bars.

"Give it to me now, give it back to me," Jickle pleaded.

"Who's that?" Barlow asked.

"Jickle Sickleon, keeper of the stone," Bargo answered. "But not any longer, because now I am the keeper of the stone."

"Congratulations, Mr. Lynden," Ang said, as he clapped his hands, and walked down the stairs. The creature sank back into the darkness of his cell. "You've passed the first test."

"Test?" the confused Woblo asked.

"You don't think I'd let you just walk in here and save your friends, do you? I wanted to see if you'd try, and you did. You're wasting your talent with the Shudolin, Bargo. You and I could rule this entire land. We have the power. Think of all the riches you could have, and you could be human again."

"What is he talking about?" Barlow asked.

"Just think of it. You can rule as our king, and Lilly could be your queen." Ang stated.

"What's Lilly got to do with this?" Barlow asked.

"I have no desire for riches or fame, or to rule anything," Bargo said. "And certainly not with you. Now, let us pass, or I'll destroy you as well."

"Foolish Woblo," Ang reiterated. "You can't destroy me. The same power which controls the gem protects me as well. I am immortal, as you have already seen."

"Not if I can reach your heart with my blade."

"Silly Woblo! You are no match for me," he said, as he drew his sword. "Give me the stone, or I'll kill your cousin here and now."

"I'll use the stone against you," he said, as he pointed it at the Elf with no result. In haste, Bargo placed it back in his bag, and drew his sword.

"The stone will not harm me here, for I am a disciple of

Garlock, and evil protects these halls," Ang said, as he swung his sword at him. He ducked, his sword connected with Ang's, and the evil commander threw him to the ground, and laughed. "Some wizard. Before you can use the stone's powers, you have to know what they are, and obviously Glam was a poor teacher. Now, give me the stone, or he dies."

"Bargo, don't do it," his cousin warned.

Ang pointed his sword at his cousin's chest, and pushed him back to the wall where the Woblo was. Bargo, disgusted and discouraged, handed his sword and the gem to the Elf, reluctant to do so.

"Now back in the cell, both of you," Ang said, as they followed his order, and he shut the door. "Thank you for everything you've done for me, Mr. Lynden. You helped me eliminate Vladimir and his men, found the stone for me, and delivered Glam as my own personal prize. He'll be pleased to know his future wizard is feeble and inadequate, and the Shudolin will become the new Licaria."

"I hope you rot in the underworld," Bargo said.

"The underworld will become all of your new home. And Garlock will rule once again. Otul Liathra." The gem grew white again, and the lock fused. "Now that I have what I want, your friends will die a long painful death, slowly starving to death, and tortured, while you're down here, a floor below them doing the same, and there will be no one to save any of you."

The Woblos sank to the floor in despair, as they watched Ang leave the chambers and laugh in delight. Barlow turned to his cousin, and placed his hand on his shoulder.

"Bargo, if you knew this stone was so important, why did you give it to him?"

"He would've killed you, and I couldn't live with myself if that happened."

"Well, now none of us are going to live. And what's Lilly got to do with this, anyway?"

"She's here, above us."

"Lilly?"

"Yes, there is more to her than meets the eye. She's some kind of mercenary."

"Lilly?"

"Yes, Lilly. Anyway, they all depended on me, and I let them down. We'll never get out of here now. I wish I never got involved in this mess."

"Same here. I wish I never got mixed up with the soldiers looking for the king. Everyone was killed except for me."

"They would have never kidnapped you, if they hadn't thought you were me."

The two of them glanced around the cell, and then at each other in silence for a few moments, and then Bargo began to cry. Barlow, being the soldier he was, turned to his cousin and friend.

"Do not fret, my friend. Things are not as dire as they seem. We still have hope, and hope will help us survive."

"But how?" sobbed Bargo. "Without the stone, all is lost."

"Then we must find a way to get it back. Even if we have to dig our way out pebble by pebble."

CHAPTER NINETEEN:

THE DEFILEMENT OF THE WEAPON

A floor above, Glam and the others remained locked in their cell, watched by four guards. Barton paced back and forth, nervous about what was to become of them. Lilly and Glam sat on the floor, and tried to think of a way out of this predicament.

"Do you think Bargo has a chance of getting us out of here?" Barton asked the Elf.

Glam rubbed his hand across his face and let out a sigh.

"I suppose he could, if he could only remember the words."

"He's always had an excellent memory," Lilly said. "I really don't know why he's having problems now."

"The stress is overwhelming to him, I'm sure. He will get it, but it's a shame he hasn't had the time to properly train for his craft."

"His craft?"

"To be a wizard, of course."

She began to laugh a hardy chuckle, and shook her head.

"I'm willing to buy the stone is magic, or sacred, or whatever you want to call it, but Bargo a wizard? Surely, you must be joking?"

"You, especially, I would expect to have more faith in him," Glam scolded. "I just hope it's not too late."

"Too late for what?" Barton asked.

"To stop Ang from retrieving the stone from our friend," their Elven commander said.

"But you said yourself he would have to give it willingly and freely," Lilly said.

"Yes, but he'll resort to trickery to make him do that. Bargo must be strong, and resist his demands, even if it means the lives of his friends. The stone must be protected at all costs, or it will fall

209

into the hands of evil."

"Do you think he's capable of that?" Barton asked Lilly.

"No," she answered, as she bowed her head in doubt and despair. "He will not allow his friends to be harmed. If I know anything, he has compassion."

"And it's his compassion that has made him weak," Ang said, as he walked down the steps, and stopped in front of their cell. "Hello, Glam, I have some interesting news for you. I have your two Woblo friends locked inside a cell downstairs right now. Bargo has done exactly what his friend Lilly thought he would do, and gave up the stone."

"I knew you shouldn't have relied on him to keep it," Barton barked. "Now we're all dead."

"Not quite yet, Mr. Barton," Ang said. "If any of you wants to reconsider your position toward the Shudolin, now is the time to do it. I will give anyone of you 1000 gold pieces to join my army of Licarions."

"I wouldn't take 10,000," Glam said. "And neither will anyone else here."

"Just an offer. Very well, then. Since I know Glam can't wait to see what I'm going to use the gem for, I will let you all live for a while longer. I'll have the guards bring him up to the royal chambers so he can see the true power of the stone. The two of you will remain here."

He was brought up to Glamara, who was pleased Ang retrieved the stone from the Woblo. He also brought Bargo up as well, but left Barlow below in his cell. Glam was surprised he was there, but relieved he was still alive.

"Bargo, I hoped you would have been stronger," he told him, as the two stood next to each other. "I told you not to give up the stone for anything."

"I know you did," the Woblo said. "But I couldn't let him kill my own flesh and blood either. Can't you understand that? "

"Of course I do."

"And why didn't you tell me the stone has no power here?"

"It was wrong of me to expect you to understand the old Elven ways, and I'm sorry for not disclosing certain information to you."

"Welcome my friends," Glamara said, as he sat on his royal

throne made of gold. "So I hear Ang has a gift for me?"

"A gift for Garlock," the one eyed Elf corrected him. "And for the Licarion Empire. But first, we'll need the cooperation of the Woblo."

"Never," Glam barked.

"I was afraid you'd say that," Ang said, as two Licarions grabbed the Elf, and pushed him to his knees in front of the king. One of them drew his sword. "If the Woblo refuses once, cut off the Elf's ear. He refuses twice, cut off his head. Bargo, come here."

He shook his head in defiance, as the guard pulled his sword back to get a full swing of Glam's head. He moved forward to try to stop him, but was held back by two guards.

"Cut his right ear off," Ang ordered.

"No, no, I'll do whatever you say, don't kill him," Bargo said.

"Bargo, what did I just tell you?" Glam pleaded, as a Licarion hit him in the head with his fist.

"Well, that's better," Ang said.. "It's true some Elves have magical and mystic powers, but they have to be trained in such, and with the exception of Glam, I know few that are. Even though I'm trained in the black arts, I alone, or Glam alone, would not have the power to use the stone without a true wizard's help."

"But I'm not a wizard."

"Not yet. But you are still a threat to me. That's why I cannot allow the forces of good to control you, and destroy everything we've worked for. From now on, you are a disciple of Garlock, trained in the black arts."

"And if I refuse?"

"Your friends will all die."

"Our lives are not important," Glam told his friend. "The Shudolin must survive the forces of evil."

"If he talks again, kill him," Ang ordered.

"This is preposterous," Glamara said. "And time consuming. Just make him do what we need him to do, or kill him."

Ang turned back at him, angered.

"Let me remind you, your Highness, that even though you're in charge, I am the true disciple of Garlock, and he does not answer to you, only to me."

"How about we take stone from you, and send you back to

him in a wooden box?" Glamara said to the Elf. "Here, I am in charge."

"I don't wish to debate the issue any longer. Guards take him to the altar." The guards forced him to walk to the altar, where Ang placed the stone. The Woblo stared at it, and if it weren't for the guards next to him, and the chains on his wrists, he would've grabbed it, but he knew he was outnumbered. The other factor was he was terrified, and afraid to use it against Ang and the king. "Place your hand on the stone."

He placed his dagger against the Woblo's throat. Bargo followed his order in fear.

"Now, repeat after me. Cala Rica ulti Garlicio. talatu fiaris fiatia."

"Coola Rocu," Bargo began, as he fumbled the words.

"Say them right, or your friend loses his head."

"Cala Rica ulti Garlicio talatu fiaris fiata." The stone began to glow white and shimmer more than he ever saw yet.

"By the power of Garlock, destroy our enemies," Ang translated, as he waved his hands in the air.

Seizing the opportunity, Bargo grabbed the stone in haste, turned, and grabbed the Elf's hand, which held a dagger at him. He pushed against his arm, and then bit him with his beak. While he knelt in pain, Bargo jumped up and wrapped his chains around Ang's neck, choking him until he dropped the knife, and fell to his knees. Glam kicked the guard's leg, grabbed his sword, and fought off the three other guards. Ang tried to reach for the woblo, and he used the gem as a weapon by pushing Ang across the floor and into the wall, which knocked him unconscious. Bargo grabbed his sword from the Elf's sheath, and looked down at his adversary.

"That will teach you to mess with a Lynden," he said, as he kicked him in the stomach. "This one's for my dad."

"You may have beaten him," Glamara said, as he raised his sword to the Woblo. "But you are no match for me."

He was ready to slice the woblo in half, when Glam came from behind, and hit him with his shackles, and knocked him unconscious as well.

"So much for royalty. Get the keys and unchain us. We've

got no time to lose."

The two of them headed out of the chamber with swords drawn. They opened the door to face six guards, all with swords drawn upon them.

"I hope you're ready for a fight?" Glam asked him.

"Never been a better time than now."

The Licarions advanced upon them, as the swords clashed against one another; and the glimmer of steel shimmered against the torchlight. Glam stabbed two of the six, punching one, as Bargo killed one, and was struggling with the other two. His Elven friend rushed to his side to assist him, and they successfully fended off the others. They ran down to the where the prison doors were on the second floor, and where their friends were located. Bargo used the gem to burn the lock, and then held it up as he entered, which made the four approaching guards disappear. The others couldn't believe their eyes, and when Bargo and Glam came for them, they were relieved.

"Bargo, you're all right," Lilly said.

"I never doubted him for a minute," Barton said.

"Right," Lilly said in sarcasm.

"Back up, shield your eyes, and I'll break the lock," Bargo said. They followed his orders, and in seconds they were freed."

"Come on, we have to get out of here while we still can," Glam said in haste.

"What about Barlow?" Bargo asked.

"I don't mean to distress you, Bargo, but they've probably killed him by now. Even if they didn't, he's a soldier, and can take care of himself."

"He's alive. I've seen him; he's right below us."

"All right. You guys get going while it's still daytime. Get out of these caves into the open air before the evil air consumes you."

"I'm going with you. He's my cousin."

"No, Bargo, you have to get as far away from here as you can, and get back to Riverton. Send for King Glaridia, and ask for a special meeting of the council. Do not tell the prince you have the stone, and let the king know where the staff is."

"I need your help to use the stone. You're the only one who can train me."

BARGO LYNDEN

"There is another, and you will meet him soon. Someone who knows even more than me. Now go, before they discover we're gone."

They ran up the stairs and out the doorway, as Glam headed down the flight of stairs that led to the lower cells. While the others ran for their lives away from the exit gates, Bargo turned back, unwilling to let his Elven friend venture below alone.

He ran down the stairs and greeted his commander, who freed Barlow, and also gave him one of the guard's swords. Soon, several Licarions chased down after them, as they headed towards the gate. Glam fought them off, and the two Woblos ran through the exit. He narrowed the guards from five to one, who were knocked to the ground while he passed through. The last guard was quick to react, however, and stabbed the Elf in his lower stomach with his dagger. He had no armor on, and unprotected, the blade passed through his skin deep into his abdominal cavity. He turned around, stabbed his enemy's chest with his sword, and staggered after the Woblos.

Bargo saw he needed help, and he and Barlow helped him out of the area. He remembered the small crevice, and headed in its direction to seek refuge. When they found the crevice, the two Woblos helped him inside, and laid him on the floor of the cavern.

"No," he said, as he began to lose conscious. "Can't stay here. Must get out."

"Just for a little while," Bargo said. "You can't travel. You've been stabbed, and you're bleeding."

"The stone will save me."

"The stone?" Bargo asked, as he began to pull it from his pants pocket.

"No. Mustn't use it here. When we get out."

"By then he could be dead," Barlow said.

"We'll have to find a way," Bargo said, and thought of an idea. "His cape. We can use it as a stretcher."

The Woblos untied his cape, placed him on the makeshift stretcher, and left the cavern, struggling through the passages, and searching for an exit. They heard the Licarions screech in the distance, and took evasive action to travel away from them. A half hour passed, until they found a cave which led to the outside, and a bright, sunny day. They carried him close to the river, and placed him on the ground, near some bushes, concealing their location.

"Glam?" Bargo asked, as he tried to awake him, but had no luck. He took some water with his hands and rubbed it on his face, but there still was no response.

"I'm afraid we're too late," Barlow said.

"Have you got a match?" Bargo asked.

His cousin gave him a look of bewilderment.

"Trust me, I know what I'm doing."

Barlow handed him a match, he grabbed a section of the bush, and placed it on the ground. He then struck the match on a rock, and lit the small pile on fire. He stared into the flames until he heard the voice speak to him in his head. He then took the gem out and placed it over Glam's wound. By this time, he wasn't far from the world, for he lost a lot of blood, and didn't respond to their attempts to revive him.

"Viatra Calia Fior," Bargo said, as Barlow watched in amazement at the wound, which healed itself within minutes. Within five minutes, the wound was gone, and Glam was conscious and alert.

"What happened?" he asked, as he sat up.

"You were stabbed, but Bargo saved you with the stone," Barlow said.

"Thank you, my small friend," he said, as he rose to his feet, still a little dizzy. He noticed Bargo was a little weak as well. Glam steadied him. "It's an after effect of the stone. You'll need to rest. But first, we need to get away from this place."

"I thought we stopped Ang from any more destruction?" Bargo asked.

"You didn't grab the stone before you said the magic words, so you were unable to stop the spell. Soon, evil will spread throughout the land, and everything will die; first the plants will die, then the animals in the forest will die, and then the humans and Elves will die as well."

"Isn't Bashworth a little distance just up the river?" Barlow asked.

"It is indeed," Glam said.

Bargo, who wasn't so optimistic, looked in the other

direction at the large army of Licarions, which came from the caverns down about a mile south.

"Isn't that half of the Licarion Empire?"

"It is indeed," Glam said. "Quick towards the river."

The three of them ran down the hill, and through the brush and grass near the river. The Licarions saw them, but due to the light, they were a little stunned. It took them several minutes to finally adjust and ascertain their direction. By that time, they were well out of range, and moved close to the river. They figured the town was at least thirty miles up the river, and this was one time they wished there was a boat around. When they finally got to a place where they could rest, they sat down on some rocks. Bargo turned to his Elf friend, as he caught his breath.

"Why didn't you tell me?"

"I was hoping you had heeded to my instructions, and to the voice that keeps talking to you," Glam answered.

"Is that you?"

"No, it's not, and I couldn't tell you who it is. Perhaps, Garlock, trying to mislead you."

"So far, it's the only thing that's kept me alive. I wish I knew who it was."

"Perhaps it's the voice within yourself, cousin," Barlow suggested.

"I doubt it," Bargo said. "Not this voice."

"One day you will become a great wizard," Glam said. "But only if you wish to do so. And human, only if you wish to do so. The choice is yours and yours alone."

"What if I don't want either?"

"Then the staff and gem will remain in the royal palace, under the direction of King Glaridia, until another can be found."

"What about this guy you told me about earlier? Why can't he do it?"

"It needs to be a direct descendant from the true Elven royal blood line."

"What about Glaridia then, isn't he of the royal bloodline?"

"His family married into the royal bloodline, he is not a direct descendant either. Please, Bargo, once we reach Riverton and we get the staff, we can stop this disease before it starts. All you have to do is say the words to break the spell on our land."

"And then what?"

"And then you're through. As long as the staff and gem are protected, you may return to your old life."

"You don't know how good that sounds right now. I used to be bored, and say I had no adventure in my life, but now I'd just be glad to be working in the Blacksmith shop, and forget I ever saw this place. What about the other prisoners they have down there?"

"Hopefully, when Tamarka tells the proper authorities, they'll send in the army or navy in to save them. I believe when we were up on the hill, I saw some Shudolin ships near the coastline."

"I hope you're right."

"We need to keep moving. If anything, Licarions are persistent, and the moon is starting to rise."

They stood up, and began to walk down the river bank.

"What about Grassmen?" Barlow asked.

"They're seldom this far south," Glam said. "But keep a sharp eye anyway. Things haven't been the same since Ang attacked Old Monko."

"Bargo, I've been meaning to ask you, how's your father been?" Barlow asked.

"He was killed by Ang and the Grassmen back in Old Monko," Glam said in a solemn tone.

"What happened?"

"We were ambushed, and his father saved us. He gave his life for us. Bargo, would you do the same for your friends?"

"Of course he would," Barlow said.

"He must place the value of the stone above his friends, even if it means his life. Then he is worthy of becoming a wizard."

Back in the royal chamber, Glamara and Ang just awoke from being overthrown and subdued. Ang rubbed his head, as he looked at the dead guards around him. He became angry, and swung his sword at the altar.

"You let them get away?" he asked the king.

"What you mean, I let him get away?" the king snapped back. "You fail, so I go to stop your little Woblo friend. Me struck on head from behind by Elf."

"You don't deserve the title 'king.' You're a failure to Garlock's cause."

"Oh yeah? Well, maybe you like to try to take my crown from me?"

"It will be my pleasure," Ang said, as he drew his sword.

"To death?"

"Of course."

The Licarion swung his sword at the Elf, as he blocked it, moving his blade down and to the right. They unlocked, and Ang swung low, and tried to knock him off his feet. The Licarion jumped quick, kicked the Elf in the chest, and knocked him off his feet. Glamara dropped his blade to the floor, as Ang rolled out of its path just in time, and grabbed his sword, which was on the ground next to him.

Now on his feet, he advanced with his blade, as Glamara blocked his strokes, until his arms grew weak. Ang knocked the sword from his hand, while the reptilian creature grabbed him by his throat. Ang came down with his sword, and chopped the king's arm off. He then plunged his dagger with his free hand into the leader's chest, fatally wounding him, and dropped him to the ground. He raised his bloody sword high in victory.

"Now I'm the Licarion king, and Garlock's right hand," he shouted throughout the hall. Several of the creatures came into the hall to see what the commotion was. "I am your king now, Glamara's reign is over. I want you to send all of our people to Riverton, where we'll destroy the Shudolin once and for all. Man the boats, send the militia, and we'll destroy King Glaridia and his Elven kind."

He walked out of the chamber and towards the docks, where he jumped into a long boat with several Licarions. "Take me to Riverton," he commanded, as they began to row the boats out of the cave and into the river.

The sun set on the land, and as the nightfall fell upon them, so did the evil which would encompass the land for the next few days, and jeopardize everything Bargo and his friends already accomplished. It was up to him to save the Shudolin from its power, and Ang didn't know it yet, but the Woblo was up for the challenge.

CHAPTER TWENTY:

FACE OFF IN THE BAY OF DOOM

Barton and Lilly struggled to figure their way out of the cavern system, following an underground river, which led to some docks and long boats with sails. A few Licarions guarded it, but no more than the two of them couldn't handle. They hid on the ledge just above them, and Barton quickly immobilized the guard at the top of the stairs by strangling him until he passed out.

He handed Lilly his bow and the bag with arrows, and waved for her to take the guard farthest from them. She pulled back her bow and released, as the arrow went directly into the creature's neck, and he fell into the water. When the others turned, the two of them drew their swords, and jumped from the stairs to face them.

Barton's sword sliced one of them like a butcher, dismembering both his arms. Another tried to attack Lilly, but found her just as ruthless, as she kicked him in the chest, and then threw a knife into his forehead. They fought with the other two, effectively disarmed them, and rendered them unconscious. They jumped from the dock, and boarded one of the Licarion long boats with a sail.

"Get the ropes," Lilly told Barton, as he followed her command, and pushed them off.

"There'll be more coming."

"By then we'll be in Bashworth."

Two more Licarions emerged from the stairway as they left, and Lilly sent two arrows, one for each, into her targets.

"Damn, you're a great shot."

"You should see me with geese."

They emerged from the cavern, and into the Mego River, about ten miles from the town of Bashworth. Glam and Bargo diverted their enemy away from the others, which gave them at least an hour's head start. Their next step was to reach Bashworth, and try to find someone who Tamarka and Daniel had contact with in the last day or two, if they made it back at all.

Once they were out of danger from the enemy, Lilly commandeered the sail, while Barton took a short rest. He packed his pipe with tobacco, lit it, and puffed out the usual four or five clouds of smoke rings, as Lilly waved her arms to clear the air.

"Must you do that in the boat?"

"What better place than one surrounded by water?"

"Do you think Bargo is all right?"

"Glam is with him, he should be fine. He's probably not too happy he didn't follow orders, however."

"He's always been a bit of a rebel. Just like his father in some many ways."

"Did his father ever mention anything to him about the old Elven legends?"

"No, he thought they were just ancient stories made up to explain religion."

"He must have known he was a descendant of the true mystical people. Being near Elf City, he must have met somebody who knew his ancestral background?"

"Other than his Aunt Catherine, I'm not aware of anybody else."

"Well, it's not really important now. We'll be reaching the mouth of the river, and will have to head into open ocean for about a mile to get to Bashworth." He thought about the treasure they left behind in Jickle's cave. "I still wish I could have kept a few rubies at least."

"You nearly got us killed for a few rubies. Glam was right. It's nothing but blood money."

"Don't you think the rightful owners are entitled to get it back?"

"Of course, but that's for royalty and the authorities to decide."

"How do you know royalty didn't take it from someone else in the first place?"

"I trusted our king, and know he wouldn't have done that. The prince on the other hand..."

"Which reminds me, once Bargo gets the gem to Riverton,

how are they going to get the staff from the prince?"

"I'm sure they'll figure it out."

"Don't you mean, we'll figure it?"

"Once we reach Bashworth, our part of this quest is done. Bargo and Glam know what to do from there. We must let the nearest militia or naval outpost know a Licarion invasion is coming, however."

"I'm not just leaving Bargo and his cousin at their mercy with that fairy tale minded Elf. Pull over to the shore and let me out right now!"

"I can't do that."

"Well, then I'll swim if I have to."

She stood up, removed her jacket, and prepared to jump out. Barton pulled out his dagger, and rapped her in the back of the head with the handle, which knocked her unconscious.

"Sorry, Lass."

He came up on the mouth of the river, and the weather started to get rough. He manned the jib sheet with great difficulty, so he put a jackline on her and himself just in case. He then watched, as they rounded the last bank, and started into the open waters of the ocean.

The Bay of Doom was named such due to the numerous attacks by sea going Licarion vessels, and the likelihood of a ship escaping the area. This side of the Licarion Islands was their territory, even though Bashworth and Shudolin waters lied just a mile to the north. Most of their ships weren't very seaworthy, but still had enough capability to have a tactical advantage in the narrow strip of water, where the weather could be unpredictable.

It was no different when they entered the bay, as Barton immediately spied three Licarion ships heading towards them from the south. He caught the wind, and followed it, tacked to the north, and tried to outrun their pursuers, as well as keep out of range of their arrows and catapults.

"Just a little further," he told himself, as they closed in on the seaport of Bashworth.

The Licarions, persistent, gained on the smaller vessel, and several of its crew launched a barrage of arrows. Barton used the boom to deflect some of the projectiles from the vessel. Waves

BARGO LYNDEN

flushed over the side, and the boat began to fill with water, as a large piece of iron from a catapult fell into the floor of the vessel. He didn't want to abandon ship yet, just a quarter of a mile from the shoreline, so he tried to plug the hole with Lilly's jacket, which helped a little, but water still leaked through it once it saturated into the fabric.

Just before he gave up hope, a Shudolin naval clipper emerged around the next peninsula. The Licarions proceeded towards the vessel, even though it was close to one hundred feet long, and twice the size of their vessels. The Shudolin ship fired a catapult towards one of the Licarion ships, which caused it to shatter into timbers, as it crashed through its side. The other two fired catapults at the large clipper, but they were ineffective, and splashed into the water beside it. After the second one's mast was destroyed from a projectile, the third retreated back to its own territory. By this time, the long boat was half full of water and sinking.

Just when Barton grabbed Lilly, and prepared to leave the boat, the large clipper turned around and headed towards them. Once within range, the crew threw a rope down to them, Barton tied it around Lilly's waist, and they hauled her up. The boat full of water, Barton left it to sink, and climbed up the side of the ship, as a man with a black beard and scraggly hair helped them on board.

"Welcome aboard," he said. "Looks like we caught you two just in time. We'll send the lass below deck, so her injury can be attended to.

"I have some urgent news for the captain," Barton said.

"That would be Captain Newlander. He's below with the pursor, and Leuitenant Garkee."

"Lieutenant Garkee is on this vessel?"

"Yes, below, in the Captain's quarters."

Barton walked across the deck, and down the stairs to the cabin area, through a couple of large sleeping rooms, and into the captain's quarters. Barton knocked on the door, and he heard the captain's voice, as he let him in.

"Morning Captain Newlander," Barton said, as he saluted him. "My name is Horatio Barton, I am under command of the Royal Guard for the King. I regret to inform he has been captured and killed by the Licarions."

"Oh. Boy," he said, as he sat at his desk. "That means the prince is in charge. I am well aware of his pretentious, destructive nature. Lieutenant Garkee has informed me of your mission, and if there's any way we can help, we will."

"What about my cousins?" Joe Garkee asked. "Are they alive?"

"As far as we know," Barton answered. "They were with Glam. Even if they are, they're still in danger. Ang is heading towards Riverton with the whole Licarion Army."

"We'll head over to the mainland to inform the forces there, and also let Fort Shendlekend know," the captain said.

"Sir," Barton said. "There's something I have to tell you that must not leave this room."

"I trust both my men as well as I do you. Continue."

"This is not just about the king's kidnapping, it is about an ancient Elven legend. Have you ever heard of the Gem of Rebolin, or the Staff of Varlana?"

"I'm not a religious man, but I know it has something to do with the god Rhiatu."

"Well, it's not just a myth, it's real. I've seen its power with our own eyes."

The captain laughed.

"You're expecting me to believe in magic?"

"That's exactly what I'm expecting you to do," Barton answered.

"Those Elves are all the same, with their ancient rituals, and their magic spells."

"He's telling the truth, Sir," Joe Garkee interrupted. "I know an Elf who's seen both the gem and the staff and their power. My cousin is supposed to be the chosen one as his apprentice."

"Apprentice for what?"

"To become a wizard, Sir."

"I've heard enough of this nonsense," the captain stated. "I'm willing to buy the Licarion invasion, but not the rest of these wild tales. I'm a busy man, and I don't have time for this."

"Just keep them off my back until I reach Riverton," Barton said. "Is that too much to ask?"

"No, I guess not. We'll drop you off over to Bashworth, and

inform the militia. They'll barricade the trails to the north and south of the city, and I'll see to it you're provided an escort to get you to Riverton."

"I'll do it, Sir," Joe Garkee said.

"No, Lieutenant, I need you with me. If there is going to be an invasion, I'll need you here."

"It will just take a day or two, and then I'll come back down here."

"I know you're compelled to help your cousins out in any way you can, but an order is an order."

"Yes, Sir."

"Besides, the Shudolin may need a new General one day, and I wouldn't want to deprive them of one of my best officers."

"Yes, Sir."

"We'll be docking soon. Once we do, take our guests over to the militia headquarters and debrief him. After that, they'll be free to go. Make sure he gets an escort to accompany him to Riverton, other than you."

"What about Lilly?"

"She can fend for herself," Barton said. "I'd like to get back and get my money. I will still get my money?"

Joe Garkee frowned at the scraggly, tattered man in disgust.

"You haven't changed at all over the years have you? Still the same, selfish Horatio I've always known. You barely get out of Licarion Territory alive, and you're still wondering about getting your damn money? If Glam said you're getting paid, he will pay you when he gets to Riverton. Isn't that sufficient?"

"I guess."

"Sir, if you could send Lilly back on a coach with two guards, I'd appreciate it. Do not let her leave their sight, and make sure she's not armed."

"I wasn't aware she was so dangerous," the captain said. "She looks harmless; beautiful, but harmless."

"Oh, she's far from harmless," Barton jested. "She has a dark side."

The large vessel pulled into Bashworth Harbor, and parked at the first of ten docks. The men tied the mooring to the docks, and lowered the gang plank, where they exited the vessel. The captain informed the admiral in charge of the upcoming invasion. The ship was scheduled to go back to the Licarion Islands within an hour to join the rest of the fleet. Joe was to take Barton over to the militia office, and then get back on the ship. When they came in the office, the quartermaster greeted them, and they shook his hand.

"Good afternoon, Sir, Lt. Garkee," he said. "What can I do for you today?"

"We're in need of a few favors. We just got off Captain Newlander's vessel, and explained to him that the Licarions are planning an invasion. He sent us over so Mr. Barton, a member of the Royal Guard can be debriefed, and said you would provide him with a couple of militia soldiers, supplies, and horses to help him get back to Riverton.."

"Seems odd a member of the Royal Guard needing protection. But I guess it won't be a problem."

"We'll also need a large militia regiment to meet the Licarions. They're on their way here now, as we speak, fully armed and ready for battle."

"I have seven hundred men stationed here. And I can send for another thousand, but they won't get here until tomorrow."

"Tomorrow will be too late," Barton answered. "They'll leave this city in ruins by then. Unless, you pull the naval vessels closer to land, and use them as a backup."

"The admiral will never agree to that. It would leave the Bay of Doom open to attack from the north side."

"Fort Shendlekend can handle that end," Joe said. "Right now, you'll need to protect the city by land because that's where most of them are coming from."

"Very well. I'll inform the militia here, we'll put up a barricade south of here."

"You'll also need a north flank, in case they decide to approach from that direction."

"Of course."

"And I'll need some weapons," Barton added.

"I have several swords, shields, bows and such in other room. Take what you need. I will notify General Thompson of the situation."

"Thank you," Barton said, as they walked to the next room. He handed the man a bow, a sword, a shield, and about ten arrows. He walked them outside, and called one of his men over to the office.

"Round up two of our best men, and come back here." He nodded, and they waited for about ten minutes, until two men came back with four brown horses. Barton turned to Joe Garkee, and shook his hand.

"Good bye, Lieutenant. Thanks for everything."

"You just make sure my cousins get back in one piece."

"I will."

They mounted their horses, and started to leave, when they noticed a commotion over by the docks. A disgruntled Lilly fought to get away from two sailors, as she punched one in the face, and kicked the other in the groin. She reached for the sword from the fallen one, grabbed a horse from another man who passed by, and mounted it. She then ran away at a full gallop, right past them without so much as a blink.

"Oh, for crying out loud," Barton said.

"You know we're going to have to go after her?".

"Why?"

"You know damn well why."

Barton nudged his horse to proceed, and headed down the road, followed by the two militia men. Lilly raced down the south road out of Bashworth, and towards the direction of her Woblo friends. Little did she know, but the road would lead her to a path of fear, despair, and the hardest decision she would ever have to face.

CHAPTER TWENTY ONE: BATTLE OF BASHWORTH

Lilly raced out of town, and down the south road that led into Licarion territory. The dirt path ended at the river, just about ten miles away. Barton and the two guards were just behind her, and caught up to bring her horse to a full halt.

"Get out of my way," she told them, as she pointed her sword at Barton's chest.

"Please, Mrs. Tumberhill," Joe Garkee told her. "We need to leave the area and let the militia handle this."

"Listen," Barton said. "I'm sorry about the tap on the head, but he's right. This is no longer our fight. We need to go home now. The Licarions will be here any minute, and we'll be right in the middle of the battle."

"Maybe you want to be a coward and run, but my place is to fight by my friend's side, and die by his side, if necessary."

Barton thought about what she said, and turned to the guards.

"I can't let her do this alone," he said.

"Ten minutes ago, you were asking me why we were going after her." Joe said.

"I know what I said," Barton said. "And it was cold. I kind of miss that fur ball myself. If Mrs. Tumberhill wants to help her friend, I think we should give her a hand."

"I think you're both out of your minds," Joe said. "But Glam would never forgive me if I left you on your own. We'll head over through that hill to the west to get a better view of what's going on. The militia should be heading this way by nightfall. That's when the Licarions will attack. I'll probably get court martialed for this, but it is what it is." He turned to his two militia soldiers. "Get back and help the forces at Bashworth. I'll take care of it from here."

The soldiers nodded, and headed back in the direction of the city.

"Do you notice something strange around?" Lilly asked.

"Like what?" Barton asked.

"It's the middle of Junatra and the vegetation is dead and brown," Lilly said. "It should be green."

"Now's not the time to be worried about that," Barton said. "Maybe it's a disease of some kind."

"It's a disease, all right," Joe said. "A disease of evil. Ang must have somehow put a spell on the land when he had the stone. We need to get Bargo and the gem to Riverton before it's too late. If the forces of evil are allowed to overrun Riverton, we'll all be doomed."

"Then we've no time to lose," Barton said, and bolted ahead on his horse.

Glam and the two Woblos were only ten miles away, on the other side of the river. They could hear the Licarions just up the bend, and feared they might be using long boats, which gave them the advantage of speed. They needed to get to the other side somehow, but the current was such, they feared they would drown. Woblos were light in the water, and a good current could send them miles down the river.

They had no rope with them, so they found a point on the river where a large dead tree fell, but wasn't quite all the way across. Glam went across first to make sure it would hold their weight, and the Woblos followed behind. Glam jumped from the end of the tree into the water, as Bargo leaped into his arms. He helped him on the land, and did the same for Barlow.

The Licarions were no further than a couple of miles behind them, and gaining ground. On foot, they wouldn't be able to outrun their enemy, and would ultimately have to face them. They just hoped the militia would be waiting on the other side of the territory, just two miles to the north. Once they reached the other side, they ran across the field, and sought refuge under a tree. Glam took out his periscope, and focused it towards the river.

"They're coming up the river on long boats," he said. "And it looks like Ang is leading the pack."

"How many of them?" Barlow asked.

"A couple hundred," Glam answered, as he turned the scope towards the hill to the west. "And another thousand coming down from the hill."

"One thousand?" Bargo asked.

"Keep moving," the Elf said, and the two Woblos followed him, while he ran toward the territorial road.

The Licarions emerged from the countryside in a frenzied rage, as the sun set on the land. The landscape was littered with a sea of green reptiles running across a brown landscape. Their spears were held high, poised for attack, as they headed towards Shudolin Territory.

The trio continued to run until they came to a hill. "To higher ground," Glam yelled, and ran up the hill. The others followed him, and they hid behind some rocks, as the army of Licarions ran right pass them, and down the road towards the town of Bashworth.

"They must not have seen us," Bargo said to him.

"Oh, they saw us all right," Glam said. "But their orders aren't to come after us, they're to go straight to Bashworth. Ang will look for us personally. We have to get all the way up the hill to get a better look."

They climbed to the top, and could see the ocean and beach below them on the other side. There were several Shudolin ships nearby, as well as Licarion, getting ready to do battle at sea. Ang was about a half mile to the south, coming up the road with several Licarions. In the midst of them were Tamarka and Daniel; tied, beaten and tired, but still very much alive.

"Damn," Glam said, as he gritted his teeth.

"They never made it back," Bargo said. "They were captured before they could tell the militia."

"Well, unless Lilly and Barton made it there, the city has no idea what they're up against," Glam said.

"What about if I use the stone against them?" Bargo asked.

"You are not to use it unless absolutely necessary," Glam said. "Its power is too great to use on a whim. Part of the secret of the stone is not letting others know it exists. Too many people are susceptible to its evil nature. Besides, I have a better idea. It will require some risk, however. Barlow, I want you to get their attention, and bring them up this hill. Bargo, take this bow, and cover him."

The two woblos followed their instruction, as Glam aimed an

arrow at one of the passing Shudolin ships, which caught their attention. They began to fire back at him, as Bargo and Barlow emerged to the top of the hill.

"Come on, run to the north," Glam ordered, as they ran across the top of the hill. The Licarions ran behind them, as the ship started to fire catapults of round, metal projectiles at them. Ang emerged with his horse to see what the commotion was, but galloped back down when he found they were being attacked by the clipper. "Keep going, I'll catch up."

"No, Glam, you'll be killed," Bargo said.

"Trust me," he told him. "I'm just buying a little time for reinforcements to arrive."

Glam ran down to free Tamarka, and fired his arrows at the Licarions guarding them. Ang ran after him on his horse, traveling ahead of the other two, with his sword drawn. Glam faced him, without any armor, as Ang swung with full force, and knocked him off his feet, the two weapons connecting. The one eyed Elf turned his horse around, Glam came to his feet, and the other Licarions came up from behind him, ready to pounce upon the Royal Guard member.

"Don't touch him," he told them. "He's mine!"

Glam readied himself, as Ang approached him again. He pulled his adversary from the horse and onto the ground. While he was down, he kicked him three times in the stomach, and then once in the face. The Licarions came over to help Ang to his feet.

"Never mind me, get the others," he ordered.

The Woblos ran, while they led them through a barrage of arrows from the bay. Several of the Licarions were killed, with the creatures right behind them, and Bargo and Barlow had a tough time navigating without catching an arrow themselves. They took a breath, and hid behind some rocks.

"Glam's going to killed down there," Bargo said to his cousin.

"And so will we if we don't keep moving. Bashworth is just about five miles up the river. We'll follow the coast."

"I can't just leave him," Bargo said.

"He'll be all right," Barlow stated.

Just then, three familiar faces appeared to the north from the brush that lay ahead of them. A young woman with blonde hair on a brown horse appeared from out of the foliage, a Woblo, and an older gentlemen carrying a sword.

"Bargo," Lilly said, as she jumped from her horse to greet him. Bargo ran to her, and hugged her tight.

"I'm so glad to see you," Bargo said. "All of you. Glam is down there fighting Ang, and they have Tamarka and Daniel."

"There's a militia heading here from Bashworth soon," Joe said. "We've got to get them out of here."

They raced to the edge of the hill to see where their friends were. Glam now faced Ang again, as he waved the sword at his old adversary. He slashed Glam's chest, and drew blood, while the Royal Guard defended himself from his advances. He found himself at a stalemate with him, as each one matched each other's move by striking the blades together. He struck Ang across the jaw with his fist, and swung his sword towards his neck. He quickly moved to the right, and landed his sword into Glam's arm, causing an inch gash. He dropped the sword to the ground, and Ang swung again, knocking him off his feet.

In an unpredictable moment, Lilly bolted her horse down the hill towards him with her sword high in the air.

"Lilly, no!" Bargo yelled to her, as Joe held him back from the edge of the hill.

She swung her sword at his head, but Ang blocked it, grabbed her by the hair, and threw her to the ground. She fell in a cloud of dirt, and her weapon fell a few feet away from her. The evil Elf kicked it away, as Glam grabbed him around the neck, but was thrown over his head and onto his back. Ang kicked him in the ribs three or four times, until Lilly rose, and scrambled for her blade. He backhanded her to the ground, picked up the sword, and threw it twenty feet away.

Bargo watched in horror, as he gripped the gem tight, and it began to get white hot in his pocket, almost burning his leg while it glowed. He knew it was summoning him to use it, but he was afraid if he did, Glam would be angry with him.

"Stay here," Barton told them, as he started down on his horse as well.

Lilly tried to grab Ang, but he choked her until she fell to the ground. He was ready to stab her, when Barton thrust an arrow into his right arm. He dropped his saber, as the man quickly freed the two Elven guard members. He turned and fired two more arrows at some Licarions, who threw spears at him, but missed. He cut the Elves' ropes with a hunting knife, and they made their way up the hill."

Glam knocked Ang to the ground, and held a knife above him, ready to stab him. The one eyed Elf kicked him, rolled him over, and jumped on top of his nemesis. Barton came from behind him, and swung his sword to behead him, but Ang turned quickly, waved his arm with magic, and Barton fell off the horse.

By this time, the militia met their enemy just about a half mile up the road, and were engaged in full battle. Ang saw the commotion, and stabbed Barton in the stomach. He went to finish off Lilly, when another arrow hit him from Joe's bow above.

Glam tried to grab his long time foe, but he threw him to the side, and slashed his leg. Determined to get the stone, Ang mounted his horse to climb the hill where the Woblos were. Tamarka and Daniel joined them at the top, while Joe sent another arrow into Ang's arm. The horse bucked him, and he fell to the bottom of the hill, unconscious.

"Let's get out of here," Glam said, as he helped Barton up the hill. Lilly rose to her feet, shaken but still breathing, grabbed her sword, and followed them up as well.

By this time, the Shudolin Army advanced on the Licarions, but were outnumbered. Fortunately, the naval brigade landed one of the clipper ships, perched on the hill, and began to fire flaming arrows at the enemy in the fields below. The napalm explosions frightened the creatures, as they ran and scattered in several directions. When Ang awoke, he found himself alone, and in the midst of the chaotic battle. He ran away to seek refuge, in the same direction the others had just gone.

They traveled to a secluded spot on the hill, away from the battle, and closer to Bashworth. From what they could see of the sea battle, the Licarions were losing, with several of their ships going up in flames, or sinking. It was the land battle where the Shudolin was having trouble, and the Licarions were advancing on Bashworth rapidly by way of the north path.

Lilly and Glam helped Barton lie down on some moss. He

was dying, and they were still at least three miles away from the city. They ripped strips of their clothing and placed them around his and Glam's wounds. Most of the Elf's injuries were superficial, and only flesh wounds, but Barton suffered internal injuries, and was losing his battle to survive. He began to lose consciousness about a mile back from the moss.

"Will he live?" Bargo asked.

"It's hard to tell," Glam said. "If we can stop the bleeding, he might."

"What about the stone?" Bargo asked.

"It will not work with him," Glam said.

"Why not?"

"Bargo," Glam said, reluctant. "There's also something else I forgot to tell you. I'm not like other Elves, I'm of a special breed."

"What's that supposed to mean?"

"I am from a class of Elf called the Dhriatu. We are an ancient people, and there are only a few of us left. Two, as a matter of fact."

"Who is the other one, Ang?"

"It's not Ang, but I can't disclose his identity until this mission is over. We do not heal like others, we heal quicker and in some cases heal when others will not."

"Then what is Ang, if he's not a Dhriatu?"

"An abomination of the Elven kind. He was a descendant from Garlock himself."

"But I saw the power of the stone heal you," Bargo said. "It must be able to save him."

"Lilly is right in some ways, I'm afraid," Glam said. "I've misled you to believe the stone is all powerful, and so far we've only seen simple tricks."

"But I am to become a wizard," Bargo said. "You said so yourself."

"Now see what you've done," Lilly said, still weak from her struggle with Ang.

"I'm telling you I can do it," Bargo said. "But first, I have to look into the fire."

He walked over to the edge of the hill overlooking the bay, about twenty feet away.

BARGO LYNDEN

"What in the Underworld is he doing?" Barton asked weakly, as they bandaged him.

"I'm not sure," Tamarka said.

Bargo looked out at the burning Licarion and Shudolin ships, and into the fire. He could hear the voice from the fire recite the words 'viorta rhiala santu,' which meant 'heal thyself.' He then turned around, and pulled the gem from his pocket. He knew exactly what to do now, almost like learning a long forgotten skill which came back to him.

He knelt beside Barton, and placed the stone on Barton's wound.

"Hi there, little fellow," he said to him, as he awoke briefly.

"Hi, Barton," the Woblo said, as he smiled. "Try to lie still."

"Bargo, this is a waste of time," Lilly insisted. "You can't save him."

"At least let him try," Glam told her, as he grabbed her shoulders and looked into her tearful blue eyes.

"Viatra Calia Fior," Bargo proceeded, as the stone grew white and bright as the sun. The others turned away, and it lit the dark night sky like a beacon of hope in a moment of despair. In a few moments, the wound healed and Barton fell asleep on the soft moss. Bargo turned toward the group, who couldn't believe their eyes. "You were saying?"

"Bargo," Glam said in amazement. "Excellent, you are indeed the wizard of the prophecy."

Even Lilly was at a loss of words, as she lay beside Barton, not happy at all about the prospect of his new career.

"As soon as we return to Riverton, and settle this mess out, we can start you for your real training," Glam said. "But as for tonight, we're pigeon holed here. Tamarka, you, Daniel, and Lieutenant Garkee can keep watch tonight. Make sure the battle stays down in the valley. We don't want anyone coming up here until we can vacate the area, especially Ang."

"Do you think they'll overtake Bashworth?" Barlow asked.

"That, my friends, is the 500 gold piece question."

Bargo spent most of the night awake, worried for their safety, and what was to become of his homeland if they should fail. He had a strong feeling of uneasiness in his gut, as he stared at the fires across the landscape towards the sea, and a voice called to him, but it wasn't from the fires. It was a feeling of impending doom, even greater than the fall of the Shudolin, coming from across the ocean, and a place called Bereuka Island.

CHAPTER TWENTY TWO:

<u>SHOW ME THE WAY TO GO HOME</u>

Barton slept through most of the night, despite the commotion in the valley below him. The two Elven guards and Joe kept watch all night, but there was no sign of Ang. They noticed, however, that their worst fears became reality, as the Licarions successfully overtook the Shudolin Militia, and the city of Bashworth itself was engulfed in flames. Glam turned to his friends in despair, as he dropped the edge of his sword into the ground. He pulled out his periscope and looked down at the smoking ruins.

"We've failed," he told them. "I knew we would be too late to save them."

"We did our best at warning them," Barton told them. "They were just outnumbered."

"As are most men who don't believe in the power of true evil," the Elven commander said. "Well, we best get moving on towards Riverton. The Licarions are heading north. We have to find a sea going vessel to beat them to Riverton. Once we get the staff, we can stop them once and for all."

"Which reminds me, how are we going to get the staff, if it's guarded by the prince and his guards?" Lilly asked.

"I've thought about that, and I have a plan, but we'll discuss that later, after we've dealt with Ang."

"Do you think Ang is with the Licarion Army heading north?" Barton asked.

"No, he's still around here," Glam said, as he looked down at the surrounding area. "He's waiting for an opportunity to get the stone. We're just lucky he didn't come last night. He'll try to use the stone to seal the fate of the Shudolin."

"I thought you said Bargo was the only one capable of magic?" Barton asked. "The only one to possess the power of a

BARGO LYNDEN

wizard? Ang pushed me off my horse without even touching me."

"I was afraid of that," Glam said. He's had contact with the stone. If he gets a hold of it again, there will be nothing to stop him. That's why under no circumstances should Bargo give it to him, even if our own lives are at stake."

"Don't worry about that," Bargo told him. "I've learned my lesson. I will defend the stone until my death."

"The true sacrifice for one's friends is the real power of the wizard and his instruments," Glam said.

"You're asking him to give up his life for all of ours," Lilly sneered. "None of us asked for this."

"And neither did the people of the Shudolin ask for their prince to kill their king, or the Grassmen and Licarions to invade their homeland. We can no longer afford to be selfish, Mrs. Tumberhill."

"Well, why don't you face him then?"

"I can try, but I don't possess the power to kill him; only Bargo does."

Barton began to giggle again, but held himself back.

"Forgive me," he remarked. "I didn't mean to laugh, but Bargo is no match for Ang. Three of us took him on, and he still managed to overtake us."

"The odds have changed," Glam said. "Bargo has changed."

His friends stared at him a moment, now understanding what Glam meant, as the small creature walked towards the edge of the hill overlooking the charred city. He held one hand on his sword, and the other on his pocket, as the stone began to glow white again.

"He's calling me," Bargo said. "I have to go now."

"Then we're going with you," Lilly said, as she followed.

He started to walk down the embankment, as the others trailed close behind him. While descending, they found the charred body of the prince's messenger.

"Well, at least the Prince doesn't know his father is dead yet," Glam said.

They turned their eyes back towards the city, and Ang emerged from behind the ruins, with about thirty Licarions behind him. Once they reached the bottom, they faced their adversaries in what was left of the main street. Ang waved his arm, and they rushed toward the eight allies with their swords drawn.

Lilly pulled out her bow, drawing arrow after arrow, until she shot at least six of them. Barton waved his sword at the crowd of reptilian beasts, stabbing one in the stomach, and two in the chest. Glam, with usual precision, took out at least ten of them, with body parts flying in every direction. The other Elves and Woblos were no less efficient, as they finished off the rest of them, leaving Ang all alone to face all of them.

"Why must I be surrounded by incompetence!" he shouted in the air, as he drew both his swords. "Who wants to die first?"

"The only one who's going to die here today is you, Ang," Glam said.

"Not by your sword, old friend," he told him.

"I will not kill you, but he will," Glam said, as Bargo drew his sword, and stepped forward.

Ang laughed an evil laugh.

"The Woblo?," Ang asked. "You must be joking. He's a kind and gentle creature, he won't kill me. He's as much a coward as his father."

"Do not speak of my father that way," Bargo sneered. "He's a better Woblo than you'll ever be an Elf."

"That's good," Ang said to him. "Let your anger guide you. Revenge is sweet, and you'll soon taste the sweetness of evil; the power it possesses, and the riches you can have. Just give me the gem, and let me show you the way."

"Nice try, Ang, but your manipulation won't work anymore," Glam said.

"Perhaps he needs a little motivation," Ang said, as he waved his hand, and a red light from his fingertips lifted Lilly in the air twenty feet above them. "Give me the gem, or I'll drop her like the stone in your pocket."

"No," Bargo said. "Let her go."

"Don't allow him to control you, Bargo," Glam told him. "Use the gem."

"But I don't know the words," he pleaded. "There is no fire to guide me."

"You don't need them, it's within your mind. Think hard."

BARGO LYNDEN

"But think quick, because your time just ran out," the one eyed Elf said, as he let her go.

"Fira giola aratu!" Bargo shouted, as Lilly floated softly to the ground.

"Enough of the magic show," Ang said, as he started towards the group. "Prepare to die, Woblo."

He swung his sword down at the four feet Bargo, who blocked the first sword with his shield. The second one he blocked with his weapon, and pushed him twenty feet away and onto his back. Shaken, the Elf rose to his feet.

"You surprise me, young one. You are stronger than I imagined. But you will die just as easily."

"I'm tired of your talk, Ang. Let's get on with it."

One thing which amazed Bargo was he no longer feared him, and knew he could complete the needed task when the power of the gem stood behind him. Ang rose to his feet, grabbed his saber, then walked back over to his adversary, and circled him.

He swung again, with a force so powerful it broke the Woblo's shield in half. Bargo blocked the second swing, and his blade went into Ang's arm, but the mail armor protected him. He backhanded the Woblo, which sent him to the ground. Lilly was tempted to jump in, but Barton held her back.

Bargo rolled over, as the Elf dropped his sword to the ground, just missing him. Bargo kicked him hard, and he flew four feet in the air, and onto the dirt. The others found it difficult to see due to the smoke in the area, and drew closer to the brawl.

The two of them rose to their feet, and Ang swung again and missed, while Bargo struck him with his sword in the back. He quickly turned, and put a gash into the woblo's right leg. He fell to the ground in pain, as Ang descended the weapon again, but Bargo placed his hand out, and the Elf again flew in the air.

He tried to get up, but Bargo ran towards him, and kicked him in the jaw. Without a sword, the Elf grabbed a log, and hit him in his side. Bargo fell next to him, and the Elf tried to choke him while they were both on the ground.

"We have to help him," Lilly said. "Before he gets killed."

"We cannot interfere," Glam said. "He must fulfil his prophecy."

"Damn your prophecy," Lilly said, as she drew her sword.

Bargo found himself in an awkward position, as he tried to reach for the gem or his sword, which were both on the ground now. Ang went to reach for the stone, but Lilly swung her blade at the Elf. He turned quick, grabbed her arm, broke it, and threw her to the ground. When he let go, it gave Bargo just enough time to grab his sword, and thrust it right into his enemy's chest.

Ang rolled over onto his back in agony, as he tried to pull the blade from his chest. Bargo pushed so hard it went through his armor and into his lung and rib cage, but not his heart. He yanked the Elven blade from his body and lay there, as he tried to rejuvenate his health.

"Bargo, put the sword through his heart," Glam said, as he helped Lilly over to Barton, who put her arm in a sling. Bargo hesitated as Ang lay there in pain, as if something wasn't right about killing an Elf; for some of his best friends were Elves. "Do it, before he gets up again!"

"Bargo, please have mercy on me," Ang gasped. "Can't you see I'm a dying man?"

"No you're not," Bargo said, as he decided he needed to do this to save the Shudolin. "Not yet."

He thrust the sword into his heart, as a bright red flare flew up into the dawn sky, and released a force so powerful it knocked all of them off their feet. When the light disappeared, all that was left was his cloak, bones, and ashes from the rest of his body on the ground. Bargo went to reach for his weapon, and Glam placed his hand over his on the handle.

"No. It must stay in the ground until you say the words."

"But I don't know the words."

"The words are Fiarta Rhiala Ziathia. "Repeat them."

"Fiarta Rhiala Ziathia."

"Now you can take your sword out."

"What do they mean?" He asked, as he removed the sword from the ground.

"It means, my small friend, once we have Glaridia and the council remove the prince from power, you are the new king."

"Me?"

"How's that possible?" Barton asked. "A knight, I could see, but a king?"

"There is no king at the moment," Glam said. "And with Bargo's newfound power, he's the logical choice."

"A king and a wizard in the same day. Imagine that."

"But right now, we have to take care of the matter at hand," Glam said. "Which is getting back to Riverton. I saw a small fishing vessel at the dock. Our task is not over yet. We have to get the staff in order to stop the evil spell upon our land and the Licarions approaching Riverton."

"How long do you think we have?" Barton asked.

"The Licarions should be there in a couple of days. We can be there in a day by sea, if the weather holds out. But first, Medicine Man, you need to heal Lilly's arm."

"Yes, Sir," Bargo said to him. Glam placed his hand on his shoulder, and looked into his eyes.

"You'll never have to call me Sir again. You've earned the right to be called whatever you want, even king."

"Thank you." He placed the stone on Lilly's arm, as he recited the words, and the pain was gone.

"Thank you, Bargo," she said. "I'm sorry I didn't have faith in you. I just couldn't bear to see that monster try to kill you. I had to do something."

"I understand. And thank you, as well."

They walked down to the dock through the smoking village, sad about the events which occurred here, but relieved they survived the ordeal. They just hoped all was well with the people back in Riverton. They climbed inside the thirty feet fishing vessel, which was similar to a herring boss ship, only smaller. Being able to relax for the first time on their journey, Bargo, Lilly, Tamarka, and Daniel decided to get some much needed sleep in the cabin below. The ship's aroma reeked of a fresh catch, but none of them minded, considering how tired they were. Glam and Barton stayed on deck, and Joe Garkee manned the sails. As Glam took the wheel, Barton lit his pipe, and smoked the last of his tobacco.

"Did anyone ever tell you that's a dangerous habit around wood?" Glam asked.

"Yes. My mother used to hate it when my father did it."

"So what made you start?"

"I don't know. I guess I just picked up his bad habit."

"Do you realize that's the first time you've even talked about your family since I've met you?"

"It's something I really don't like to think about. My father was abusive, and my mother enabled him. I had to become my own man, and I'm better for it today."

"Except that you're a loudmouth and a thief as well."

"You are absolutely right. "I shouldn't have taken any of the treasure, and I've been a bit of a bastard. I put all of our lives at risk, and I'm truly sorry for that. You know, the funny part of it is, I never had very many friends, until I met you guys."

"Well, we all need friends. "Even if we sometimes don't think so. And I'm sorry I struck you."

"You are a wise man, even if Mrs. Tumberhill doesn't think so."

"She just doesn't understand the old Elven ways. Most of what Bargo must learn, he must do so in total secrecy. It is an advantage few people know the old white magic that was taught eons ago."

"I understand it," Lilly said, as emerged from the cabin below. "I just didn't believe it until I saw it with my own eyes. But even though I believe what I saw doesn't necessarily mean I believe Bargo should become a wizard, or a king, for that matter."

"His destiny will call him, and when it does, it will be up to him to decide who and what he is," Glam said. "He cannot be both; if he's a king, he must protect his homeland, and if he's a wizard, he cannot be a king."

"He's a Blacksmith, just like his father before him, and he needs to go back to that life."

"Yes, but what will his life be without you as his bride? He loves you; anyone can see that."

"As I told him, I'm a married woman. And he's still a Woblo."

"Not for long, if we get the staff."

"As you say, that is his decision. How long before we reach Riverton?"

"About twelve hours. We have a good headwind, and the water's calm."

"Well, at least something's finally going our way," Barton replied.

"In the morning, we'll get together and come up with a plan," Glam said. "I'm sure by this time, the prince has upped his security, and has several guards around the palace."

"You said earlier that Ang was a descendant of Garlock? What is he, a great-great grandson, or something?"

"Not exactly. He was his son."

"His son?" Lilly asked.

"Yes." Glam answered.

"Wouldn't that make him over 900 years old?" Barton asked.

"He was immortal. Until Bargo stabbed him in his life force with the magic sword. He must train now, so he can destroy Garlock in the same fashion."

"I thought Garlock was locked inside his own castle?" Barton asked.

"He is, but he will not stay that way for long. There is already one who will fuel the evil which will unlock the doors, and revive his tyranny.

"Who?" Barton asked.

"I don't know at this time. But I will soon. Perhaps the voice from the fire he keeps hearing."

"You don't really believe that, do you?" Lilly asked.

"I believe in all things which seem unbelievable."

"He'll never agree to such a venture."

"You may not know your Woblo friend as well as you think you do. When the time comes, we'll let him decide."

"Fair enough. But don't expect me to be clicking my heals for joy."

The rest of the night was uneventful, as the cool, early summer wind took them two hundred miles up the coastline. The sun rose upon the water, and they could see the harbor city of Riverton in the distance, and the open ocean behind them. The whitecaps signified the coldness of the liquid, and the smell of fish scent migrated through the ocean air. It would surely be a day to remember, but one they would rather soon forget.

CHAPTER TWENTY THREE: CONFRONTATION

They awoke to some breakfast of fresh fruit left on board, and a few hard, but edible biscuits. They washed it down with stale ale, sat up on deck, and discussed their plans for the day. Bargo was the first to dig in, and even though he was one of the smallest, he was the most hungry. He was rather fond of the cantaloupes, which weren't common to his area. There was something about their sweetness which made him partial to their taste.

"Here's the idea I came up with," Glam told them. "The prince isn't expecting us to return, but he is expecting Vladimir. When we come to the gate, I want Barton and Lilly to walk by, and act like you're having a domestic dispute."

"That won't be hard," Lilly jested. Barton frowned, but remained silent.

"While you attract the guards, I want Daniel and Tamarka to tell them they have important news from the Royal Guard, and insist to see the prince. Tell them it involves Vladimir. Bargo, you come with me, and we'll slip in the back while the rest of you keep as many guards busy as you can."

"What about us two?" Joe asked.

"I appreciate both your help, but your part of the assignment is over, and once we make landfall, you're free to go."

"But he's our cousin, and we stick behind family," Barlow said.

"There is nothing you can do to help us at this point," Glam said. "Once we get the staff, the rest is up to Bargo."

"I'd still like to help," Joe said.

"Do you think your plan will work?" Barton asked.

"It better," Glam answered. "It will be our only shot at it. And being in the middle of the day will not help our task., but we must get the staff by sundown, or the Shudolin is doomed."

"We'll have to dock on the west side of Riverton to avoid

being seen by the royal guards," Tamarka suggested.

"Right you are, Tamarka. I just hope Barton was right in his assumption it was the true staff. Otherwise, our efforts could be in vain."

"I know what I saw," Barton said. "It looked just as you described it. I just don't understand why he would keep it in the trophy room, where everyone could see it."

"To display his victory over others. "He's well guarded and he knows it; he would never suspect someone to steal it."

"No one would be foolish enough to steal it, except us," Barton said.

"What about talking to Glaridia and the council?" Lilly asked.

"Lieutenant Garkee, if you can send someone to Elf City, and let them know what's going on?" Glam said.

"Of course," Joe answered, pleased he was of some use before he returned to Bashworth to get reprimanded by Captain Newlander.

They entered the bay and mouth of the Swift River, and the familiar site of marinas and sailboats. They docked at a small marina on the west side, and Barton tied the ropes to the cleats on the dock. They exited the boat, received the usual strange looks at their tattered appearance, but were thankful to see human beings again. They ducked down the nearest side street, and huddled together as a group. Barlow and Joe each gave their cousin a hug goodbye.

"Good luck, Bargo," Barlow said. "And thank you. Thanks to all of you."

"Your welcome," Bargo said. "But I couldn't have done it without my friends."

"Good luck with your wizardry instruction," Joe said, as he shook his hand. "Or becoming king, whatever you decide."

"And good luck with your Captain. I'm sure he'll give you a break once he finds out the truth of what's going on."

"Let's hope so. Be careful, cousin. If you ever get back to Woblo Town, say hello to Aunt Catherine for me."

"I will. And say hello to your mother for me."

"You bet. It's been a pleasure meeting all of you, although it could have been under better circumstances."

The two Woblos left them, headed towards the nearest militia office, and Glam turned back to the group.

"The palace is about five miles from here. Try to not look suspicious until we get there."

"And how do we do that?" Lilly asked. "None of us have bathed in over a week."

"Try not to huddle together. The Elves can stick together, a little ways ahead of us, you and Barton behind them, and Bargo and I will follow up on the rear. If anybody asks, tell them you're homeless, and looking for a little food or money."

"It wouldn't be too far from the truth," Barton jested.

"Okay, we'll meet in front of the palace in a half hour," Glam said.

They went their separate ways, and Bargo walked with Glam, still gripping tight to his sack with the stone in it. There was a feeling in his bones this wouldn't be as easy and straight forth as the Elf thought it would be, and they underestimated their opponent.

"Glam, I've been thinking a lot about what you said. And I've decided even though my father wanted me to be a Blacksmith, I'd like more out of life. I feel I no longer have a place in Woblo Town for me."

"Does Lilly know you feel this way?"

"I haven't told her how I feel about it."

"So what are you saying, do you want to be king?"

"By the power of Rhiatu, of course not."

"Then you must want to be a wizard? Bargo, before you decide, there's something I have to tell you."

"Whatever it is, I'm sure it won't change my mind about how I feel."

"I'm afraid it might," Glam said, as he placed his right hand on his left shoulder. "Bargo, after we get the staff and remove the curse on the land, your job as a wizard will begin."

"I know that."

"But it will be more than just learning spells and magic. There will be a great task involved; one where you may not return."

"What do you mean?"

"Remember when Christopher and I told you about how

Garlock was locked inside of his castle?"

"Yes, what about it?"

"I have reason to believe this will not be over even if we remove the spell. We have a few years before it happens, but I believe another disciple will take Ang's place, another Licarion king will rise out of the mountains, and evil will once again raise its ugly head. We need to be ready."

"I've defeated one evil disciple, what's another?"

"That attitude will cause the darkness of evil to invade your heart. You must be humble, as well as self preserved. Besides, it's not the disciple you need to kill. We need to attack the evil at its source."

"Garlock? But how?"

"That's not important right now. Your instructor will show you how."

"And my instructor is?"

"All in due time, my small friend, all in due time."

When they arrived at the palace gate, they met in some trees just south of the entrance. Lilly and Barton went ahead, while Bargo and Glam went around to the south end of the grounds. When they reached the gate, the three guards in the front watched, as Lilly started to walk by. Barton followed behind her, and in front of them, she turned around and slapped his face.

"I told you not to talk to me that way," she said, to initiate the dispute.

"But, sweetheart, you know I didn't mean it," he said. "I just wanted you to listen to me for a change."

One of the guards approached the couple, a little annoyed.

"Would you mind taking your argument somewhere else?" he asked.

"How would you like it if your husband called you a lazy wench?" she asked him.

"I wouldn't," the guard said. "But you can't bring your argument here, in front of the palace."

"Isn't the king married? Maybe he understands women better than I do."

"Maybe if you weren't such an idiot, you would understand me," Lilly reiterated.

"Why you little bitch," he said, as he tried to grab her. Two of the guards grabbed him, as he swung at her, and she did the same, tying up the third guard.

The two Elves walked through the gate during the commotion., as several other guards tried to stop them as well.

"We have urgent news about the chief's advisor," Tamarka said. "We're from the Royal Guard and need to see him right away."

"What's the nature of your news?" he asked.

"I don't need to answer to you, I'm a Royal Guard member."

"If you can't tell me, then you need to leave"

"Get out of my way, peasant," the Elf said, as the two of them got involved in a brawl with the guards.

During this time, Glam and Bargo sneaked around back to the south wall. Glam threw a rope with a grappling hook to the top, and Glam quickly shimmied up the wall. Bargo waited, and then followed behind, although not as quick, after he waved his hand all was clear. One of the guards heard the hook, and walked along the top of the wall. When he bent down to look over the side, Glam grabbed him by the collar, and threw him twenty feet to the ground.

He looked all around to make sure no other guards were looking, and jumped on a tree next to the wall. He helped Bargo, who did the same, almost falling to the ground, and losing the gem out of his pocket. A guard heard the rustling, and walked over to look in the tree. Glam held his finger to his lips, as they remained motionless. After the guard couldn't see anything, he walked away.

There was an open window above the tree line, maybe twenty feet at the most, and Glam thought if he could attach a line to an arrow, he could launch it into the open window. He waited until the guards passed the area, while he could still hear the commotion at the front gate, and then shot the arrow into the open window. He waited a minute to see if anyone noticed, pulled it to see if it was anchored, and tied the other end taught to a branch on the tree.

"Wait here," Glam told him. "No matter what happens, don't move. Understand?"

"Yes," the Woblo answered.

Glam shimmied himself with the rope, and stopped for a

moment, as a guard passed under him. He then climbed into the room, which was one of the guard's bedroom. He walked toward the door, and hid on the other side of it when he heard someone coming. The man walked in, which happened to be the same guard Barton met in front of the trophy room, and he held a knife to his throat.

"Where's Phillip?"

"He's down in his study."

"Take me to him." Glam let him go and pushed him out the door.

They walked through the long hall, and down the stairway to the next floor. The prince's study was at the end, and he stopped him just short of the door.

"Go in there, and tell him Vladimir's here."

"Sir?"

"Just do it, and don't let on it's me, or I'll put a knife right in your back."

"Yes, Sir," he said, and opened the door. The prince looked up at him, angered.

"Didn't anyone ever tell you to knock?"

"Sir, Vladimir's back, and he'd like to see you."

"Well, why didn't you say so? Send him in."

He stepped aside, as the Elf walked in, and his look went from cheer to disgust and anxiety.

"You?"

"Yes, Phillip, me."

"Maurice, that will be all," he told his guard, who nodded, and walked out.

"You were expecting Vladimir to return, after you eliminated all of us. But you didn't count on Ang and the Licarions fouling up your plans. You see, Vladimir was under equipped to handle such a mission. You did succeed in killing your father, however."

"My father's dead?"

"Don't act so surprised. It's what you wanted, isn't it? He suffered a long, agonizing death at the hands of ruthless beasts, which is more than can be said of you. You're the real beast, the player of pawns, the prince of evil himself."

"Save the speeches for diplomatic advisors. I did what I had to do. My father never would have let me command this kingdom, even after he died. He'd let that Elf king run it before me."

"As right he shouldn't. Your father was a good man, and a good king. He wasn't greedy, and he respected everyone. It's a shame he raised a brat like you."

"What do you want? Money? Women? A small kingdom of your own? Name it."

"You know what I want, and you're going to take me down to it?"

"I don't know what you're talking about/"

"There are ten thousand Licarions on their way up the north road towards this city as I speak, ready to destroy your kingdom, and place Ang's evil spell upon the land. You have the one thing that can save us from them, and you're going to give it to me. Let's go to the trophy room."

"Just give me a second, I have to get a key to open the case," he said, as he reached toward a cabinet behind him. He grabbed the dagger on the wall next to him, and threw it at Glam, who moved to the left just in time to dodge it. Phillip grabbed a fencing sword from its wall mount, and jumped over his desk, as the Elf raised his weapon to defend himself. He backed out into the hallway, as two guards came from behind him. "Kill him!"

He knocked one guard off the balcony to the ball room below, and the other he knocked down the stairs. Phillip pushed him down the stairway as well, and Glam rolled to the bottom, dazed and bruised, but still coherent. The prince raced down the stairway, and kicked him in the ribs while he was down. Glam rolled over, and held his sword up, as the prince tried to reach his chest with his blade. The Elf kicked him with his right foot, and pushed him back.

"It's a shame I'll have to kill my best guard, but I guess that's the spoils of war," Phillip jested. "I have twice your skill level, and half your age."

Glam tried to run towards the trophy room, but was cut off by Phillip, who just missed Glam's head. He ducked, and pushed him against the doors, they opened, and the trophy room was breached. Phillip fell to the ground, his blade broken in half as it fell. Glam walked towards him, as Phillip rose, smashed the glass case behind him, and then grabbed the staff off the wall with both hands.

He pointed the staff at the Elf, who dropped his weapon, for he knew the power of the staff was greater, and now faced failure. He backed up into the main entrance hall, as the prince approached him, threatening him with the weapon. A blue light came from the end, and Glam fell to the floor, paralyzed, on his hands and knees in pain.

"Feel the true power of the staff," the prince told him. "Feel the power of evil shooting through your veins, and slowly crushing you, until you're nothing but a hollow shell."

Just then, the prince felt a strange feeling of pain himself, as a knife lodged into his back. He dropped the staff to the floor, and when he did, the light was gone, and Glam felt tired, but okay. A small friend helped him to his feet. They watched Phillip writhe in pain, as he lay in his own blood.

"You talk too much," the Woblo told him, as he reached down and picked up the staff.

"I thought I told you to stay outside?" Glam asked.

"You know me, I never listen if it means adventure."

"Well, I'm glad to see you, anyway. Let's go outside and finish our mission."

They started towards the door, as the guards brought in the rest of their party. They were pushed out into the open, as the guards met Glam.

"Sir," the main guard said. "These people were out front creating a disturbance."

"I know. I told them to. Glaridia will be arriving in two days to take over temporarily until a new king can be found. The prince has been found guilty of conspiracy to overthrow the king. Since he's almost dead anyway, there'll be no trial. There is more than enough evidence to prove he's guilty. Until such time, I'll be in charge here, understand?"

"Yes, Sir."

"Now if you'll excuse us, we have work to do," he said, and the party stepped outside into the large front courtyard. Glam and Bargo walked down the path, and the Elf directed the others to stay back. He turned to Bargo, and placed his hand on his shoulder. "Take out the stone, and place it on the end of the staff."

NICHOLAS T. DAVIS

"But it doesn't look like it fits," he said, as he looked at both of the instruments.

"It will fit."

Bargo placed the stone on the end, and the blue crystal was drawn to the staff like a magnet, and began to glow.

"Now raise the staff to the sky, and repeat the words Caila Ziatra Fiala Rhiatu, rhialian epocha apala tan. By the power of Rhiatu, release the evil upon this land."

Bargo had trouble with the words at first, but after repeating them several times, he raised the staff toward the sky and recited the command. A bright blue light emerged from it, traveled miles into the air, and straight to where the Licarions were. They felt the sting of the staff, as several were burned by its heat, while the rest retreated into the Bacon Hills.

"It is done," Glam announced. "The Shudolin is free once again." He then turned to his Woblo friend. "If you decide to become a wizard, you must never let this weapon fall in the wrong hands ever again."

"Yes, Sir."

"What did I say about that?"

"Yes, Friend."

The trees began to turn green again, and the birds began to sing, as if it was a new beginning for them. The group was relieved they were successful in their task, and felt a new beginning upon the land. Bargo turned back to his friends, they smiled, and he felt for the first time in his life, most important of all.

253

CHAPTER TWENTY FOUR: THE TRUE VALUE OF LIFE

Two days later, there was a huge feast at the castle for the heroes, as they waited for King Glaridia and the other council members to arrive. Lilly wore a beautiful dress once worn by the queen before she passed away. Bargo wore his usual khaki pants, white shirt, and brown vest. He proudly wore his Elven sword by his side, and used the staff as a walking stick. Barton wore the best suit his money could buy, after receiving the modest 100 gold pieces he was promised, minus the 5 he owed Bargo. He knew it wasn't the treasure he hoped for, but it sufficed. He received something much more valuable than money-friends.

The food was varied, between different meats, vegetables, and fruits, along with nuts and berries as well. Glam invited everyone in the castle, and even apologized to Maurice for pointing a knife at him. A good time followed with dancing and music from the royal band, and a small Woblo with a brand new banjo. He felt like he'd been reborn, and although he was saddened by his father's death, he discovered who he really was, and what he was destined to become.

He wasn't the only one in mourning, and wouldn't be the last. Glam missed his old comrades, Thomas, William and Christopher, and couldn't help but feel hate in his heart. He knew even if he could, he would've been unworthy to use such a powerful weapon. It needed a true wizard, one incapable of revenge or evil thoughts.

Then there was Lilly, torn because of Bargo's feelings toward her, and the love for her husband. She didn't want to hurt him, and she still loved Bargo like a brother, but knew it could never be. The thought of an animal wanting to be her lover didn't appeal to her in the least bit, even if he did become human someday. Her world would soon be torn apart even more the next day, upon the return of the messenger with King Glaridia.

Barlow, who saw him one final time, said goodbye again to

his cousin, and the others, and headed back to his militia unit, who's new job was to rebuild Bashworth. He was placed in charge of the unit, and also promoted to Lieutenant, along with cousin.

The next day was rainy; the first rain they'd seen in a week, and the sound of thunder echoed through the palace walls. The Elven coach arrived about 10:30 that morning, and King Glaridia entered, with a face of gloom upon his face. The news of losing his beloved neighboring King Timothy broke his heart; they had been like brothers, and ruled together in peace for many years. He entered the Council Room, as Glam, Tamarka, Bargo, and Daniel entered as well, and they all took seats. Glam rose, and addressed the council.

"Council members," he said. "I appreciate all of you coming on such short notice, and under such dire conditions. As all of you know, Ang and his army of Licarions recently destroyed several villages along the north path. With the Gem of Rebolin, and the Staff of Varlana, we were able to squash the evil bestowed upon our land. Unfortunately, the prince was involved in a plot to overthrow his father's regime, and to eliminate certain members of the Royal Guard. I regret to say, the prince was successful, and the king has since passed away, which leaves us without a ruler. Since Glaridia cannot effectively rule both kingdoms, we need to appoint a new king of the Shudolin. Our savior, Bargo Lynden is the logical choice, but he has refused. Any suggestions, or possible replacements?"

"How about you, Glam," Bargo suggested. "You would make a great king. You're wise, you know both kingdom's histories, your honest, and your authoritative when you need to be."

"Don't be ridiculous," Glam said. "It's bad enough I have to do Chris' job."

"Perhaps the Woblo has a point," the Elven king replied. "Why can't you become our new king?"

"I'm not really cut out to be king," he said.

"And you think I am?" Bargo asked.

"All right, you win. I'll try it out for one year. If it doesn't work out, I'll leave it for someone else."

"Anyone opposed to the idea?" the king asked, as the room remained silent. "Then it's settled. All hail, King Glam of the

Shudolin." They stood and bowed to their new leader, as Glam smiled in gratitude.

During this time, Lilly walked in the courtyard, admiring the royal garden; with its marigolds, lilies, snapdragons and daffodils. After the council session ended, Tamarka greeted her in front of the palace, carrying a piece of folded paper in his hands, and a long look of despair on his face. He handed the paper to her as he approached her.

"I received this from a courier from Woblo Town," he said. "I'm very sorry, Mrs. Tumberhill."

She read the message, which stated while her husband was plowing in the field, his heart gave out. By the time anyone found him, he was dead several days. She tried to get extra money so he wouldn't have to work so hard, and he wound up pushing himself anyway. She dropped the note to the ground, at a loss of words, as Tamarka placed his hand on her shoulder.

"I'm all right," she lied. "Thank you for bringing this to me, Tamarka."

She sat down in the grass and cried, as Bargo came out the front door, and into the courtyard.

"What's wrong?" he asked.

Infuriated, she rose to her feet and looked down upon the Woblo.

"You had to wish it, didn't you?"

"Wish what?"

"Lawrence is dead," she sobbed. "You said it would happen, and it did. You and that damn magic."

"I'm sorry," Bargo pleaded with her. "I don't know what to say. I didn't mean for it to happen, it was a what if question."

"I don't think you and I should see each other any more," she told him, sorrowfully.

"Lilly, I'm sorry," he said. "Would it help if I said if you need anything, I'm here for you?"

"No, it wouldn't," she said. "I don't want you there for me."

"What if I decided to become human? Would I be there for you then?"

She shook her head, and cried harder.

"Just leave me alone," she said. "Go and become a wizard, if that's what you choose to do. I don't ever want to see you again."

"I just want you to know I love you," he told her, as he placed his hand on her shoulder.

"I know you do," she answered. "But I think right now I don't feel the same, and even if it wasn't your fault, you still implied it, and I don't think I can forgive you for that. Goodbye, Bargo."

She hugged him one more time gently, and then walked off the castle grounds, and down the streets of Riverton. While she did, Glam came out as well, and stood by the new apprentice. He watched, as she left the area, and placed his arm around the Woblo.

"How did she take it?" he asked.

"Hard," Bargo said. "You mean, you knew?"

"Of course I knew," Glam said. "I never mentioned it for security reasons, but I do have a few special powers of my own, you know."

"I know," Bargo said. "I think I've always known you did, ever since I met you."

"What about the other part of the prophecy?"

"What's that?"

"The part when you become human again," he said. "Perhaps someday she might change her mind about you."

"I don't think so," Bargo said. "She never really was in love with me. She thought of me as a pet, or a child."

"I think you're wrong," Glam said. "I think she does love you, and she just doesn't realize it yet."

"Nonetheless, I don't want to change," Bargo insisted.

"Oh?" Glam asked.

"I'm happy to be who I am, and what I am about to become," the Woblo said. "And that is a wizard of the Shudolin."

"Then let's get started," the Elf said, as a hooded elf emerged from the palace doors to greet the two of them. He wore a dark gray cloak, and carried a sword identical to the one Bargo was wearing. "Bargo, this is Galong, the only surviving member of the order of the Elven Dhiartu wizardry. He is the extra Elf I had observing us. He is aware of every move we made on the journey, and knows all of what occurred."

"How do you do?" Bargo asked.

"I do fine," he said, as he shook the Woblo's hand.

"Your voice wasn't the one I heard, was it?"

"I'm afraid not," the cloaked Elf said. "It must have been either Rhiatu's or Garlock's, trying to deceive you."

"I'll never know who it was," Bargo sighed in disgust.

"Maybe you aren't supposed to know who it is," Glam said. "Perhaps it is the merely the voice of reason."

"After your training you will know the answer. Shall we begin, young one?"

"You are my guide," Bargo said. "And my teacher."

Bargo was saddened by the fact Lilly rejected his sympathy, but happy he found his place in the Shudolin. His father's shop remained closed, and the Woblo Town community were both shocked and heartbroken at what happened to the Lyndens. Some blamed Bargo for his supposed selfishness, and others understood why he left, but everyone was still in mourning over Jeremiah's death.

Lilly never went back to the farm, and took a job as a barmaid in Riverton, working for a friend of Glam's. She arranged to have it sold, for her old life there was over, and she wanted no connection with it. It was Lawrence's dream to have a sprawling farm, but she knew by herself it would be an almost impossible task, and really couldn't afford to pay for farm hands. He was a good husband to her, and she could never live her life the same without him.

Part of her still loved Bargo, but she knew things would never be the same, now that she knew how he felt. The thought of him becoming human wouldn't change her feelings for her husband, and he could never provide emotionally what she needed, even if he was.

She was still mad he followed his dream to become a wizard. She always felt he was needed back at the Blacksmith shop, and with the closure of the shop, the thriving business went sour, and most people felt its absence. The nearest place was one hundred miles away, and the Blacksmith was nowhere near as experienced as Jeremiah or Bargo was.

Barton took a job in Riverton as well, working at a local stable. Now that the fighting ended, mercenaries weren't in as big a demand. It was time for him to put away the sword, and take out the pitchfork to bail hay. He sometimes wished he found someone to start a family with, but knew it would've never worked out. He drank and smoked too much, and loved his ladies, when they were interested in him. Most decent women would look the other way when he passed, and he was usually stuck with either a drunken wench hiding from her husband, or a prostitute. At any point, he knew he was a simple man, and just wanted a simple life from now on.

Back in Licarion country, they were left without a leader, and hid deep within the caverns of the Dagar mountains; frightened, defeated, and without a purpose. There was one particular Licarion named Glazar, however, who would soon become a pivotal figure within the Licarion community. When Ang's reign ended, the Licarion was just a youth, but would soon take on the Shudolin with a vengeance not seen since the reign of Garlock himself. Glam, due to his special talent, knew this, and also knew there was a dark presence at the edge of the horizon which would free the evil sorcerer from his stronghold of bondage and imprisonment.

Deep within the caverns of the Licarions, in the total darkness of the cold, damp, dank prison, a small half bred creature cried where no one could hear. His claws dug into the stone wall, as he tried to dig his way out to escape, and he shook the cell door with a force surprising strong for such a small creature. While he did, he recited the words over, and over, as his red eyes glowed in the darkness.

"I will find you Bargo Lynden," he sneered. "And I will get it back, because you took it from me. And when I do, you will sorry, because you will feel the true wrath of my master."

THE SHUDOLIN, ELVEN KINGDOM AND LICARIA

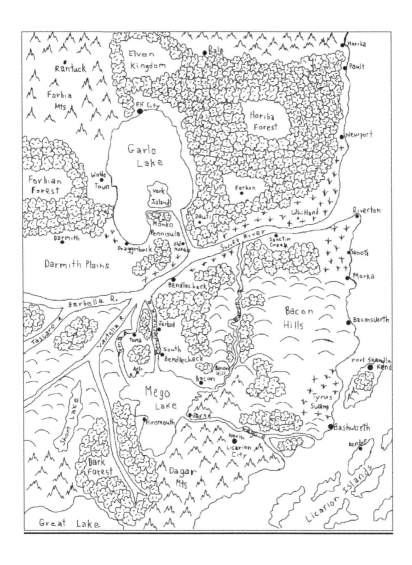

OTHER BOOKS BY NICHOLAS T. DAVIS

SCIENCE FICTION

Dimension Lapse, © Copyright 2014

Dimension Lapse II: Return To Doomsday, © Copyright 2015

Dimension Lapse III:Dimensional Breakdown© Copyright 2016

CHILDRENS BOOKS

Tobias Meets A Friend, © Copyright 2015

Wacky Wild Tales © Copyright 2016

ABOUT THE AUTHOR

Nicholas T. Davis lives in East Syracuse, NY, has been writing since he was 12 years old, motivated by his seventh grade teacher and his love for literature. He has been married to his wife, Nancy, for 15 years, and has a daughter, Kelly, from a previous marriage. His father was a protestant minister and maintenance worker for Syracuse University and his mother was a homemaker, and he is one of eight children.

He worked as a cleaner for a psychiatric hospital for 26 years, writes in his spare time, oil paints, and is a part time musician. He is the author of a science fiction series, and also has two children's books. Bargo Lynden is his first fantasy novel, and the beginning of a series. For more information on what his next project will be, please visit his Blog, or Facebook page.

WHERE TO FIND NICHOLAS T. DAVIS

BLOG: ntdavis18dotcom.wordpress.com
FACEBOOK: https://www.facebook.com/NTDAVIS
DIMENSIONLAPSE
Email: ntdavis18@verizon.net
Twitter: Nicholas T. Davis @ NICKTDAVIS18

Made in the USA
Columbia, SC
07 June 2018